D1387610

KILKENNY COUNTY LIBRARY

Murder at Rough Point

Books by Alyssa Maxwell

Gilded Newport Mysteries

MURDER AT THE BREAKERS
MURDER AT MARBLE HOUSE
MURDER AT BEECHWOOD
MURDER AT ROUGH POINT

Lady and Lady's Maid Mysteries

MURDER MOST MALICIOUS
A PINCH OF POISON

Published by Kensington Publishing Corporation

MURDER AT ROUGH POINT

ALYSSA MAXWELL

KENSINGTON BOOKS
www.kensingtonbooks.com

KENSINGTON BOOKS are published by

Kensington Publishing Corp.
119 West 40th Street
New York, NY 10018

All Kensington titles, imprints, and distributed lines are available at special quantity discounts for bulk purchases for sales promotion, premiums, fund-raising, educational, or institutional use. Special book excerpts or customized printings can also be created to fit specific needs. For details, write or phone the office of the Kensington Special Sales Manager: Attn. Special Sales Department. Kensington Publishing Corp., 119 West 40th Street, New York, NY 10018. Phone: 1-800-221-2647.

Library of Congress Card Catalogue Number: 2016933899

Kensington and the K logo Reg. U.S. Pat. & TM Off.

ISBN-13: 978-1-4967-0328-6
ISBN-10: 1-4967-0328-6
First Kensington Hardcover Edition: September 2016

eISBN-13: 978-1-4967-0329-3
eISBN-10: 1-4967-0329-4
First Kensington Electronic Edition: September 2016

10 9 8 7 6 5 4 3 2 1

Printed in the United States of America

To my honorary cousins, Benay, Deena, and Robin.
Thanks for including me! I love our girls' time and only wish it happened more often.
Robin, the quilt in Chapter Two is for you—of course! But I fear my words could never do justice to your beautiful craftsmanship.

Chapter 1

Newport, RI
September 1896

"You will come down from there this instant. *Now*, sir." I clapped my hands for emphasis, but to no avail. The individual whose disorderly bulk presently concealed the newest tear in the leather seat of my buggy merely tilted his head at me with an infuriating mixture of defiance and incomprehension.

That look begged the question: How could I *possibly* object to his accompanying me? Yes, well. Such had been my morning thus far. The same individual had earlier spilled water across the kitchen floor and managed to fold the doormat in half so that upon entering from the garden, I'd first stumbled over the mat and then slid sideways across the wet floorboards. These acrobatics culminated with the bumping of my hip on the edge of the kitchen table.

While I did not find this latest antic any more endearing, it was not, however, entirely unexpected.

The rays of an uncertain sun seeped through lacy cloud

cover and the sharp tang of low tide permeated the air and settled on my tongue. I stepped closer to the buggy and unceremoniously took hold of a bold red collar. "I must be off, and you, good sir, must vacate this seat immediately."

Patch, a brown and white spaniel mix and Gull Manor's newest and unruliest resident, whimpered sadly and resisted my gentle tug for all of a second or two. Then, with a growly whine, he hopped down onto the footboard and from there sprang to the ground beside me.

I bent to stroke his sweetly rounded head, which reached just above my knees. The curling fur slipped like warm velvet between my fingers. "There now, your job is to keep Nanny and Katie company while I'm gone. Be sure no harm comes to them." Did he understand me? Oftentimes I believed he did. On this occasion he licked my hand and took off at an uneven lope, his shaggy ears flapping and his curling tail feathering in the breeze. He bolted out of sight around the corner of my sprawling if somewhat ramshackle house that had once belonged to my great-aunt Sadie.

I was not about to waste the opportunity, for who knew how long it would be before Patch remembered that Nanny, my housekeeper, and Katie, my housemaid, were fully capable of taking care of themselves. I climbed into my gig and clucked to my old roan hack, Barney. He lurched into a halfhearted stroll. Barney only knew one speed, but his leisurely pace was just fine with me today as I hadn't far to go.

My front lawn, which had recently benefited from the attentions of my uncle Cornelius Vanderbilt's gardeners, showed tinges of yellow and brown, a sure sign that autumn had arrived. Though the elms and maples on the perimeter of my property remained heavy with summer growth and showed only hints of the blazing colors to come, the hawthorn, boxwood, and azaleas closer to the house already looked tired and thin.

Despite the fading summer and my trials with a naughty, nearly full-grown pup, my spirits ascended with each of Barney's labored steps. Mr. Millford, editor-in-chief and my employer at the Newport *Observer*, had called last night with a new assignment for me, one that promised nothing in the way of danger. That in itself came as a welcome relief, for I'd had enough of danger back in July. Yet neither was this to be one of Bellevue Avenue's extravagant fetes, about which I had written countless frivolous columns about gowns, jewels, tableware, and decorations. No, for once I would neither be threatened by murderers nor secretly bored by frippery, and, best of all, I had been asked for specifically. *Asked for*. By name. It seemed I was establishing a reputation as a journalist. Finally.

One question did niggle at the back of my mind, but I resolved to ignore it. Why contemplate vexing riddles in the face of my good fortune?

As we left Gull Manor behind, a sturdy ocean breeze threatened to lift my hat right off my head. I placed one hand on the crown of my straw boater and turned my face into the gusts, letting my eyes fall half closed while I enjoyed the heady promise of a story of substance, the likes of which Newport hadn't seen in far too long. Decades, actually. I didn't even mind when the gull feather, dyed blue by Nanny to match my carriage dress, worked loose from my hatband and fluttered away. More than a decade ago, the intelligentsia—artists, writers, and philosophers—who had once inhabited our city in such great numbers had fled before the onslaught of the industrial barons such as my uncle Cornelius. Suddenly they were back, at least a small number of them were, and it seemed they wanted me to be the means through which they announced their return.

Me.

"Barney, do you realize this could be a new beginning, not only for me as a reporter, but for Newport as well?" I let him have his head, and while this only encouraged him to slacken the pace, we'd arrive at our destination in plenty of time. Barney knew the way to Bellevue Avenue as well as he knew his way into his own cozy stall.

For it was to Bellevue that we headed, but where the avenue made its ninety-degree turn north toward the opulent mansions that stretched along its length, we took a sharp right onto the curving driveway of Rough Point, the estate owned by Uncle Cornelius's youngest brother, Frederick. Here was no palazzo like The Breakers, or Italianate villa like Beechwood, or the neoclassical variation of Versailles's Le Petit Trianon that was Marble House.

With its granite façade trimmed in red sandstone, diamond-paned windows, and crenellated accents, Rough Point seemed a transplant from the English countryside, at least those whose pictures I had seen in books. Three gabled wings jutted out imposingly from the main structure, while a fourth gabled wing set at a slight angle from the rest made up the kitchen and service quarters. Heavy double doors beneath a Gothic arch stood framed by Ionic pilasters, forming an entrance that seemed to convey a forbidding message: Enter if you dare. Sitting on relatively isolated grounds near the southern tip of Bellevue Avenue, with rear lawns that heaved and tumbled to the Cliff Walk's rocky precipice, Rough Point had been aptly named.

And yet, for all that, I smiled as Barney brought the buggy closer. Perhaps Rough Point spoke to a dark and defiant part of my nature, one that allowed me to endure danger and death without giving way to despair. Perhaps. At any rate, I had never felt the disquiet here some of my young Vanderbilt cousins experienced. Gertrude termed the place oppressive, Neily called it archaic, and Consuelo feared the shadows no amount of sunlight or electric illumination could dispel from its mahogany interiors.

At the sound of another vehicle crunching along the drive behind me, I looked back and was surprised to see Uncle Frederick's brougham being brought up from the carriage house. A moment later the front door opened, and both Frederick and Louise Vanderbilt stepped outside. The pair had vacated Rough Point at midsummer, and I had not realized they'd returned. A man with dark hair slicked close to the scalp, angular, European features, and a pencil-thin mustache followed them. I recognized him as their estate manager, Howard Dunn, who handled legal and financial matters on Uncle Frederick's various properties. As if he were a footman or butler, he carried a valise in each hand.

Aunt Louise saw me and waved. A tall woman with tightly curled hair and a slim figure envied by her sisters-in-law Alice and Alva—and explained by her never having borne children—she always seemed genuinely pleased to see me. "Emmaline, I'm so glad you arrived before we departed. Another few minutes and we would have quite missed you."

"I'm glad I had a chance to see you, too," I said, but I couldn't help a slight sinking in the pit of my stomach. Here I had believed the individuals renting the house for the next two weeks had specifically asked for me to report on their activities. But now I suspected it had been Frederick and Louise who had recommended me for the job. I hadn't achieved distinction as a journalist after all; I merely had thoughtful relatives.

Matters could be worse, I supposed. Either way I had an opportunity to distinguish myself as a reporter in matters other than fashion and frippery.

"I thought you'd left after the tribulations of the summer," I continued as Uncle Frederick handed me down from my carriage.

"We most certainly did," he replied. "Who could bear such vulgar disorder here, in what is supposed to be a peaceful summer enclave of garden parties and festive balls? This past summer, combined with the town's rabid need to keep up with the Joneses, only served to reinforce our decision that Newport is not for us."

I hid a grin. Though I couldn't fault his motives when it came to murder and mayhem, it had been Uncle Frederick's plans for Rough Point eight years ago that had, in large part, changed the nature of Newport's summer cottages forever. Before then and with only a few exceptions, our visiting socialites had been content with Newport's very New England shingle style of mansion with the occasional exception of an Italianate villa or Gothic revival cottage. It had been the startlingly lavish blueprints of Rough Point that prompted a covetous Alva Vanderbilt to erect high walls around her newly acquired Bellevue Avenue property to prevent anyone from glimpsing her triumphant Marble House until its completion. That in turn spawned the rebuilding of The Breakers to its palazzo-inspired glory. Now, Newport boasted one palatial tribute to the owner's ego after another, with more in the making.

But of course, I wouldn't remind Uncle Frederick of all that. I believed him sincere in having grown weary of constant one-upmanship. Of his two older brothers, Uncle Frederick most resembled William, but perhaps with kindlier eyes, and a great, dark mustache that curled beyond his cheeks. "We returned only to see our renters settled in," he told me, "and to pack up any irreplaceable treasures. Now we're off again to New York."

Their driver brought the carriage to a stop beside us. Mr. Dunn, having silently held the valises this whole time, moved to load the cases onto the rear of the vehicle. A footman came out of the house with two more bags and piled them on top of the others, then proceeded to strap them all in place.

"You've been spending less and less time in Newport. If you stop coming altogether, I'll miss you terribly," I said truthfully. Of all my Vanderbilt relatives, Frederick and Louise were the most apt to accept me as I was, and suggested they find a husband for me much less frequently.

The wind stirred the silk flowers adorning Aunt Louise's wide-brimmed hat, set at an angle over her carefully arranged curls. She gestured with a lace-gloved hand. "I know how much you love Newport, Emmaline." She smiled at me. "But couldn't you love it a teensy bit less, just enough to visit us in Hyde Park? You would love it there. This ocean with its constant winds is so unsettling to the constitution. The countryside at Hyde Park is ever so much more tranquil, like a Charles Baker or Thomas Cole painting. So idyllic and soothing and . . . well . . . civilized. We'd so love to have you there. And our neighbor's youngest son—"

"Thank you, Aunt Louise, perhaps someday. But I have responsibilities here. A household to maintain, and employment."

"Speaking of which, we're glad you've been asked to report on whatever it is these bohemians plan to do." Uncle Frederick flicked a disapproving gaze up at the house. "You'll help Mr. Dunn keep an eye on things for us, won't you?"

"Yes," his wife interjected with some degree of agitation, "and alert the authorities should things get out of hand."

"Out of hand?"

"Yes, you know how these freethinkers are with their modern ideas of art and poetry and theater. As if the traditional and established needed fixing." Uncle Frederick gave a dramatic shudder.

"Of course," I promised rather absently. My thoughts fixed on what he'd just said. *We're glad you've been asked to report* . . . Was he merely trying to conceal his and Louise's hand in my being here? Or *had* their tenants truly asked for me? I brightened at the prospect and with unfeigned enthusiasm said, "Can you tell me a bit about this group? Who they are, and their respective art forms."

"Mr. Dunn will apprise you of all of that, dear." Aunt Louise patted my cheek. With a careful tilt of her head to avoid our hats from colliding, she leaned and kissed me good-bye. "We really must go. Our luggage has gone ahead and our steamer is waiting to set sail. Adieu, Emmaline!"

Uncle Frederick kissed my cheek and squeezed my hand. "Good-bye, then, Emmaline. Come see us in Hyde Park sometime."

With that he helped his wife into the carriage and climbed in after her, leaving me with a sense that their departure seemed rushed. With her smiling face and broad hat filling the open window, Aunt Louise called out another good-bye and added in a breezy tone, "It just occurred to me you might be familiar with one of the guests, at least by reputation. Mrs. Edward . . ."

The carriage jolted as it followed the curve of the drive, and the rest of Aunt Louise's disclosure became lost in the rumble of wheels and the creaking of leather suitcases. I watched until the brougham reached a stand of elm trees and disappeared from view.

I turned to Howard Dunn, the estate manager I knew only vaguely, for I'd never had reason to say more than good day to him when we had met previously. Despite his carrying valises to the coach today, his was not a service role here but rather an administrative one. I opened my mouth to question him about the guests, but he spoke with a twitch of his mustache, so thin it might have been sketched in ink.

"Do come inside, Miss Cross, and I'll apprise you of all you need to know. Some of our guests are already here. Others should arrive by this afternoon." With no further attempt at pleasantries, he turned and led the way into the house. Apparently he found me beneath his regard.

The vestibule and foyer of Rough Point left one with a distinct sense of disappointment. Smallish, rectangular rooms with stone flooring, white walls, and coffered ceilings, the entryway rather underwhelmed the first-time visitor. Especially if one had visited, say, Marble House, with its golden Sienna marble entry hall and grand staircase, the eighteenth-century Venetian-painted ceiling, and generous views of the veranda and expansive rear grounds. No, one would not enter Marble House and experience the slightest twinge of letdown.

Here, it was as if the architects, Peabody & Stearns, hadn't deemed this foyer of great importance and perhaps even added it as an afterthought. Ah, but before taking many steps, the visitor entered Rough Point's Great Hall, a room of stone and marble that stretched two stories high, with an upper gallery that ran the full length of the room, and opposite, a rotunda of soaring windows that confronted a carefully sculpted scene of lawn and rock and sea. One had a sense of stepping back in time and across the ocean, to the charmed manorial world of the English countryside. Dark marbles and darker woods defined the interiors of Rough Point, creating those shadows Consuelo so abhorred, and lending a Gothic atmosphere to the place that might have leaped out of a Brontë novel.

Unlike Marble House or The Breakers, Rough Point sprawled from one end to the other, with the majority of rooms on the first and second floors facing out over the ocean. It was across the house that Mr. Dunn led me, through the Stair Hall, dining room, and through a heavy door to the servants' wing. His brisk stride didn't cease until we reached the butler's pantry with its locked storage cupboards and equally locked safe. Multiple scheduling boards decorated the walls, and an imposing desk that boasted a telephone dominated nearly a third of the room. He bade me sit, and then ran through a list of instructions rather as a butler might have conveyed the house rules and daily duties to a new housemaid: quickly and tersely. If he thought to intimidate me with the importance of his position, I might have informed him that I had dealt with Newport's most formidable butlers and housekeepers in the past with little or no permanent bruising. I held my tongue. He went on to explain that I would come and go each day, conduct interviews, view artwork-in-progress, and report on the retreat only once it had concluded and the artists had gone.

This last puzzled me, but I assumed the group had its reasons. Mr. Dunn then escorted me back across the house, leaving me alone in the drawing room to mull over the information while he went off to manage last-minute arrangements. I was instructed to wait, though for what I received no clue. I drifted through the room, making note of the changes since the last time I'd visited. Ming vases, an original Gainsborough, and other priceless items had been supplanted by expensive but not irreplaceable pieces, just as Uncle Frederick had said. He and Aunt Louise were taking no chances with their beloved possessions.

I returned to the central seating arrangement and sighed. That niggling question from earlier had been answered, for I had wondered how a group of artists, never known for possessing wealth, had raised enough funds to lease an estate like Rough Point. Mr. Dunn had confided that one of the guests was no starving artist, but an English baronet with a fortune at his disposal. I found his inclusion in such a group both unusual and interesting, and looked forward to interviewing him.

Wondering how long I would be consigned to the drawing room and what I might be waiting for, I stared at a fire screen I hadn't seen here before, an elegant piece in carved, gilded wood holding an embroidered design on gold silk. It was a bright spot in this room, which, like the rest of the house, boasted the same dark floors, thick mahogany moldings, and deep, coffered ceilings.

"Your reputation quite precedes you, Miss Cross. Mr. Dunn informed me of your arrival, as I asked him to. I've been looking forward to meeting you again."

Even after more than a decade, I recognized the voice. I also realized it belonged to the person whose name had not fully reached my ears as Aunt Louise and Uncle Frederick drove away. I also understood now why Uncle Frederick had used the term *keeping up with the Joneses*. For a member of that very family, the daughter of George and Lucretia Jones, was here beneath this roof, in this very room with me. It was her family's wealth and extravagant lifestyle that had inspired the saying that had grown so prevalent most people had no idea where it originated. But I knew, and I struggled to compose my feelings.

How ironic that an individual I might most wish to avoid—whom I had for the most part avoided through the years—would be the first to greet me today.

I turned to face Mrs. Edward Wharton. Some ten years my elder, she and I had met once before, only briefly, before my mother shooed me away. *Run to Nanny, Emma,* she had said, *and let the grown-ups visit*. It had been at our house on Walnut Street in the Easton's Point neighborhood by the harbor. I had scraped my knee, badly, and sought my mother's attentions. But she had company, and I'd been too young to understand the significance of such a visitor entering our modest home. Too inexperienced to grasp that my father's Vanderbilt roots combined with his growing reputation as

KK371268

an artist had garnered the notice of one of society's wealthiest young women. Edith Wharton.

"Do you not remember me, Miss Cross? I suppose it *has* been many years, and you were so very young at the time."

Oh, I remembered. I remembered how my child's heart had detested her for putting such an avid light in my mother's eyes, when her own daughter so rarely achieved the same level of enthusiasm. I hadn't understood the reasons then. I hadn't understood that this woman would become one of my father's most ardent patrons, so essential to an artist's career, and that eventually she and others would persuade my parents to leave Newport for the intellectual stimulation of Paris. But even if I had comprehended all those years ago, all it would have meant to me was that this individual could purchase my parents' attentions while I could not.

I drew a fortifying breath, forced a courteous smile, and summoned the professionalism I so prized, and which I'd lost, utterly, at the sound of this woman's greeting. "I certainly do remember you, Mrs. Wharton. I hope you've been well?"

"Come, let us sit and become acquainted." She went to the lovely Regency-era sofa set at a perpendicular angle to the hearth, its gold pin striping setting off larger bands of burgundy and cream and picking up the gold silk design of the fire screen. She patted the cushion beside her. "I'm a great admirer of yours. I'd hoped we might discuss our literary tastes and writing techniques."

I was taken aback and could do little to hide the fact. "You follow my Fancies and Fashions page?"

"Well, yes, there is that." She brushed the notion aside with a flutter of her carefully manicured hand. "But your news articles, your reports on the terrible goings-on in Newport these past two summers. I must tell you I'm exceedingly impressed that you convinced your editor-in-chief to allow you to write those articles. Nellie Bly would be proud of you, I should think."

I confess to experiencing a tiny thrill at being compared to the journalist I most wished to emulate. Nellie Bly, who wrote for the *World* in New York, had exceeded boundaries no female journalist had ever crossed before. "I confess it wasn't easy. Mr. Millford resisted my efforts at every turn, as did my fellow reporter at the *Observer.* Ed Billings attempted to step in each time and claim the byline for his own." As soon as I'd spoken, I wondered why I'd confided such details to her.

"And yet you persisted, didn't you, Miss Cross?" She didn't wait for my answer. "I believe you have grown into a woman of substance. And your style! It is much to be envied."

Puzzled, I swept a glance downward at my blue carriage dress. It had once belonged to my aunt Sadie, was years out of date, but Nanny, my housekeeper and surrogate grandmother, had refreshed its appearance with jet buttons and, more recently, satin trimmings. Still . . .

Mrs. Wharton must have guessed the train of my thoughts, for presently she laughed, a light, easy sound. "No, Miss Cross, I don't mean your fashion style. That is neither here nor there. I refer to your writing style. I don't know if you are aware, but I've written a good deal of poetry, and I'm currently working on a manual of interior design I plan to call *A Decoration of Houses*. That is why I'm here, you see, and I'm hoping . . . well . . ."

She hesitated, seeming uncertain for the first time during our little tête-à-tête. I waited, wondering what she could possibly be leading up to, and took the opportunity to take in details that, in my shock of recognition, had eluded me.

She was dressed simply yet expensively in a cream skirt and, in the current trend that emulated menswear, a gray silk shirtwaist topped by a crisp white collar and a smart black bowtie. A tailored black jacket completed her outfit, the sleeves fashionably wide at the shoulders and tapering to tight cuffs at the wrists. The effect was both masculine yet unmistakably feminine. Confident. There was nothing frilly or superfluous about her, and the ease with which she moved in the outfit aroused my envy.

Yet Edith Wharton was not what I would consider a beautiful woman. She had rather plain, even features, large, earnest eyes, and a small, thin mouth that, in its resting position, did not encourage the viewer to expect more than a polite smile.

"What I hope," she elaborated, "is that you might deign to look over a bit of what I'd written and give me your honest opinion. Perhaps advise me where and how I might adjust my prose for greater impact."

I believe my mouth might have dropped open. She in turn looked apologetic, as if she supposed I would say I was far too busy and dismiss her request out of hand. "If you wish," I said, "I'll be happy to take a look, but be forewarned, Mrs. Wharton. I'm merely a journalist. I have no experience with writing books."

Briefly, almost guiltily, I thought of the manuscript buried in a drawer in my desk at home. Ah, but I had progressed very little before I realized no fictional scenario could ever compete with the realities I'd witnessed these past two years, and the prospect of even trying had become a trite endeavor to me.

"My dear, a journalist is exactly what I need to banish the poetess in me. I wish to be taken seriously, to be seen as having valid opinions in matters of taste and style." Mrs. Wharton hesitated, absently fingering the bowtie beneath her chin. "I have aspirations beyond my interior design project. Did you know I've tried my hand at playwriting, and I believe I might have a novel in me. Perhaps several. But I must hone my craft before I plunge in."

"I'd be happy to help you if I can, Mrs. Wharton . . . And honored." How extraordinary. This was not how I would have envisioned such a meeting, and most surprising, after years of resenting Edith Wharton, I found myself quite liking her. Admiring her. And finding in her a kindred spirit of sorts. "Mrs. Wharton, I must ask. Was it you who asked for me to report on this retreat?"

Her smile brought a trace of beauty to her otherwise plain features, yet I detected some glint in her eye that hinted at more than her next words revealed. "I did. I hope that's all right. Perhaps it was a bit presumptuous of me."

"Not at all. Thank you." A bit of my former elation returned. Still . . .

"No, thank *you*, Miss Cross. I acted out of completely selfish motives, and this is an opportunity of which I plan to take full advantage, if you'll allow me."

"I can see no reason why not." I fell silent as I studied her a moment. It seemed highly odd to me that this woman, who could easily gain access to some of the most creative and brilliant minds of the day, would seek my counsel.

She obviously noticed my pensiveness. "Is something wrong?"

I slowly shook my head. "No, but . . . is there any other reason you wished me to be here?"

"Such as what, Miss Cross?" Again that evasive look in her eye. "Perhaps you underestimate your talents."

"May I ask you . . . why lease Rough Point when your own Land's End is so close by?" I referred to the property she and her husband inhabited in the summer months, on Ledge Road off Bellevue Avenue at the very southern tip of the island. Land's End was a blend of Colonial and Italianate styles, with steep gambrel roof lines that gave the appearance of a great beast crouched at the edge of the land.

"There is a very good reason for that," she said. "Anonymity. If we were to open Land's End, my mother and other relatives would be on us in an instant. As it is, they don't yet know I've returned to the country. We wish this retreat to be exactly that, Miss Cross. Peaceful, contemplative, and productive. Oh, but here is our Miss Marcus." She gestured to the doorway and the woman entering the room.

I admit to having yet a second unprofessional moment. Like an unseasoned schoolgirl I rushed to my feet and met the woman in question before she'd closed even half the distance between us. "Miss Marcus, what a thrill. I've had the very great pleasure of seeing you perform in Providence, oh, nearly three years ago I believe it was. You were in—"

"*La Traviata*, wasn't it?" Her skirts swayed as she spoke. She wore lavender silk jacquard with a pale green pattern of dogwood and bamboo—swaths of it draped elegantly around a generous figure, with flowing sleeves and a lacy décolletage cut daringly low for this time of day.

"Yes," I confirmed, hearing my own eagerness and helpless to do anything about it. "Opening night. I went with my Vanderbilt cousins, Cornelius, Alice, and—"

"Yes, I don't often perform in Providence, and I remember that opening night." She pouted full, pink lips—rouged, if I wasn't mistaken—and awakening dimples in either cheek. "It rained dreadfully and I feared no one would come."

"A little rain could not have kept us away, Miss Marcus. You were divine."

She tipped her head, her blond curls caught up in a beaded band sporting a tulle bow at one side. "I'm sorry, I don't believe I heard your name."

"Josephine, this is Emma Cross." Something in the way Mrs. Wharton spoke my name once again raised my guard. My reporter's instincts reared up inside me, banishing the starry-eyed admirer of renowned opera singer Josephine Marcus.

I returned to my seat beside Mrs. Wharton and removed

my tablet and pencil from my purse. "Will you be performing in the area while you're here, Miss Marcus? The Casino, perhaps?" I couldn't contain the hopeful note in my voice, although I knew full well the social Season had ended weeks earlier and it was a rare performer indeed who could be coaxed to entertain our local populace.

"No, I'm here to calm my nerves and enjoy a bit of sea air." Miss Marcus sat opposite us. Whereas Mrs. Wharton perched properly upright with the straightest of postures, which I attempted to emulate, the opera singer reclined against the cushion at her back—a woman who sat as she pleased and, I guessed, did as she pleased, convention be damned. "I'm afraid I'll be no use in providing gossip for your newspaper article, Miss Cross. The spring and summer seasons have left me quite diminished."

"I don't write a gossip column, Miss Marcus," I told her as politely as I could, although the very word raised my hackles. "My Fancies and Fashions page is about styles and trends and follows society activities during the Season."

"That's not all Miss Cross does, Josephine." Mrs. Wharton went on to describe the more harrowing tales I'd retold in print. Then she and Miss Marcus traded pleasantries of the sort people do when they know each other well but haven't seen each other in recent days. I listened, jotted down a note or two that might be of interest in my article, but my attention was momentarily drawn elsewhere.

The drawing room looked out onto a covered veranda and the main terrace, both of which overlooked the sea. Two men presently came up the terrace steps. They were young men, not yet thirty, I estimated, and they were laughing. When one stumbled on the top step the other reached out to steady him with a firm hand. This only elicited more laughter. Then they sobered and traded quieter words.

I had a good look at them then. One was all darkness—hair, eyes, even his complexion, which possessed a smooth olive sheen particular to Mediterranean climates. He again raised a hand, this time to push a mop of thick curls off his forehead. That hand was large, the fingers long and slender, and beautifully tapered.

But it was when the other turned in my direction that my breath stopped. Where the first was dark, this man was light—hair, eyes, skin, and even the way he held himself and the way he moved, as if he might at any moment grasp the breeze and fly out over the ocean. The fanciful notion nearly made me chuckle out loud. Here I had thought I had regained my professional perspective. But his was an artist's face surrounded by wavy light brown hair, or at least the sort of face artists loved to capture, with its chiseled cheekbones, strong chin, and intelligent brow. And yet the mouth—the mouth was soft, gently bowed, almost feminine in its lushness. . . .

"Ah, that's Vasili and Niccolo you see out there, Miss Cross." Miss Marcus's grin was feline and, I thought, cunning. "They've been out exploring the Cliff Walk. Thank goodness neither went over the side."

The men entered the veranda, first sitting to remove their boots and step into shoes before opening the drawing room doors to come in. They seemed startled at first to see Mrs. Wharton and me, and greeted us with brief bobs and good mornings. They continued through to the Great Hall, their steps echoing off the high ceiling.

"I assume they're part of the retreat," I said. "Who are they, may I ask?"

Josephine Marcus looked almost sorry for me. Mrs. Wharton said, "My dear, that's Vasili Pavlenko—the pretty one with the light brown hair."

"And the delicious figure," Miss Marcus added in a stage

whisper. "He's perfect—absolutely perfect from head to toe. But then, ballet dancers usually are."

"A dancer," I mused. "How wonderful."

Mrs. Wharton's hand came down on my wrist, startling me with its abruptness. "No, dear. Not any longer. Vasili sustained an injury that prevents him from dancing professionally ever again. It is his great sorrow. He's now a choreographer with the Imperial Russian Ballet. Do not mention his past unless he brings it up first."

"Thank you for warning me. I won't. And the other . . . ?

"The dark one is Niccolo Lionetti." Miss Marcus wrinkled the perfect slope of her nose, but rather than a negative gesture there was something proprietary in her expression, though she elaborated no further.

"Is he a dancer, too?" I asked.

"Goodness, no." Mrs. Wharton laughed again in that easy way she had. "Niccolo plays the cello, and quite beautifully, I might add. He's in demand in every major city in Europe. I expect the same will soon be true here in America once he's played on a few stages."

"I see. And whom else can I expect to meet?"

My question sent furtive glances back and forth between Edith Wharton and Josephine Marcus. Mrs. Wharton said casually, "There is Sir Randall Clifford, of course. He's interested in buying Rough Point."

"I didn't know it was for sale." Indeed, Mr. Dunn hadn't mentioned that very pertinent fact, nor had Uncle Frederick and Aunt Louise.

"Nothing is certain yet," Mrs. Wharton explained. "I'm sure it's no secret to you that they've grown tired of Newport. One cannot blame them for wishing to unload the place."

"No, I don't suppose so." My thoughts turned inward. I couldn't help thinking about how much had been lost to me already, and how much more stood to be lost. My cousin Consuelo, gone away and unlikely to return to Newport anytime soon; Cousin Neily—dear Neily—also out of the country indefinitely; and his sister, Gertrude, had left as well, having married Harry Whitney in August. My childhood home on the Point had been sold—to a man who, despite my every resolve, held a significant part of my heart, and now he was gone as well with no definite plans of returning. Then there was Uncle Cornelius, victim of a stroke during the summer, from which he might never fully recover. On top of all that, I barely saw my brother Brady these days, working as he was in New York City at the offices of the New York Central Railroad.

Was I about to lose another piece of my world? I tapped my pencil on the open page before me, so hard the point splintered and a tiny shard of lead went flying toward the hearth. "Is that everyone?"

Another question answered my own as a gentleman I hadn't seen previously strolled in from the Great Hall. With one hand in the pocket of his smoking jacket and the other held dramatically out to his side with the fingers curled upward, he spoke in a heavy French accent. "*Quoi*, Mademoiselle Cross? Has no one told you?"

Chapter 2

I *knew* Miss Marcus and Mrs. Wharton had been withholding something. A suspicion began to take root. "Tell me what? Is there something else I should know?"

Mrs. Wharton was on her feet in an instant. "Miss Cross, this is Monsieur Claude Baptiste. He is a stage director. Claude, come and greet Miss Cross properly. She'll be spending a good deal of time here with us over the next two weeks."

"*Oui, très bien.*" He crossed to me and with a little bow, took my hand and raised it to his lips. "A pleasure, mademoiselle." He didn't hold me in his attentions for long, for presently he addressed the other two women. "Have either of you seen Vasili?"

"He just passed through a moment ago," Miss Marcus told him. Her eyes narrowed and that catlike smile flashed again. "With Niccolo. Didn't you pass them along the way?"

"*Non*," came his stiff reply.

"Check the billiard room," Mrs. Wharton suggested brightly. The Frenchman nodded and went on his way.

I longed to demand what that had been about—why the

exchange left me feeling puzzled and uneasy. But it wasn't my place to question these people about their private affairs. That would have been overstepping my professional boundaries. As if she heard my silent musings, Mrs. Wharton once more sat beside me and placed her hand on my own, as if she and I were fast friends, confidantes.

"I've just had the most splendid idea. Instead of you traveling back and forth every day to check up on our progress, why don't you stay on? You can dash home now and pack a bag, and this way you can truly immerse yourself in our artistic world, so to speak."

It didn't take a genius to recognize her effort to distract me. "Mrs. Wharton, please, what is this secret—"

Her hand tightened around mine. "All in good time, my dear. Please trust me. Yes, there is still a surprise or two—" She broke off and darted a quick glance at Miss Marcus. "But I can promise you, all will be revealed. Now, will you stay?"

"I have responsibilities at home, and there is my job . . ."

"Nonsense. If you're needed at home, you can be there in a matter of minutes. I believe the telephone wires have been extended to Gull Manor?" When I nodded she raised an eyebrow in acknowledgment of my rapidly dwindling protests. "As far as your job is concerned, the Season is over, Miss Cross. Surely you'll miss no urgent soirees in the next two weeks."

"I suppose not."

"Good. Then do stay. We'll have more chance to become better acquainted, and I'll have ample opportunity to run my ideas by you. As I said, my book is about interior design, and who is more familiar with Newport's grandest homes than you—besides their owners, of course, but most of them have left until next Season."

My better judgment, along with my reporter's instincts,

wished to demand full disclosure about these surprises Mrs. Wharton spoke of. Yet I found myself caught in a spell woven by this unexpected favor she showed me. And I must admit, rather ashamedly, that thoughts of how she might advance my own career may have rendered the tiniest influence on my decision. "Yes, all right. I'll go home now and pack what I'll need."

"Yes," Miss Marcus agreed. "Go now so you'll be back by luncheon, and you can meet everyone all at once. We're a lively group, Miss Cross. I'm sure we'll all confound you with our chatter and arguing—yes, we're prone to arguments every hour of the day—but it's all in good fun. We're the best of friends. Comrades, all."

I didn't know quite what to make of that speech, so I smiled and came to my feet. "I'll be off then."

Mrs. Wharton stood as well. "I'll come with you, if I may. Did you know my husband and I can see your estate from the upper windows of Land's End? I've always envied you your vantage point, there on your little peninsula. I'd love to see the view from your perspective."

That Edith Wharton might have gazed across the distance to Gull Manor slightly unnerved me, as did the notion of her walking through my front door into the house's undeniably shabby interior. "My home is no estate, Mrs. Wharton. It's quite ramshackle as you'll see."

She merely grinned. "Let's go."

Somehow I weathered her foray into my home, though I cringed at every step she took over my increasingly threadbare rugs, and gritted my teeth when she sat on the faded settee in my front parlor. Worst of all, perhaps, was Nanny's pinched lips as she stiffly greeted my guest, for Nanny, too, remembered the day of Mrs. Wharton's visit to our Point home. It was Nanny who had held me when I cried that day, and she who had distracted me from my woes by handing me a freshly baked cookie, patching my knee, and taking me for a walk to pick wildflowers. I wished for an opportunity now to whisk her aside and explain that I no longer considered Mrs. Wharton the enemy, but no such opportunity presented itself. I packed quickly and my guest and I climbed into one of Uncle Frederick's smaller buggies that had followed us over, driven by the footman I had seen earlier, a handsome young man of towering height named Carl Davis. I knew him only vaguely, although his father, Hank, worked for Stevenson's Livery in town. Barney might as well remain at home in familiar surroundings, since I would not be needing him during my sojourn at Rough Point.

"Your home does not disappoint, Miss Cross," Mrs. Wharton was gracious enough to say as we left Gull Manor and my embarrassment behind.

"You're too kind," I murmured in return.

"Not at all. It's plain to see Gull Manor is the home of a young woman of independent means, and that, my dear, is worth more than all the satin brocade and fine velvets a fortune can provide. You are very lucky."

I thanked her and left it at that. I didn't doubt her sincerity, but I found her statement oddly naïve. If Mrs. Wharton and others like her truly felt that way, why didn't they shun their satin brocades and fine velvets in favor of a simpler life? Such individuals touted ideals, but were perhaps unwilling or unable to make the sacrifices to achieve those ideals. They didn't understand that for someone like me, there were no sacrifices. There was only life, which I lived as I must.

When we arrived back at Rough Point, Howard Dunn met us in the Stair Hall. "Luncheon will be served in half an hour." A twitch of his miniscule mustache suggested he perhaps found something distasteful in having to convey this information. I waited until he disappeared into the dining room before turning to Mrs. Wharton.

"Mr. Dunn is the estate manager, if I'm not mistaken. Why is he acting as the butler? Has Mr. Johns taken ill?"

"No, we asked for as little service staff as possible." She and I climbed the stairs, and at the half landing, beneath the portraits of Aunt Louise and Uncle Frederick that gazed down on us from opposing walls, I stopped her with a comment.

"I admit that surprises me greatly." As far as I knew, Mrs. Wharton had always been surrounded by servants, just as my Vanderbilt cousins were, or Mrs. Astor or any other member of the Four Hundred.

"This is to be an artistic holiday, Miss Cross. Having too many servants about would only be distracting. All we want is for someone to cook our meals, discreetly serve and clean up, and leave us to ourselves." Stained glass showered a rainbow of colors from the mullioned windows above us, bringing vivid life to the browns of the woodwork, the dark Persian rug, and the velvet sofa set into the wide bay of the half landing. Mrs. Wharton shielded her eyes from the brightness and preceded me to the upper half of the staircase. "You'll be surprised at how well we can do for ourselves. You might even mention it in your article. An artistic quirk, if you will."

I agreed that would make an interesting addition to the article. I followed her up, noticing how, as soon as she reached the top, her pace slowed, became almost dragging as she turned to the right and led me past the main bedrooms and through a doorway that had been propped open with a brass doorstop. Here the corridor jogged to the right and became narrower, while polished parquet woodwork gave way to plain floorboards. I judged we were now above the kitchen and pantries, and I followed Mrs. Wharton into a small bedroom furnished in utilitarian oak. A maid had placed my bags on a double bed framed in brass and was presently unpacking. Like the footman, I didn't know her well. In fact I recognized her only from my past visits to Rough Point. She placed a folded pile of my cotton underthings into a tall chest of drawers, followed by stockings and a few light scarves.

"I hope this will do and you won't see it as a slight," Mrs. Wharton said. "As a relative of the owner you should have one of the better rooms, but I'm afraid they've all been claimed. We all decided Randall should have Frederick's bedroom, since he's interested in purchasing the house."

"This is lovely," I assured her, and meant it. A bright quilt draped the bed, the morning sunlight animating a patchwork design that reminded me of stacks of books turned this way and that on library shelves. Such a coverlet would never have been found in the main bedrooms, but its homey touch made me smile and reminded me of the one I made with Nanny's help when I was twelve. Admittedly, mine paled by comparison. I also realized this quilt constituted the room's only source of heat, as there was no fireplace or heater. But there needn't be, I supposed, in a house used only in the summer months. A sturdy wardrobe, a plain dressing table furnished with a kerosene lamp, and a simple chair completed the room's luxuries and provided all I would need.

The maid turned to me. "Shall I hang your gowns in the wardrobe, Miss Cross?"

"I can manage, thank you."

She was a slim woman not many years older than myself, with small hands that darted quickly as she went about her tasks with barely a sound. She organized my toiletries in the dressing table and slipped out of the room so discreetly I didn't notice until after she had gone. If these artists wanted as little intrusion as possible, this woman would certainly perform her job well.

"I'll help you hang your gowns," Mrs. Wharton offered.

"That's all right. There isn't much to hang." Indeed, I'd brought one evening gown suitable for dinner, a muslin day dress, and a couple of skirts and shirtwaists I could wear interchangeably. I unpinned my boater and set it on the end table beside the bed, then sat to remove my lace-up boots and slip on the low-heeled house shoes I'd brought, a tad worn but with a lovely embroidered design. Lastly I removed my carriage jacket and replaced it with a tasseled scarf I tossed around my shoulders. "There, I believe I'm ready for luncheon. Shall we go down?"

From the doorway, a throat cleared. "Not just yet, Emma."

I gasped and nearly stumbled over my own feet. This was the second time today I'd utterly lost my equilibrium at the sound of a voice from my past.

"This is your surprise," Mrs. Wharton whispered. "I'll have Mr. Dunn hold lunch another twenty minutes or so." She hurried out of the room, leaving me to face this startling development alone.

Could an additional twenty minutes possibly be enough? Could two hours? Somehow I found the presence of mind to open my mouth. "Father?" For it was indeed my father who had spoken. A figure clothed in apricot muslin stood behind him, tentatively gazing over his shoulder at me. "Mother."

"Darling, we're here because we longed to see you." My mother reached across the sofa we presently occupied, she at one corner and me pressed against the armrest on the opposite side. We had traded embraces, but the distance that had separated us these four years could not be breached simply by occupying the same room again. Perhaps it was ungenerous of me, but I wanted explanations for this sudden and secretive appearance and so far none had been forthcoming, including my mother's present claim. The words were correct enough, but as for the sentiment behind them . . . Instinct told me there was much more to this reunion.

My father looked on from his stance near the front-facing window and uncharacteristically said little. I believed I understood why. Upon first seeing him moments ago, I had called him *Father*, a distinct departure from Dad, as I had typically addressed him in the more modern, familiar way. Now the word simply wouldn't form on my tongue. I would have liked to attribute the change to my having grown up in the ensuing years, and not to any simmering resentments on my part. *Father* felt more natural to me and I decided not to examine my motives too deeply.

Sunlight from outside framed him from behind, while the room's shadows obscured his features so that I couldn't guess what he might be thinking. Still, my brief view of him in the more revealing light of my bedroom had showed a few more wrinkles around his eyes than I remembered, a more silver sheen to his hair. He did, however, move with a young man's vigor that reminded me of his friend, Jack Parsons. The memory made me sad, so I forced my mind to concentrate on the present. I continued my perusal of my parents.

Mother's waistline had thickened a bit and a few light lines scored her forehead, but that was to be expected. Although my parents were now in their late forties, time had treated them well. Mother's sandy blond hair, so like my half brother Brady's, was pulled up in a chignon with a fringe of curls hanging loose to frame her face. The apricot day dress suited her coloring, especially her hazel eyes that mirrored my own in color. I could easily imagine candlelight shedding at least a decade from her actual age.

"Why didn't you send word you were coming?" I asked, not for the first time. "Why the furtiveness?"

"Furtiveness? Oh, darling." Mother's arm, draped across the sofa back, slid lower until her hand covered mine. I perceived an instant's hesitation, as if she couldn't quite decide whether or not to leave it there, before her fingers relaxed. "We wished to surprise you, that's all. And I see we succeeded."

Yes, they had. A suspicion of just this scenario had entered my mind several times this morning, but each time I dismissed the idea as too outlandish. Then again, earlier this summer they had wired me in hopes of my convincing Uncle Cornelius to extend them a loan. An emergency, they had said.

I slid my hand out from beneath my mother's with a feigned need to adjust my collar. "Does this have anything to do with your telegram in July?"

"How suspicious you are, Emmaline." Father stepped away from the window, moving closer and standing in front of the coffered mahogany paneling that lined the walls. I saw him more clearly now, and I found his smile forced, his gaze evasive. "Aren't you happy to see us?"

I breathed in and let it out slowly. "Yes, yes, I am. Very much so. I'm sorry if it seems otherwise but you did shock me with your abrupt entrance. Did you stop in on Brady in New York before heading north?"

"No, we didn't know he was there." Father fiddled with the shade of a porcelain figurine lamp on the table beside him. "We'd hoped to find him here."

I shook my head in bewilderment. "I haven't seen you in almost four years. Don't you realize you might have missed seeing me as well? I might have been away."

"Emma, darling, you never leave Newport." Mother

made the very notion sound ridiculous. "We knew you'd be here. Where else would you go?"

Italy sprang to mind. Derrick Andrews was in Italy. . . . But even as the thought formed, I cast it aside. If Derrick and I were meant to be together, we would be—when the time was right. My chasing him halfway around the world when he had pressing responsibilities there would only complicate matters.

"Perhaps Brady can make the trip up before we leave," Father said.

"I'm afraid that's highly doubtful on such short notice, especially as Uncle Cornelius is still unable to work and Neily is in Europe on his honeymoon. Brady is needed at the New York Central. Unless you intend staying longer than the duration of your retreat, or you make the trip back to New York afterward, I don't believe you'll see Brady at all."

"Perhaps we'll do just that," Mother said brightly. "We'll spend a few days in New York."

I narrowed my eyes at her. "How long *are* you planning to be in Newport, or in the country for that matter? Does this mean you've wearied of Paris?"

"We haven't exactly decided yet." She played with a fabric-covered button on her sleeve. "When our friends mentioned the trip, your father and I knew we had to take advantage of the opportunity to see you."

"With what funds?" I wouldn't let it go. Couldn't. I wasn't being the best of daughters, but something simply didn't *feel* right about this visit. "In July, all indications were that you were short of funds."

"Oh, that." Father waved a hand. "Yes, it's true we were rather in straits at the time and your mother . . . well . . . she panicked. But I've since sold a couple of paintings and everything is fine."

"But now maybe you can explain something, sweetheart."

Mother slid a few inches closer on the sofa. "Why are you staying on at Rough Point? You live nearby, and I'm sure you have plenty you must see to every day at Gull Manor. And don't you prefer solitude when you write your articles?"

My articles. Had Edith Wharton been untruthful? Perhaps it had been my parents who asked for me to report on the retreat—not someone who knew of me by reputation, but my own mother and father, well-meaning but unintentionally reducing a professional triumph to a vast disappointment. With an inner sigh I let my hopes of becoming the next Nellie Bly flitter away.

I concealed my letdown with a shrug and answered Mother's question. "Mrs. Wharton convinced me it would be a good idea to stay and . . . how did she put it? Ah, yes, and immerse myself in your artistic world."

"Perhaps Edith should learn to mind her own business," my father murmured.

Mother glanced over at him. "What was that, dear?"

"Nothing."

I pretended I hadn't heard him. "Will you be painting while you're here, Father?"

"I certainly plan to. Would you care to sit for me?"

Mother's face lit up at the suggestion. "Yes, Emma, you must. Let your father capture you as you are now. Darling, you've grown so beautiful. But still, I wonder at the wisdom of your staying at Rough Point."

"Why? Is there something I should know about your friends, Mother? Or perhaps something you don't wish me to know?"

"Oh, they're a lively bunch, to be sure," she replied, evading the question.

"Yes, Miss Marcus mentioned that earlier. But she certainly didn't indicate I'd be in any sort of peril." I said this only half jokingly, for my curiosity and determination to uncover facts had indeed led me into peril in the past. Mother and Father didn't know that. I had always glossed over such details in my letters.

"You might find us distracting," Father said, "when you're writing."

"That shouldn't be a problem. While I'm here, I'll primarily be taking notes. I've been instructed not to submit my article until the retreat is over." I paused to study them both. They were trying their hardest to appear natural, but there were volumes being left unsaid. I was more confused than ever. Why have the *Observer* send me here by day, only to send me packing each night with flimsy warnings of distractions and unruly friends?

I stood, prompting Mother to assume a look of mild alarm.

"Where are you going?"

I smiled down at her and offered my hand to help her to her feet. "To luncheon, of course. You do realize the others must be famished by now." And since I thoroughly doubted I would be enlightened any further at the present time, remaining upstairs would serve no good purpose.

The group, now complete with all nine of its members having settled in, gathered for luncheon in the dining room, which faced the rear lawns. Unlike Gull Manor, which occupied a promontory only yards above sea level, Rough Point sat high on the cliffs, away from the briny reek of low tide. Open windows admitted cool breezes that carried the distant lull of the ocean and the hum of bees in the elaborate flowerbeds closer to the house.

Although I had been allocated a servant's bedroom, my role had subtly changed since I had first entered the estate. This morning I came as a journalist to write about the retreat

around the table for approbation, which she received from several quarters, though not all. The Whartons appeared appalled at this turn in the conversation, and Niccolo Lionetti looked apologetic, as though he'd like to agree with Miss Marcus but had never yet experienced the disdain of his audience. Vasili Pavlenko, the fair-haired former dancer, grumbled something into his hand, and though I couldn't be certain I'd have wagered the Russian words were an oath, and a vehement one at that.

I couldn't have been the only one who heard, but the others pretended they hadn't. Father set down his fork. "It does happen, Randall. The only cure is to keep working at your craft."

"If I might ask—" Ask *again,* I thought—"What is your craft, Sir Randall?"

"It is—was—"

"*Do* stop the dramatics." Josephine thrust her napkin to the table and tensed as if about to push back her chair and abandon the table. A throat-clearing stopped her; it came from Niccolo. Their gazes met across the table, hers sparking with anger, his dark and calm. He raised an eyebrow, smiled slightly, and Josephine slid her napkin back into her lap.

Thoroughly flummoxed, I wished to demand that these people explain themselves. Mother caught my eye, rolled her own a little, and shook her head. I relaxed. After all, I had been warned, hadn't I? I'd grown accustomed in recent years to the meticulous manners of my Vanderbilt cousins and other members of the Four Hundred. I had little experience of artists, and I supposed one must accept their stormy temperaments as part of their charms. Although the idea of describing this bunch as *charming* produced a chuckle I barely managed to stifle.

"My dear, I am a sculptor very much in need of new inspiration." Sir Randall gestured to the scene outside the windows. "I am hoping to find it here on your rocky island and your steep cliffs."

"I'm sure you will, Sir Randall. Those same views are what inspired my father to become a painter. Aren't they, Father?" For some reason he avoided my gaze and Mother let out a strained giggle. The others went right on eating. "Of course," I continued, "there must be equally stunning views all over Europe. What brought you all to America?"

"I have concerts in Philadelphia and New York, signorina," Niccolo said in his lyrical accent. "I am to be playing at the Car-ne . . . Carneggy . . ."

"Carnegie Hall?" I supplied, and he nodded happily.

"And I am considering bringing my new staging of *Carmen* to your Metropolitan Opera House." Claude Baptiste raised his wine goblet, his hawkish nose almost touching the liquid as he sipped. "Do you care for opera, Miss Cross?"

"I do, though I don't often have the pleasure." A thought occurred to me, and eagerly I asked, "Is that what brought you as well, Miss Marcus? Will you be Monsieur Baptiste's Carmen?"

Once again, as if it were a gauntlet, Miss Marcus threw her napkin to the table. "No, I shall not be." She slid her chair back and sprang to her feet, and with her blond curls dancing and her bosom jiggling, she swept from the room.

"Oh, dear . . . I'm very sorry. . . ."

"Never mind, Miss Cross." Mrs. Wharton took a roll from the silver basket and passed the rest to me. "As Josephine herself told you earlier, we are a lively group."

My father raised his glass. "To our lively group."

When luncheon ended the group scattered. My parents, as well as some of the others, had unpacking to finish, and Niccolo retired to his room to play his cello. Even through his closed door, the deeply sweet notes drifted through the upper hallway and down the stairs. I stood alone for some minutes in the Stair Hall, my hand resting atop the banister's ornamental finial. As I listened, I thought how incongruent his playing was to the contentious meal I'd witnessed. There seemed to be a dynamic I didn't understand at work here, that didn't resemble anything I'd encountered before. My Vanderbilt relatives argued, certainly, and this summer one of those arguments had yielded dire results, but there were always reasons one could point to, sources of the discontent. This group, however, seemed to thrive on discord. I believed they enjoyed it. Did it provide fuel, perhaps passion, for their art? I wondered, and then doubted as I considered their continual evasiveness. Something was wrong here, and my journalist's heart yearned to discover what it was.

Voices from another room at first blended with the plaintive notes of Niccolo's cello, but after another moment they became quite distinct from the music. The sound drew me to the doorway of the dining room, which should have been empty at this hour. It was far too early for Mr. Dunn and Carl to be setting up for dinner, and there was no reason for guests to be in there. Yet when I peeked in I realized the voices did not emanate from the dining room at all, but from an adjoining office that faced the front lawns.

"Randall, no one was pandering to you, I promise," a female voice said. "Your work is brilliant. No, do not rumble at me. Your sculptures have shown cunning and innovation. If anything, you are ahead of your time and your recent audiences have failed to understand your meaning."

"I don't know. . . ."

I tiptoed into the westernmost end of the dining room, but did not crane my neck to peek around the elaborate moldings framing the office doorway. I didn't have to, as I recognized both voices well enough.

"I do know," Mrs. Wharton said, "and furthermore, I

think you should buy Rough Point. Stay away from Europe for a time. Americans are much more amenable to change. In fact, we embrace change and progress in a way your stodgy Europeans never will."

"Ah, Mrs. Wharton, you cannot convince me you find the Parisians stodgy." There was a touch of laughter in Sir Randall's voice.

Mrs. Wharton laughed as well. "You are correct, but Paris is an altogether different matter. I—"

"Is that my wife I hear?"

If the voice behind me wasn't enough to send my heart thudding in my throat, the hand that gripped my shoulder and drew me aside prompted me into a defensive stance. My fingers stiffened, and I very nearly resorted to a self-defense tactic I'd learned last summer by thrusting them tips-first into the Adam's apple of the man who had sneaked up on me. The act would have sent my attacker coughing and stumbling backward while I prepared to strike again, but I forestalled my assault as I recognized, not an imminent threat, but merely Teddy Wharton.

"I—uh—that is . . ." I stuttered as I groped to explain why I had been standing near a doorway listening in on his wife's conversation. Yet here before me was not the mild gentleman I'd met during luncheon. He wasn't merely inquiring as to the whereabouts of his wife. He clearly seethed, his eyes sharp and bright against the room's dark woodwork. I thought all that anger must be directed at me, yet before I could utter another word, he strode past me into the office.

"Edith, I've been searching for you. What are you doing here?"

"Teddy." Mrs. Wharton sounded surprised, but not unduly disquieted. "Randall and I were discussing his future. Help me persuade him to stay on in Newport."

"Randall's future is his own concern. Come. I need you elsewhere."

I seized the opportunity to turn and flee. My pattering steps took me across the Great Hall and into the drawing room. Would Teddy Wharton think I'd been eavesdropping—as indeed I had been? But what had sent him in pursuit of his wife in such a rude manner? Surely he couldn't think she and Sir Randall . . .

Suddenly I regretted my snooping. I had hoped to glean some clue as to what drove this odd group with its many idiosyncrasies, but had I simply made my presence known and joined in Sir Randall and Mrs. Wharton's conversation, I might now be able to provide Mr. Wharton with proof that his wife's moments with Sir Randall had not, in fact, been a tryst.

Chapter 3

Having decided I would do best to mind my business when it came to the domestic affairs of Rough Point's current inhabitants, I took my pencil and tablet and sought the relative privacy of the library. Of the first floor's public rooms, this was the only one that overlooked the drive and front lawns, and I understood why my relatives had chosen this location for their library. The view here of trees and flowerbeds elicited a peacefulness conducive to reading, while the rear vista of windswept hillocks, rocky cliffs, and restless ocean inspired one to toss down one's book in favor of a brisk tramp across the promontory.

I selected an armchair that faced an open window. To my right, French doors that opened onto a covered piazza filled the room with sunlight but still couldn't quite banish the shadows hunched in the corners of the room. I began making notes on the only uncontroversial topic I could think of: my impressions of Niccolo Lionetti's cello playing.

I hadn't been writing long when Sir Randall shuffled in from the drawing room. He stopped when he saw me. "I thought

I'd search out a good book, but I don't wish to disturb you, Miss Cross."

"Not at all. Join me, please." My pencil came to rest. "I was just attempting to capture in words the essence of Signore Lionetti's talents, and failing miserably, I'm afraid. Perhaps you'll tell me a bit about your sculptures."

"I suppose that is why you're here, isn't it?"

He ambled over and chose an armchair set at a comfortable angle to my own. The open windows admitted the heady perfume of late-season roses, and the light breeze stirred my hair. In the room's tranquil environment I felt comfortably at home, but it seemed to take an effort for Sir Randall to settle in. He tugged here at his tie, there at his cuffs. Finally, he regarded me with a careworn expression.

"What would you like to know, Miss Cross?"

"Well . . ." I picked up my pencil again. "Sculpture seems a much more rigorous pursuit when compared to sketching or watercolors. What first attracted you to the endeavor?"

He gave a small laugh, as if he found my question amusing. "My mother dabbled in the arts, Miss Cross, and she encouraged me to explore. I was hopeless with paints, but stone, clay, wood—I somehow had a knack for creating lifelike images."

"And from what I gathered at luncheon, you've been successful at it."

"Yes, for a time. But I grew weary of lifelike images. I thought, what is the point in portraying something as we might already see it in nature? It is merely a copy, an imitation. Rather like photography, which has its uses but in my opinion is no kind of artwork."

"And so you changed your technique?"

"Right you are, Miss Cross. Have you seen the work of the Impressionists?"

"You refer to the paintings? Yes, of course." My parents

had taken me to an exhibit in New York years ago, and there had even been a collection here in a Newport gallery. "My father admires them greatly."

"As do I, Miss Cross." His fingers opened and closed around the arms of his chair, and his foot thudded repeatedly against the rug in a bout of nervous energy. "They sparked a new passion in me, and I began to experiment with more abstract designs, new proportions, angles not typically found in nature."

"It sounds exciting." I quickly made note of the terms he used to describe his methods.

"It *was* exciting . . . until the first exhibit. The others tried to convince me one cannot be discouraged by one poor showing, and so I weathered on. But the response was the same everywhere. The audience *loathed* my new work, and the critics agreed." He released a breath, gazing down at his feet as he shook his head.

"I'm so sorry." I groped for something useful to say. "You could always return to the sort of sculptures people liked."

"Move backward, to what now feels hollow and pointless?"

"Oh." My own spirits sagged. My father had had days like this, I suddenly remembered, when he'd felt devoid of both talent and a future as an artist. I hadn't been able to be of much comfort to him then, and I doubted my ability to counteract Sir Randall's downheartedness now. So I merely said, "Then you should continue with what you love, for yourself, and the critics and everyone else be damned." I said this last word in a whisper, and hoped Sir Randall would take no offense.

"Good heavens, my girl, you *are* Arthur Cross's daughter, aren't you?" A chuckle became a guffaw, a sound that carried the first authentic enjoyment I had heard from his lips. "Yes, yes, that's exactly what I should do. Good heavens."

He slapped his thighs and came to his feet. "I believe I'm going to have a sherry, and then take a stroll down to that Cliff Walk of yours. Would you care to join me in either?"

"As a matter of fact . . ." I had been about to accept his offer of a stroll, when a streak of brown and white outside the front windows caught my eye. Rising ire pushed me out of my seat. "I'll have to join you in a bit, Sir Randall. There is something I must attend to first."

"Is something wrong, Miss Cross?"

"Indeed there is."

"Patch, come here this instant!"

With energetic leaps, that brown and white blur I'd glimpsed from the library darted past me a third time. I stood with my hands on my hips and arranged my features into my most disapproving expression, until my itinerant pup grew tired of trying to coax an obviously stubborn human to play. He bounded over to me on the gravel drive and jumped several feet in the air before returning to all fours and nudging my hand with his snout.

I refused to give in. "No, I will not pet you! You're supposed to be home. How did you get here?" Though his soft brown eyes showed no trace of guilt and beamed only love up at me, the answer was obvious. "You followed me when I returned here with Mrs. Wharton, didn't you, you sneak? And then you hid so I couldn't bring you straight home."

My accusations only prompted Patch to sit and lift a front paw, a trick Katie had spent hours teaching him. When I didn't lean to "shake his hand," he waved the appendage and tilted his head, ears flopping to one side, as if to make his message clearer to this rather dimwitted human before him.

I sank to a crouch. "You're a very bad boy, you know that." But while my words chastised, my tone did not, and soon Patch rolled onto his back and presented his belly to be scratched. I obliged. As with orphaned babies and young women in crises, it appeared dogs were yet another weakness of mine. And how does one remain angry with an exuberant, silky-furred creature with great floppy ears and a warm, soulful gaze that proclaimed you the most important being in all the world?

"I'm beginning to think you're part fox terrier." I increased the speed of my ministrations until Patch's eyes rolled backward in bliss. "You're certainly as clever, determined, and naughty as one." To his dismay I stopped petting him and pushed to my feet. "But what to do with you?"

With a quick roll he achieved a four-footed stance and gave a breathy little *woof*.

"The house is full of people, I'll have you know, and I am hardly in a position to ask them to tolerate an unexpected visitor."

His tail wagged furiously.

"I suppose I might ask the staff if they'd mind looking after you while I'm busy. *If* you promise to behave."

As if comprehending my meaning, he stilled his tail and primly sat.

I pursed my lips as I regarded him. "Come along. We'll telephone home to let them know you're safe and then I'll make arrangements for you to be fed, not that you deserve it, you minx."

In a moment he was up and vaulting across the lawns, first in the wrong direction, then doubling back and dashing out ahead of me when he understood my direction to be the kitchen wing. But I found myself lagging behind. Faintly, for Niccolo Lionetti's room lay on the other side of the house, delicate notes sang their way through the open windows. I felt as though gossamer, fragrant petals rained down around me, encompassing my being and blotting out everything but the wondrous melody—Vivaldi, I thought it must be—rendered by the Italian's skillful hands. I marveled at the sheer beauty of it, despaired of ever being able to describe it in words, and found myself wishing the sound would never cease.

Patch barked to regain my attention and broke the spell. In the service wing, I found Mr. Dunn and explained the situation, whereupon he promised to inform the cook, the footman, and the maid that a bowl of scraps should be set out for him each day. I then used the telephone in the butler's pantry to apprise Nanny of the situation. She tsked at the same time she chuckled. I could all but see her smile.

After chastising Patch to explore the grounds but stay out of trouble, I made my way back across the house to the library. Several voices greeted me, Sir Randall's among them.

I also heard Josephine Marcus. "All this moping ill suits you, Randall, and will avail you nothing."

"But that is what I'm trying to tell you, Josephine. I've done with moping. I've gained a new perspective—"

"Since luncheon?" A mocking burst of laughter followed. "Pray, tell us, what brought on this miracle?"

"Josephine, do not belittle Randall's change of heart. It is a good thing, a thing to be encouraged, no?" At the sound of the exotic voice I realized I had no longer heard Niccolo's perfectly formed notes as I walked through the house. He was now in the library with Miss Marcus and Sir Randall, and seemed to be mediating an argument between the other two.

I hesitated before joining them. What right did I have to intrude upon matters I knew little about and had no stake in? My job was to report on the creativity of the group, not compose a scathing gossip column.

"One would almost believe you don't wish to see me roused from my doldrums, Josephine."

Snide female laughter answered Sir Randall's observation. "I wish to see you move on and stop whining. Either be successful or accept your failure."

"Josephina, that is most unkind—" Niccolo said, but even as I silently applauded him, Sir Randall interrupted.

"I don't need you to defend me, Niccolo."

I knew so little of these people. In all likelihood their contention was so deep-rooted, no one person could be held to blame, neither Josephine nor Sir Randall. Yet, perhaps because Sir Randall had identified me as my father's daughter—yes, that still meant something to me—or perhaps because I understood what it was to aspire to greater things than people expected or wished to expect, I could not stand by and watch a man maligned for the ambitions of his heart.

I swept into the room. "Sir Randall, I apologize for my sudden departure earlier. I hope we might further discuss your artwork. I'm fascinated by your ideas about form and your abstract interpretation of reality, and I'm very much hoping you'll begin a new sculpture before you leave Rough Point. I would so enjoy the pleasure of familiarizing myself with your process."

With a thrust of my chin I dared Josephine Marcus to utter a contrary word. Her mouth had twitched as I spoke of *form* and *interpretation*, as if she found it ludicrous to attach such importance to Sir Randall's work. My gaze shifted to Niccolo Lionetti. He looked relieved to see an end to the prickly conversation. I wondered why Sir Randall had not taken kindly to the musician's attempt to mediate. Perhaps Sir Randall had merely been angry enough to lash out at anyone.

Except me, apparently, for in a kindly voice he said, "My dear, I would be delighted to hear your opinion on my work. But I must first find my inspiration."

I smiled and nodded, and then in an attempt to diffuse the

situation, I turned my attention to Niccolo. "Your playing is wonderful, signore. I don't know much about music other than that I enjoy it greatly. I do hope you'll perform for us some evening."

"I would be honored, signorina. Perhaps tonight."

With a possessive gesture, Josephine slipped a hand into the crook of his arm. "You have been doubly treated, Miss Cross. The cello you heard Niccolo playing was made by Signore Domenico Montagnana. Do you know what that means?"

Was there a challenge inherent in her question? A touch of condescension? I refused to react to either. And luckily for me, I had once attended a parlor concert at The Breakers that featured a Montagnana violin. "It means the cello in question is among the finest in the world, on a par with those made by Antonio Stradivari."

Her nostrils flared, a sure sign of disappointment that she had not bested me. Yet her hauteur persisted. "To put it in simplistic terms, yes. But it is so much more than a mere instrument. It is a mingling of souls, Miss Cross, that of its maker and of the musician." A glowing passion ignited behind her eyes, an unfeigned fervor that took me aback. "But perhaps that is a bit too poetic for your reporter's tastes." She lifted an eyebrow, having clearly judged me unable to grasp such a concept.

Perhaps she was correct—perhaps my musical sensibilities had yet to develop sufficiently for me to fully appreciate the communion of musician and instrument, but that was something I hoped to remedy, at least in part, during the course of the retreat. "I am grateful for the opportunity to expand my tastes, Miss Marcus." I turned to the young man. "Do you own the cello, signore?"

"*Mio Dio.*" He pressed a long-fingered hand to his breastbone. "The instrument belongs to my patron—"

"Who shall remain nameless, Miss Cross." Miss Marcus

tightened her hold on Niccolo's arm and pressed closer to his side. "At the gentleman's insistence. You understand."

Her inference, of course, seemed to be that she knew the identity of this patron, but that I was not worthy enough to be trusted with the information. "I understand the need for discretion, Miss Marcus. My article is to be a cultural piece, not an exposé."

Color suffused Sir Randall's face as he eyed Miss Marcus and Niccolo. I thought of Sir Randall and Mrs. Wharton talking together earlier in the office, and how Teddy Wharton had stormed in to break up their tête-à-tête. I could not but conclude jealousy had been a factor. Was the same dynamic at work here? Did envy run rampant among this group?

Good heavens, I began to believe myself inadequate to the task of deciphering these people's social entanglements. Once again I resolved to focus on their art and nothing more.

"Sir Randall, would you like to take that walk now?"

He surprised me with a shake of his head. "If you wouldn't mind, Miss Cross, I'd prefer to walk alone for now."

I said nothing, merely stepped aside so he could pass. He was halfway across the drawing room when Josephine called out to him.

"Perhaps you'd like Niccolo and me to accompany you." A little sneer curved her rouged lips. Niccolo, perhaps unconsciously, raised a hand and pressed it to hers. A caution?

An awkward moment ensued while Sir Randall regarded the pair with ill-concealed distaste. Then he continued on his way. The terrace doors closed quietly behind him. I watched him descend the patio steps outside and disappear until he reached the rocky upswell in the lawn. He halted abruptly and leaned low. Had he tripped? My body tensed in preparation of hurrying outside to offer assistance. But no, swirls of brown and white leaped into view and flashed in the sun. Patch had apparently introduced himself to Sir Randall. Judging by how the pair continued toward the Cliff Walk together, Patch's overtures of friendship had been readily accepted.

I smiled. If anyone could lift a person out of his doldrums, as Sir Randall had put it, my boisterous pup certainly could.

A whisper behind me doused my smile. Miss Marcus was leaning to speak into the young Italian's ear. I was reminded of naughty schoolchildren telling secrets in class and felt little compunction about interrupting.

"Why are you unkind to him?"

She looked baffled for a moment, while Niccolo assumed an expression fast becoming familiar, one of innocence mingled with slightly perplexed incomprehension, as if he didn't quite understand English in all its nuances—which I was fairly certain he did.

Miss Marcus's frown cleared. She made a two-fingered gesture, prompting Niccolo to reach into his inner coat pocket. He slid out a silver case and flicked it open. Miss Marcus plucked a pre-rolled cigarette from a nearly full row. Was she trying to shock me? Respectable women didn't smoke, at least not openly, but I had seen it before.

Niccolo took one for himself and scraped a wooden match against the striker on the side of the case to light both. I was never fond of tobacco smoke, and the clouds swirling about their heads quickly set my nose itching. My gaze went instinctively and pointedly to the piazza outside the library's French windows, but the other two failed to take the hint.

Miss Marcus puffed several times, most of the smoke thankfully drifting out the open windows behind her. "You misunderstand, Miss Cross. I don't mean to be unkind to Randall, but to encourage him." She puffed again, sending out fluffy white clouds while Niccolo exhaled long streams of gray through his nose. A pair of dragons, literally and figuratively.

"If you'll pardon me for saying so," I persisted, perhaps unwisely, "he was feeling encouraged until you said those things to him."

She simpered and smoothed her skirts with little flicks of her hand. "I'm afraid you don't understand our Randall. He isn't like the rest of us. For one, he isn't a professional, not in the sense I am, or Niccolo or your father. Our livelihood depends on our art, whereas Randall has a fortune and an estate back in England."

As Niccolo nodded his agreement, I shook my head. "I don't understand what difference that makes to a person's self-confidence."

"My dear, the rest of us understand the ups and downs of an artistic career." To my vast irritation, she leaned forward and flicked the ash at the end of her cigarette into a lovely Capodimonte vase, carved with lifelike ribbons and flowers. Though not terribly invaluable—for Aunt Louise had emptied the house of its true treasures—it was a darling piece and certainly not intended for the use Miss Marcus currently assigned to it. "We grasp the ebb and flow of an artist's popularity," she said with a haughty sniff. "Randall doesn't. His sculpture and his ego are intricately tied together."

"And a professional artist's isn't?" If anyone possessed an unduly large ego, I thought, it was the woman before me. Still, I couldn't deny a growing interest in hearing more about the inner workings of an artist's psyche. Such details would add substance to my article. First I pushed the porcelain vase out of reach and replaced it with a more suitable silent butler of etched silver with an ivory handle. Then I took a seat facing the pair.

"Perhaps at first, when we are young and starting out," she said after another contemplative waft of smoke. "But experience makes us wiser, Miss Cross. Randall began dabbling in the arts much later in life, and being a man used to having his way with a snap of his fingers—the European nobility is like that, you see—he simply isn't equipped to accept those momentary lapses in public interest. Besides, his latest works have been rather hideous." She turned to Niccolo for consensus, but the young man only shrugged and smiled apologetically at me.

I raised a quizzical eyebrow. "And you feel disparaging him is an effective means of urging that acceptance?"

Miss Marcus snuffed out her cigarette and came to her feet. I'd clearly gone too far, been too impertinent. "You know, you very much remind me of your father, Miss Cross. It must be the Vanderbilt in you." She didn't bother to elaborate on what traits she felt were characteristic of my father's side of the family. She looked down at her companion. "Come."

As if *she* had snapped her fingers, he surged to his feet and together they went, where I didn't know or care, for all that I had been a great fan of the opera singer until approximately ten minutes ago. I probably wouldn't be obtaining much more in the way of artistic insights from Miss Marcus, if she deigned to speak to me at all again. So be it. Sir Randall might be a member of the English nobility, a wealthy man used to having his way, but something in him—vulnerability, sadness, a sense of brokenness—aroused an instinct that made me rear my head. Call it a demand for fairness. Call it plain stubbornness. A Vanderbilt trait? Yes, and one that had served me well through the years.

Even so, a small part of me wished this story had been given into the inept hands of my nemesis at the *Observer*, Ed Billings. Having to make heads or tails out of this situation would have served him right.

In the meantime, I picked up the Capodimonte vase and brought it to the kitchen for a good soak.

* * *

With a knock, Mother opened my bedroom door and peeked in. "I thought I'd see if you needed any help, darling. What are you wearing?" Her eyes lighted on the individual who had arrived in my room about twenty minutes earlier. "Edith. I didn't realize you were in here." Mother's expression begged for an explanation, though her breeding would not permit her to ask.

I saw no reason to keep her in suspense. "Come in, Mother. Mrs. Wharton was just reading a passage in her manuscript to me as I dressed."

"I see." Mother assessed the other woman, perched with her very upright posture at the edge of the bed. She attempted a smile. "I didn't know the two of you were so well acquainted."

"We aren't really," Mrs. Wharton said, setting the pages of her manuscript aside. "Until this morning we had never spoken more than those few words of greeting when I met your daughter all those years ago. I had seen her at various functions here in Newport, of course, but never had reason to speak directly." Her brow furrowed as she shifted her gaze to me. "Now that I think of it, it seems rather odd that a society reporter never found an opportunity to interview me. You weren't avoiding me, Miss Cross, were you?"

I turned back to the swivel mirror above the dressing table and patted my simple coif, a braid coiled at my nape. "Not at all," I lied. "Merely happenstance, one I'm very glad has been rectified."

"And I, too." She looked from me to Mother, still hovering near the threshold and looking uncertain. Mrs. Wharton rose and retrieved her manuscript, hugging it to her. "I'll leave you two alone. I'm sure you have quite a number of matters you'd like to discuss."

I continued inspecting myself in the mirror. I wore the one and only evening dress I had brought, consisting of tiers of beaded lace topped with an embroidered silk jacket cinched tight at the waist, both of the same champagne color.

"That's lovely." Mother moved farther into the room, as if she had needed Mrs. Wharton to vacate the space before being able to stake her own claim. As she took in my attire, her gaze once again assessed and questioned.

"It's one of Cousin Gertrude's," I explained, giving a tug to straighten the jacket and allow the wide lace collar to fall evenly over each shoulder. "From the House of Rouff. She virtually emptied her dressing room before shopping for her wedding trousseau this summer."

"And it all went to you?" Did a slight twinge of envy accompany the question? Perhaps, but the longing in her eyes didn't seem directed at the dress, but at me. Did she resent the place my father's relatives held in my life? Did she believe they had supplanted her and Father in my affections?

Perhaps my parents should not have stayed away so long, then.

I hid my thoughts by smiling at her through the mirror. "No. Much will be tailored for Gladys, and other pieces were dispersed among younger cousins and even the servants."

"Servants, in dresses like that?"

I straightened and turned around, my chin held a notch higher than was typical. "Perhaps they do what I do with many of Gertrude's castoffs, which is to sell them. Just two or three of those dresses will keep Gull Manor in coal and kerosene for the winter. The rest will provide many a hot meal at St. Nicolas Orphanage. But this"—I smoothed my hands down the jacket's lace and satin front—"I can wear as an ensemble or without the jacket, or pair the jacket with other gowns. It will serve well when I need to look my best."

"You certainly do tonight, darling. We have some time before dinner is served. I'd hoped we might talk, just the two of us."

"As a matter of fact . . ." I gestured to the bed, and we sat side by side. "What can you tell me about Josephine Marcus and Sir Randall?"

"I beg your pardon?"

"I mean about the rancor with which Miss Marcus treats Sir Randall. I witnessed a bit of a tongue lashing today, and I fail to understand it. Is there a long-standing contention between them?"

"I see." She sighed. This was not the conversation she'd hoped to have with me—that much was obvious. But neither was I ready for mother-daughter confidences. It was too soon, and I sought the safety of a more neutral topic. "Don't judge Josephine too harshly. She has her own disappointments to contend with, though she won't speak of them. It's made her generally resentful. I believe when Sir Randall expresses his own frustrations, it grates on Josephine no end."

"Isn't her career going well?"

"It *was*. But things have begun to slow for her in Europe." Her gaze darted to the door and she lowered her voice. "Can you keep a secret?"

"Always, I assure you."

"Josephine was hoping Claude Baptiste would cast her as Carmen at the Metropolitan Opera House. It would mean a triumphant American homecoming for her."

"Monsieur Baptiste told me he was only *considering* staging the production in New York."

"Claude likes to tease. He pretends to hesitate, but everyone knows in the end he'll accept the Metropolitan's offer."

"But he won't cast Miss Marcus? Why ever not?"

"I don't know, neither has confided in me. I reach my conclusions judging by Josephine's demeanor. If Claude *had* agreed to cast her, she would have told us by now. Josephine is not one to play coy, not when it comes to her career."

"Interesting . . ." In a single afternoon I'd witnessed discord between the Whartons, Sir Randall, Miss Marcus, and even Niccolo Lionetti, for I hadn't forgotten Sir Randall's retort when the young musician attempted to intercede on his behalf. And now the stage director, Claude Baptiste, apparently made up part of the unsavory mix. I couldn't help but wonder about the former dancer, Vasili Pavlenko, of whom I had seen so little thus far. What kept him so busy in his rooms all afternoon? For that matter, I really hadn't seen much of Claude Baptiste either. Neither man had shown his face downstairs since luncheon.

What kind of associations had my parents made in Europe? And with so many resentments between them, what on earth led them to believe spending an artists' holiday together in this isolated house, at a time when Newport emptied of society and settled in for the winter, would yield benefits of any sort?

"Mother, why *are* you all here?"

At that moment the dinner gong sounded from downstairs. To my frustration, Mother smiled and rushed to the door as fast as her beribboned satin shoes could take her. "We'll talk more later, darling."

Chapter 4

Sir Randall didn't appear for dinner, though my father's reassurances put to rest my own and anyone else's concerns. "Yes, I passed Sir Randall coming out of his room about an hour ago. He held a sketch pad under one arm and a fistful of pencils. He said he would eat something later, that he wished to make some rough sketches of the coastline before the sun went down. Then he dashed away."

"I suppose he found his inspiration, then, though one wonders where a sculptor can find his muse in all that water." Josephine Marcus's tone clearly dismissed the idea as invalid.

"One would imagine a sculptor's inspiration lies in the nooks and crannies of the cliff face," Claude Baptiste said around a mouthful of fillet béarnaise.

"Let us hope he does not lean over too far to inspect that cliff face." Josephine Marcus sniggered meanly and with a lift of an eyebrow, looked over at me. My face burned with ire, but I refused to return her gaze. Across the table from me, Teddy Wharton chortled. Mrs. Wharton looked mortified by his lack of discretion. My parents and the others went on eating as if they hadn't heard.

After supper ended, the men went into the Great Hall and moved the gilded chairs from against the walls into a semicircle in front of the room's towering bay of windows. Another chair, armless, had been centered within the bay, and Niccolo Lionetti's borrowed Montagnana cello waited beside it, safely enclosed in its case.

We had yet to take our seats and I moved into the drawing room to peer out the French doors. I saw no sign of Sir Randall against the twilit sky. It would soon be dark in earnest, and unsafe to wander the Cliff Walk. An idea sent me scurrying across the house to the servants' wing. In the dining room, Irene and Carl were cleaning away the remnants of dinner. I waited for Irene to pass by with her rattling burden of dinner dishes. I followed her through the pantry into the scullery.

"May I do something for you, miss?" she asked as she set the tray down on the work counter beside the wide sink, lined in wood to prevent delicate porcelain from chipping.

"I wondered if you'd seen my dog lately?"

She turned on the faucet. "Why yes, miss. He ate his bowl of scraps, and happy he was to have them, before setting out across the lawns. I don't know where to, miss. Is it a cause for concern? Ought I to have brought him into the servants' porch?"

"No, I just wondered . . . Perhaps Patch is with Sir Randall," I mused aloud. That the two might be together alleviated my growing fears for Sir Randall's safety. Patch might be unruly and ill-disciplined, but he had also proved himself as sure-footed as a goat, leaping from boulder to boulder along Gull Manor's peninsula. There had been times watching him when my heart had literally thrust up into my throat, so sure I had been he'd fall in the water, only to see him lithely maneuver the terrain with joyful yips and barks.

At that moment the cook, a Mrs. Harris, cried out from the main kitchen. Irene and I traded startled looks before hoisting our hems and hurrying in to see what was the matter. Mrs. Harris was chuckling when we arrived and leaning over to pet Patch.

"He's a sneaky baggage," she explained when Irene and I skidded to halts by the center worktable. "I took the garbage to the bins outside, and he must have slipped in behind me. Didn't see him until he brushed against my legs just now. Gave me quite a fright, the naughty boy."

"I'm so sorry." I circled the table and caught hold of my precocious mutt's collar. He twisted around to sniff at me and deliver a welcoming lick. "I don't have a leash—he wasn't supposed to be here, you see. But perhaps there might be some rope I could use."

"Nonsense," Mrs. Harris chided. I released Patch and he trotted back to the woman. He stood on his hind legs and placed his paws on her thighs, panting for more caresses as if his life depended on it. Such a flimflam artist, that dog of mine. The trouble was, no one at home felt inclined to teach him the error of his ways. Mrs. Harris accommodated his request with her sturdy hands and a hearty laugh. "I'll watch out for him, miss. So long as he keeps out of the larder and doesn't pilfer anything meant for the dining room, he and I shall be fast friends."

"If you're certain . . ." I felt it was a lot to ask a woman who already had enough to do seeing after meals for eight guests—or rather nine, including myself—plus the four members of the staff.

"Go on, miss. We'll be just fine. Won't we, Irene?"

The girl smiled broadly. "He's a sweetie, that's for certain."

I hesitated before returning to the main portion of the house. "Did you by any chance see Sir Randall Clifford return with Patch? They were exploring the Cliff Walk together earlier."

"A guest, at the service entrance, miss?"

I saw her point. Then again, he might enter the house this way after tramping about the Cliff Walk. "Well, thank you both. Patch, you be a good boy."

I nodded at Carl as I crossed the dining room and glanced again at the fading view outside the windows. Perhaps Sir Randall was at this moment in his bedroom changing for the evening's entertainment.

On my way back to the Great Hall I came upon Miss Marcus and Claude Baptiste standing in the recessed portion of the Stair Hall beneath the half landing. A single electric lamp illuminated the space, dimmed by a beaded and embroidered chinoiserie shade. Their tones were hushed and urgent, but three words spoken by Miss Marcus hissed their way to my ears: *production . . . Vasili . . . revenge*.

I paused in the doorway of the dining room. My mother had spoken of Monsieur Baptiste's production of *Carmen* and the fact that he would not cast Miss Marcus in the lead role. Were they arguing about it now? Mother hadn't said anything about Vasili Pavlenko *or* revenge. At the sound of footsteps treading the stairs, I looked up to see Edith Wharton descending in a lovely rose velvet evening gown. She, too, must have heard the voices, perhaps from the half landing, for she grazed me with a look of exasperation before making the sharp turn from the bottom of the steps to where the other two, oblivious of their audience, continued their debate.

Mrs. Wharton spoke in an undertone. "Josephine, dear, others can hear you. You must learn not to make such scenes."

Monsieur Baptiste pinched his thin lips together, his eyes becoming small above his hawkish nose.

"My life is about scenes, Edith," Miss Marcus said with all the melodrama of an operatic heroine. "Scenes are my vocation, or had you forgotten. Claude here certainly has, for he is determined to disregard me at every turn. It would seem the concept of friendship eludes him." Miss Marcus noticed me then, for she craned her neck to see around Mrs. Wharton and raised her voice to address me. "You may write *that* in your article, Miss Cross."

Oh dear. I deserved being called out for eavesdropping yet again. But if someone didn't wish their conversation to be overheard, they should not hold them in public places.

Once again loud enough for me to hear, Mrs. Wharton said, "Yes, well, stabbing friends in the back happens to be a specialty of Claude's. You're not the only one of us to feel the sting of his unkindness between your shoulder blades. You must remember that, Josephine."

While Monsieur Baptiste blanched, Mrs. Wharton whirled about and retraced her steps to me. She rather roughly linked her arm through mine. "Come, Miss Cross. Niccolo will begin shortly."

Before we crossed into the Great Hall, another of Miss Marcus's whispers lashed out behind us. "Admit it, Claude, it's because of Vasili, isn't it? Because you and Vasili blame the rest of us for what happened."

If Claude Baptiste responded to the charge, I didn't hear him.

"What was that about?" I whispered to Mrs. Wharton before we reached the seating area. We paused in the glow of the great stone fireplace, brought here from some Scottish castle when the house was built. Footsteps sounded above our heads in the open upper gallery. Sir Randall? The individual passed into the inner corridor before I could glance upward.

"Claude has hesitated over casting Josephine in his production of—"

"Mother told me about that," I interrupted. "But the rest. What does Vasili Pavlenko have to do with it? And y—" I stopped myself from saying *you*, but too late. Mrs. Wharton knew what I had been about to ask.

"It's all right," she said. "Back in Paris last autumn Claude and I had been collaborating on a play we were writing jointly. I thought it had been going well, until Claude abruptly told me he was no longer interested in the project. It was quite a blow to me. I'd devoted abundant time, not to mention my heart and energy, only to have Claude tell me it wasn't any good. That *I* wasn't any good. Not as a writer—he wasn't as cruel as all that. But as far as theater is concerned, he deemed my talents thoroughly insufficient."

"How unkind of him."

Even before Mrs. Wharton's expression changed to one of irony, I knew what she would say—knew what *I* would have said had our roles been reversed.

"There is little kindness or gallantry in the art world, Miss Cross, as I am certain you are aware. It is something we must be willing to accept, or we should quietly return to our garden parties and other such entertainments. Wouldn't you, as a journalist, agree?"

I nodded ruefully. "I wouldn't have it any other way. Nothing raises my hackles faster than a pat on the head from my employer. But what about Mr. Pavlenko? What has he to do with whether Monsieur Baptiste casts Miss Marcus or not?"

Mrs. Wharton was smiling broadly now. "You truly are a reporter, Miss Cross. So very curious." My face heating, I was about to apologize for my impertinent curiosity when she continued. "But in answer, I truly don't know. I suppose it's a confidence between Josephine, Claude, and Vasili. And perhaps Niccolo," she added pensively, gazing across the width of the Great Hall and over the heads of the small audience just now taking their seats. Miss Marcus swept by us and regally lowered herself into the center seat, a red velvet throne-like affair with a gilded frame and a great eagle carved at the apex of the backrest. A fitting perch, I thought, for a woman of such flamboyant temperament.

I noticed Mr. Dunn had taken up position outside the room's second doorway, which opened onto the entry foyer. Behind him stood Carl and Irene, her maid's uniform smoothed and her apron gone, craning to see over Mr. Dunn's shoulder. Her eyes were shining with anticipation, and I was glad she was permitted to enjoy the recital, albeit from outside the room.

In the bay of windows, Niccolo sat holding the Montagnana, one ear angled close to the neck as he softly plucked the strings and then leaned to make adjusting turns of the fine tuners on the tailpiece. Vasili Pavlenko, his wavy, golden brown hair mussed, hurried in from the drawing room and took a seat beside Monsieur Baptiste. They tilted their heads toward each other and appeared to trade rapid murmurs.

Mrs. Wharton lightly touched my forearm. "Shall we sit together, Miss Cross?"

Before I replied, I noticed my parents sitting, not together, but a seat apart. I gestured to the empty chair between them. "I believe my parents are hoping I'll sit with them."

"Yes, of course." Mrs. Wharton moved away to take a seat. It was when I'd settled between Mother and Father that I noticed she had not chosen a chair beside her husband, but one at the very end of the row. As Signore Lionetti continued tuning his instrument—which in itself filled the room with a beautiful melody—I glanced over at Teddy Wharton on the far side of my mother. He slumped in his chair and stared down at his feet, and I followed his gaze to a peculiar detail.

"Mr. Wharton." I leaned around my mother and spoke

quietly so as not to disturb our musician. "Have you been out walking? Have you seen Sir Randall?"

He glanced up as if startled. "What? Oh, yes, I took a turn in the garden, but no, I haven't seen Sir Randall since before dinner. He's probably back in his room by now."

I nodded, and then Mother nudged me. Niccolo Lionetti's Montagnana had gone silent. He flipped his fringe of dark curls off his forehead, adjusted his posture, and raised his bow in a graceful sweep. The sonorous notes of a Bach concerto leapt on the air, and my heart leapt with it. The notes soothed and thrilled, lulled and electrified. The soaring height of the Great Hall plucked each note skyward, to echo down on us like calls from heaven. Goose bumps erupted on my arms and traveled my back. I felt as if some magnetic force held me in my chair and rendered me entranced and immobile but for the melodic racing of my pulse.

Did the music have the same effect on the others? I stole a glance down the row at Josephine Marcus. Nearly as thrilling as the music was the change that had come over her, a physical alteration of her entire being, or so it seemed to me. Her very posture, typically careless and unladylike, more resembled that of Mrs. Wharton, as if she, too, was shored up by the music. But most striking was the change to her features, now relaxed, serene, and utterly without artifice.

The music called to me once again, yet as I turned my sights away from Miss Marcus, I again noticed Teddy Wharton's side-lacing, patent-toed half boots, and the damp grass speckling their vamps. When Niccolo Lionetti and Vasili Pavlenko had been outside that morning, they had changed their outdoor boots for indoor shoes. It was only proper etiquette. So why had Teddy Wharton forgotten such a simple courtesy?

Then Mother placed her hand over mine where it rested on the arm of my chair, and I returned my attention to the performance.

* * *

The evening's entertainment ended around ten o'clock, after several unsuccessful attempts to persuade Miss Marcus to serenade the group.

"I've been experiencing the tiniest discomfort in my throat lately. No more than a tickle," she assured us with a toss of her curls and a flash of her dimples, "but enough to warrant having a care. It's merely the change in climate from Paris to New England, I'm quite sure." She snapped open the fan she held and fluttered it in front of her face.

"In that case, I'm going up." Mrs. Wharton stood and bid the group good night. Her husband nearly tripped in his effort to follow her into the Stair Hall. He called to her but her footsteps didn't slow, prompting him to trot to catch up.

My mother, having witnessed the scene as well, glanced my way with a little roll of her eyes. As the rest of us vacated our chairs and the men began restoring order to the room, Josephine remained in her eagle-crested throne, watching Niccolo intently.

"That was lovely," she told him.

"You should have accompanied me," he replied, tersely I thought, and without looking at her. A flick of his fingers loosened the horsehair on his bow, and he stowed it in the slot meant for that purpose in the velvet-lined cello case. With the utmost care he lifted the instrument and also placed it in the case, being sure not only to flip the latches closed, but to spin the little combination lock centered between the latches.

"I'll accompany you now," she simpered, her eyes narrowing within their lashes and her bosom straining the plunging neckline of her Jacques Doucet evening gown. The dress hailed from the spring collection, if I wasn't mistaken. Apparently her flagging career hadn't yet thwarted her wardrobe.

"I'm tired." Lionetti grasped the handle of the case in one

hand and supported the long, tapering end with his other. He strode by Miss Marcus without another word.

She heaved herself out of her chair. "Well," she said to no one in particular, and wandered away.

Monsieur Baptiste bowed, encompassing me, Mother, and Father in the gesture. "Good night. Let us hope tomorrow brings more congenial tidings. Vasili?"

"I will have a cigarette first."

The Frenchman nodded and made his way to the Stair Hall. I hurried to catch up with him. He paused halfway up the lower steps when I spoke his name, stopped, and turned. His eyes were wary, his lips tighter and thinner than usual. Did he believe I'd come to ask him about his argument with Miss Marcus? I longed to know more, but that was not my present intent.

"Monsieur, would you mind very much knocking on Sir Randall's door?"

He studied me a moment in the hall's subdued electric lighting. "How very endearing, Ma'amoiselle Cross. You are worried about him."

"He is unfamiliar with the terrain here. The Cliff Walk can be dangerous."

"Do people often plunge from these heights?" Interest ignited in his eyes, and I wondered if he found dramatic potential in the notion. Would a representation of our cliffs appear in his next stage production?

"No, not often," I said, "but it does happen. Please, would you check to see that he has returned?"

A shrug formed the whole of his answer. I followed him as far as the half landing, where I settled on the velvet sofa to wait. With my chin propped on my hand I gazed out the small squares of the mullioned window. Below me on the circular drive two pinpoints glowed orange in the darkness. At first I thought they were fireflies, but an up and down movement punctuated by intermittent brightening of those tiny lights revealed them to be the burning ends of cigarettes. I pressed my face close to the window, making out the sheen of Miss Marcus's beaded gown reflecting the moonlight. The Russian dancer must have gone out front for his cigarette, and apparently Miss Marcus had joined with him. At least this time I wouldn't have to run after them with a suitable ash receptacle.

The sound of knuckles rapping on a door drew my attention to the second-floor hallway.

"Randall?" The Frenchman pronounced the *R* in the name with a rasp at the back of his throat. "Are you within?" The rapping came again. "Randall?"

After a fourth time I continued up the stairs. The Frenchman stood outside Uncle Frederick's bedroom suite, a fitting room for Sir Randall since he was considering purchasing Rough Point. Monsieur Baptiste saw me and shook his head.

"Perhaps you might try the knob?" I suggested.

He seemed to debate that for an instant before complying. The door opened easily inward. I ventured closer, though not so close that I could see inside. It would be most improper for me to intrude should Sir Randall be sleeping in his bed. I need not have exercised that caution. Presently Monsieur Baptiste backed out of the room and closed the door.

"He is not there." He frowned, the furrows reaching his receding hairline. "Perhaps you are correct to worry, ma'amoiselle."

Twenty minutes later the house had been searched and no Sir Randall found.

"We mustn't panic," Mother said to the group of us now assembled in the drawing room. My father, Vasili Pavlenko, and Niccolo Lionetti had exchanged their dinner tuxedos for tweeds and walking boots and were preparing a trek across the rear lawns to the Cliff Walk. Mr. Dunn waited outside on the terrace with the lanterns they would need. "Perhaps he began walking, lost track of the time, and turned in at one of the other properties. He might be enjoying a pleasant evening with one of the neighbors."

"With which neighbor, Mother?" I demanded. I softened my tone. "Why wouldn't he have telephoned?"

"Surely not every house in Newport has been wired for the telephones." Father attempted a cavalier smile. "And you know how the British are, sweetheart. They don't think of such modern inventions in the course of daily life. Too stuck in the old ways."

"His host would have suggested it," I persisted. "But again, which neighbor? Most of the summer set are gone by now and their houses closed up."

"Don't worry, sweetheart, we'll find him." Father placed his open palm against my cheek in a tender gesture I had once, a long time ago, been so very accustomed to, but which now felt foreign and awkward. I instinctively took a step backward, then wished I hadn't when I saw the hurt in his eyes. I tried to smile up at him but he had already turned away to address the men. "If we're all ready, let's go."

"And while you search," my mother said, "I'll have the night operator connect me to the neighboring homes. Surely someone will have seen him."

The men filed out of the drawing room onto the veranda. I hesitated for a moment, then started forward.

"Emma, what on earth do you think you're doing?"

I turned to face my mother. "I've grown unused to sitting and waiting for others to act, Mother. I'm going out with them."

"Oh, no you're not. It's too dangerous."

Mrs. Wharton came up beside her and placed a hand on Mother's shoulder. "Let her go, Beatrice. She'll be fine. Your daughter is braver and more accomplished than you know."

She aimed a disparaging look at her husband, who showed no intention of accompanying the search party.

Her declaration held me another moment as I wondered how Mrs. Wharton had reached her conclusion. Based only on my articles? Or had she learned things about me from other sources? Could she know of my perils of the past two summers? Funny, I thought, that a complete stranger could know me better than my own parents. But I summoned a reassuring smile for my mother.

"I merely wish to be on hand during the search. I'll keep well away from the edge."

Mother's hazel eyes, mirroring my own, gleamed with the suggestion of an unshed tear or two. Fear, I wondered, or pride?

Chapter 5

I didn't keep as far away from the edge as I'd promised. While my father and the others paired off and spread out along the Cliff Walk in either direction, I walked onto the footbridge that spanned a deep gorge in the cliff face. The stone half wall rough beneath my fingers, I leaned over, first on the sea-facing side of the bridge, and then the side that faced into the chasm. Moonlight glimmered on the waves, sparking silver as the tide struck the cliffs and thrust into the jagged gap where the promontory had been torn asunder eons ago. The water lunged into the unforgiving crevices, sending up a sand-ridden spray to pelt me where I stood braced on the bridge.

The others repeatedly shouted Sir Randall's name and waved their lanterns to illuminate the treacherous pathway, for their own safety as well as to search for clues as to Sir Randall's whereabouts. The aptly named Rough Point presented some of the most rugged and dangerous terrain found on Aquidneck Island.

Had Sir Randall fallen?

The relentless heave of the ocean wove a knot of tension in my stomach. I sensed a restlessness in the waves, an agitation like that of a growling dog crouched on his haunches. A storm was coming, was surely even now churning the Atlantic waters somewhere far to the east. I didn't need a sailor's report to confirm my suspicions. The Newporter in me knew.

I soon found myself alone, the men having disappeared round the curving walk to either side of the property. Again, I leaned over the wall on the landward side of the bridge. This would not be the first time the tide wedged a body into the chasm. I dreaded seeing one now, yet I could not prevent myself from searching the glistening shadows.

It was too dark, and nothing beyond rock and water revealed itself to me. I don't know how long I stood there as recollections of that day rolled like surf through my mind. In a short time, Sir Randall had somehow endeared himself to me, while Miss Marcus's callous disregard continued to rankle. Yet when I'd last seen the Englishman, he had shown signs of having rallied, of being ready to once again take up his chisel and release his inner vision.

A voice beside me startled me from my thoughts. I flinched and glanced up to see my father looking down at me with concern.

"Have you found him?"

He shook his head. "I'm afraid not. Come, there is nothing more we can do in the dark. We'll have to wait until morning and hope Randall found shelter somewhere. Or perhaps your mother will have located him by telephone."

The argument that we couldn't simply give up welled inside me, but I tamped it down. My father was right. To continue the search along the treacherous Cliff Walk in the dark would only endanger more lives. I offered another suggestion. "I think we should send for the police, Father."

He shook his head again. "They'll reach the same conclusion the others and I did: It's too dark for a search. If he hasn't appeared by morning, we'll notify Jesse." His smile was little more than a twitch of a shadow in the darkness. "How is my old friend? Do you see much of him these days?"

If my father only knew. Jesse Whyte, a detective with the Newport Police Department, was hardly an "old" friend, considering he was only about ten years older than I. But we had lived near him in the Point neighborhood of Newport, and he and my father had forged a fast friendship and had spent many an evening in our little rear garden, debating world events over glasses of wine or snifters of brandy. I had been too young to participate then, but I'd since grown up and established my own friendship with Jesse, especially in the past year. He and I had worked together more than once to solve the most heinous of crimes, my assistance at first taken under protest, but later, after I'd proved my skills of deduction, with a grudging respect in which I took pride.

I merely said, "Jesse and I have become friends in our own right."

"Good, then he's keeping an eye on you for me, and keeping you out of mischief, I trust."

I didn't reply to that.

We walked back up to the house, the others converging on us from various directions until we entered the covered veranda in a group—a pensive one. The drawing room doors burst open and Mother and Mrs. Wharton rushed out. Pensiveness became a rush of speculation.

"You didn't find him, then."

"Poor old Randall, never could distinguish north from south."

"I'm sure he's just fine."

"He'll turn up in the morning."

"He must be enjoying a brandy with one of the neighbors."

To this my mother adamantly shook her head. "I telephoned quite a number of houses up and down the avenue. Even those closed up for the winter. I spoke with several housekeepers who hadn't seen him either. No, he's almost certainly not with a neighbor."

"We'll need to keep looking then," Mrs. Wharton declared, but no one made a move to leave the veranda. In fact, outside, Carl and Mr. Dunn were just then extinguishing the last of the lanterns. "You cannot give up. He's elderly and he might be hurt, might need our assistance." She whirled about and called into the drawing room. "Teddy, go with them this time. Help them search for our friend."

Teddy Wharton gathered himself with obvious reluctance, rose from the sofa, and came out to us. "There is no sense in continuing to search the darkness."

Even standing behind her I saw how Mrs. Wharton seethed, how her right hand stiffened as if in preparation of delivering a bracing blow. Her arm remained at her side, however, and in the next moment she pushed past him into the house and strode away.

In the morning I awoke to the distant hue and cry of frantic barking and, closer, a persistent knocking at my bedroom door. Halfhearted daylight grazed the window curtains; it could not be much past dawn. Feeling annoyed at the intrusion, I pushed myself up on my pillows, at first bewildered by the lack of my great-aunt Sadie's sturdy oak furniture that should have graced the room. Then I remembered. I was not at home, but at Rough Point, in one of the servants' bedrooms. And Sir Randall . . . we hadn't found him last night. My heart knocked against my ribs and I called out.

"Come in."

Mother opened the door and poked her head in. "You'll want to get dressed quickly and come outside."

My throat tightened, and I swallowed almost painfully. Although the look on her face told me what to expect, I asked nonetheless. "Has Sir Randall been found?"

"Your father and some of the others were up before first light. Jesse Whyte and his men are on their way. Get dressed." Her hair in a hasty twist and wearing a simple shirtwaist and skirt, she came into the room and opened the wardrobe doors. "Anything will do. Here." She selected a simple muslin that buttoned up the front. "Will you need help?"

"I can manage." Yet it took me two tries each to roll my stockings on without twisting them, and when it came time to do up the buttons on my dress, my trembling fingers could scarcely grip them.

In the entry foyer I met Jesse and two uniformed policemen. "Emma." He held out his hands as if groping for something to say. He and I found ourselves in such circumstances so often it defied logic. Our experiences of the past two summers had rendered a change in Jesse, in the youthful features I had always found so endearing. Yet the changes were not physical—he hadn't aged, exactly—but rather subtle alterations in his expressions. His redhead's complexion, prone to freckling, and the mouth that smiled so easily and so boyishly—they were the same. But the keen blue eyes now held knowledge, and with it sorrow, that hadn't been there two years ago.

I went to him and touched his forearm. Through his coat sleeve his muscles twitched beneath my fingers, and I remembered that a measure of that sorrow was on account of me, and a regard I could not return, not as he would have wished. My hand slid back to my side.

"Has Randall Clifford been found?" I asked.

"He has, thanks to Patch." He hesitated, studying me

closely. "According to your father he went loping across the lawn this morning, right to the fissure out there."

"The fissure," I repeated, feeling slightly dizzy. I had leaned over the fissure last night, and had seen nothing. Had Sir Randall been there all along? Had he been alive then, when we might have helped him?

"He wouldn't stop barking," Jesse had gone on to say, oblivious of my thoughts. "I'm surprised you didn't hear him."

"My room is on the other side of the house," I murmured. But I realized I had drunk wine with dinner last night, something I was unused to doing at home. The alcohol must have rendered my sleep deeper than usual. Had the wine also played tricks with my vision, or my judgment, when I'd peered down into the frothing waves?

"I need to see him."

"Are you sure?" he asked.

I nodded and steeled myself, knowing that no matter how many times I saw a dead body, I would never grow used to it—*should* never grow used to it.

"Come, then. We'll walk out together."

I followed him through the drawing room, inhabited only by Miss Marcus clad in a vibrant, frilly dressing gown. She looked up nervously at our approach. An unlit cigarette wavered between two trembling fingers. I nodded a somber greeting and continued outside with Jesse and his men. Mother and Mrs. Wharton stood halfway across the lawn, where the land rose up like a cresting wave. They each held an arm around the other as they gazed out at the cliffs. Several more officers stood on the footbridge, while my father and the other men hovered to one side, Teddy Wharton among them. And there was Patch, trotting back and forth near the precipice and barking madly. The sight of him so close to the brink sent me running. I called to him, and without ceasing his yipping he bounded to me, jumped around my feet, and bolted back to the footbridge. His manner clearly begged me to follow.

A Life-Saving Service cutter floated some twenty yards out, and a sleek little skiff was being maneuvered into the gorge. I stepped up onto the footbridge, took in the solemn faces around me, and leaned to peer over the half wall.

A hand immediately wrapped itself around my upper arm. "Be careful, Emma. I don't need you falling as well." For an instant Jesse looked angry; then his expression cleared. He released my arm. "Sorry."

I nodded and turned back toward the chasm, searching the rocks. I sucked in a breath when I saw him. Shock lodged in my throat, trapped between my hammering heart and my clenched jaws. "Sir Randall . . ."

He was several yards down, just above the low tide line. His body hung wedged into the sharp convergence of the fissure, his torso twisted, his legs dangling and clearly broken, his arms pinned to his sides by the granite walls that held him. But his head—his head lolled backward on his neck, so that he appeared to be staring skyward with sightless eyes. A gash scored his brow, washed clean by the sea, the bone showing starkly white.

Grief and nausea rolled in a great wave inside me. Still I stood there, battling my revulsion, until the Life-Saving Service skiff passed under the bridge. The three men inside used poles to steady the boat and prevent the waves from thrusting it against the rocks. They propelled the vessel as far into the gap as it could safely go. It was as one stepped out onto the boulders protruding from the undulant waters that I roused myself. With my teeth gritted and my lips pressed together, I pushed away from the wall, and from that awful sight.

"Why did you bring her here?" My father shouldered his way past the officers with their tablets and evidence pouches and their murmurs of theory and speculation. "Jesse, are you mad, bringing Emmaline down here like this?"

Jesse's color surged. I saved him from having to fashion excuses. "It was me, Father. I insisted on coming. I had to see."

He gripped my wrists and stared incredulously down at me. "In God's name, why? You're just a girl. A child. Why subject yourself to such a horror?"

I raised my face to meet his gaze full on, and perhaps he saw something of the change I myself had seen in Jesse, for he released me and took a half step back. His brow creased as if he were puzzling out a perplexing riddle. My name broke from his lips on a whisper. "Emmaline?"

"I've changed, Father. I've grown up. So has Brady. All of us—me, Brady, Jesse—we've gone on living while you were away in Paris." I heard the sting of accusation in my tone at the same time my father winced. Perhaps I hadn't grown up as much as I'd like to think, but at least I was being honest. He started to reply. I spoke over him. "I cannot pretend I knew Sir Randall very well. But he and I spoke yesterday before he came out and I . . . I learned something about him that compels me to be here now. It's that simple."

Father swallowed, shifting his gaze from me to Jesse and back. Jesse came forward and placed a hand on Father's shoulder. "You and the others should go on up to the house now and let the Life-Saving Service and the uniforms do their work. I'll speak with you again soon."

Suicide. The word hung over the dining room, where we had all assembled after each of us was interviewed about the days and hours leading up to Sir Randall's disappearance. Patch sat at my knee. Perhaps I shouldn't have allowed him into the house proper, but my intrepid pup had essentially recovered Sir Randall's body, and now seemed held in the same web of bewilderment as the rest of us. Surely I had never seen him so subdued, nor so unwilling to leave my side. I wondered, had he witnessed the incident? If he could speak, could he answer our questions?

"Suicide," Claude Baptiste repeated. He laced his fingers together on the tabletop and stared down at them. "It is a most horrible conclusion."

"It fits," Jesse said, scrubbing a weary hand across his eyes. What was it about a tragic death that sapped all the energy from those left behind? I felt as though I'd toiled endlessly for days, could barely hold myself upright in my seat at the table. Even Patch turned his head to rest his chin on my knee. I absently stroked between his ears and down his neck.

"Can you be certain?" My father's nose was pinched, his jaws tight. He reached for the silver cigarette case lying in front of Monsieur Baptiste next to him. At a nod from the Frenchman, Father plucked a cigarette and held it between his lips as he scraped a wooden matchstick against the striker on the side of the case. I remembered him smoking the occasional cigar in days past, but I wondered when he had taken up cigarettes. Or did he simply crave a way to keep his hands busy? His first puff came out in a rolling ball of white. Then he inhaled deeply and released a stream of leaden vapor.

"Each of you has basically repeated the same story." Jesse shook his head no when my father held out the silver case to him. "You've all corroborated that Sir Randall had been deeply depressed by his recent disappointments, and several of you witnessed him walking out to the cliffs alone. So far my men and I find no evidence of foul play. We'll continue to comb the area. I've also sent two men upstairs to go through his things."

"What about that gash in his forehead?" I asked him. "Could someone have bludgeoned him before pushing him off the bridge?"

Jesse shook his head again. "I don't believe so. The wound looks consistent with his head having hit the rocks as he fell. And don't forget the waves probably thrashed him against the cliff face quite a bit before he became lodged in the crevice. The coroner will have to confirm this, but it seems the most logical conclusion."

Mr. Dunn stood apart from the rest of us, off to one side of the rear-facing windows. "May I notify Mr. Vanderbilt of your conclusions, Detective?" The estate agent stood at attention, his slicked hair flawless and his expression grim. "He will need to know of this."

Jesse mulled over the question. Then he nodded. "Yes, inform him we are still investigating, but at this time Sir Randall's death appears . . ." Again, he hesitated. "Tell him for now we are calling this an accident."

"Not suicide?" Across the table from me, Josephine Marcus puffed heavily on her own cigarette, touching it to her lips and pulling it away with nervous, jerking motions. White clouds surrounded her face like an autumn fog. Several of the guests were smoking now, filling the room with the noxious scents of an assortment of tobacco, from the mundane to the exotic, and I longed to escape into the fresh air. From my mother's taut expression I surmised she felt the same discomfort as I. "You just finished saying he was depressed. Are you doubting your own verdict, Detective?"

Jesse's gaze turned sharp. "I make no verdicts, Miss Marcus. That's for judge and jury. It does appear to be a suicide, but I see no reason to release that information to the general public, or Mr. Vanderbilt, until we're absolutely certain. For all we know at this point, Sir Randall might have slipped and fallen over the cliff. He might not have been on the bridge at all, but was washed into the gap by the waves. We have to notify the next of kin, Sir Randall's . . ." He paused, and my father filled in the missing words.

"His son, James. Randall was a widower with no surviving brothers or sisters."

"His son should be notified before news of this gets out." Jesse cast a glance at me. "It would be wrong to release details we're not yet sure of."

"I don't intend reporting on half a story," I assured him, somewhat defensively. "That's Ed Billings's style, not mine."

Jesse looked contrite. "Of course."

"What if you can never prove what happened to Randall?" Miss Marcus's question shot out like a challenge.

"We'll do our best," was all he said.

"Who was with him last?" Sitting beside my father, Mother looked tearfully around the table. "He shouldn't have been allowed to venture out alone. We knew he was terribly unhappy. Someone should have gone with him. Someone should have—"

"Beatrice." Father reached over to place his hand on hers. "There is no point in that."

"No point?" My mother snatched her hand away. "Of course there's a point. No one knows for certain what happened. Jesse just said so himself. For all we know . . ." Her voice becoming shrill, she broke off, looking disconcerted, and then gathered herself and said fiercely, "Emma should not be here. Edith should have consulted us before inviting her. Emma should leave at once before—"

"Beatrice!" My father's sharp retort made several of those around the table cringe, myself included. Even Patch let out a throaty whine. "Beatrice," Father repeated in a murmur. "That is quite enough. Please calm yourself."

"Yes, do," Miss Marcus said with a flourish of her cigarette. "Hysterics won't help anyone."

Mother's jaw flexed, and she ground out, "I am not hysterical."

A dubious claim. Mother's agitation was as plain as it was

understandable. What I didn't understand was her reference to me. Did she continue to see me as a child, too delicate to withstand the shock of a man's unfortunate death? The worst had occurred, hadn't it, so from what else did she seek to protect me?

That question gnawed at my insides until the discomfort of it grew in proportion to a mounting distrust. What were my parents hiding?

"I'm sorry if I overstepped my bounds when I asked your daughter to stay here during our retreat." Mrs. Wharton clutched the lace neckline of the morning gown she had hastily donned earlier.

Mother looked about to retort, so I quickly said, "You didn't. And the decision to stay was entirely my own."

While that appeared to appease Mrs. Wharton, my mother's posture stiffened as though she had been slapped or unpardonably insulted. By Mrs. Wharton, or me? My father reached for her hand again, and this time Mother didn't pull away. Some message seemed to pass between them, and Mother relaxed her shoulders a fraction. An uneasy silence settled over the room, broken after several awkward moments by Vasili Pavlenko.

"What do we do now?" The young man looked drained. Fatigue dragged at the pretty features Miss Marcus had admired.

Jesse, whose heightened color revealed how uncomfortable he had become in the last few minutes, pushed back his chair and stood. "I'll—uh—leave you to discuss that. I must ask that no one leave Newport in the next day or so, in case I have more questions for you." He bobbed his head in my direction and took his leave of the group. Before he had quite exited the room, however, he cast me one more glance, one that conveyed a silent message: *Find out what you can.* I blinked once in response.

"You heard the detective." Niccolo Lionetti combed his fingers through his dark curls. "We wait to see if we must be questioned again."

A sound of impatience ground in Vasili's throat. "Yes, but after that. Our plan was to stay here for a fortnight."

"We take wing the moment that policeman opens this cage." Josephine Marcus studied her fingernails. "Of course."

"And go where?" Vasili snapped.

"Wherever you want." The opera singer's features turned suddenly sharp, shrewish. "Does it matter?"

"It matters to us." Niccolo reached for another cigarette. "To those of us who are not from this country. Where do we go?"

Monsieur Baptiste shrugged. "I will travel down to New York, where there are countless charming hotels at our disposal. Vasili, you could come with me. You too, Niccolo," he added as an afterthought, but grudgingly, I thought.

Mrs. Wharton stood and leaned with her palms on the table. "Any of you are welcome at Land's End if need be, but why must anyone go anywhere? We came here to conduct an artistic retreat. If Randall indeed died for his art, don't we owe it to him to carry on as planned? Wouldn't he wish us to do just that?"

"How very poetic, my dear," Teddy Wharton said half under his breath, although I heard him clearly enough. Had the others? If so, they ignored him.

Finally, my father leaned back in his chair. "I agree, we should stay put and carry on in Randall's name, as a tribute to a good friend and an innovative artist. Anything productive that emerges from our time here will be dedicated to him. He'd appreciate that, I think."

Mrs. Wharton patted a hand lightly on the tabletop. "I believe he would, very much. We will celebrate our comrade even as we mourn him. What do the rest of you say?" She turned to me and smiled sadly. "Miss Cross, you'll have a most poignant story when all is said and done."

I didn't doubt it, although I found myself faced with an enormous hurdle. Observing and interviewing these artists after such a tragedy now seemed trite, almost cruel, when surely they would rather be left alone with their grief, which would surely be considerable once the shock wore off. But I had also made Jesse an unspoken promise to find out as much about Sir Randall's death as I could. I wondered, how forthcoming would this group be now?

The inhabitants of Rough Point went about the rest of that day in near silence. Occasional whispers traveled through the marble-tiled rooms, hissing along the elaborate woodwork. For the most part, the group scattered, sitting pensively alone or wandering the grounds aimlessly. Even at luncheon, they filled their plates and retreated to the private nooks and corners they had made for themselves throughout the house. This surprised me, for I'd have thought they would wish to keep company and trade thoughts and memories of their friend. Perhaps this was an artist's way, however. An artist's endeavors are, for the most part, solitary ones.

I took their cue and maintained my distance as well, but kept Patch with me as I moved about the house. After coming upon Teddy Wharton sitting at the desk in Uncle Frederick's office, I used the telephone in the butler's pantry to call home to Nanny. My news was met with a long silence, and then she said, "Well, I don't suppose it would do any good to suggest you come home?"

"Mother and Father are here as well." I went on to explain the artists' wish to continue their retreat in tribute to Sir Randall.

Another weighty silence was followed by a sigh. "I'm glad. Your parents have been away too long."

I didn't tell her my parents' visit came fraught with secretive undercurrents, but I let her believe the Cross family's reunion a happy one, for now.

I also used the time to mull over—and write notes on—the various responses to the morning's events. Niccolo Lionetti had seemed more concerned about where to go once they vacated Rough Point, as if he might be cast out into the street, rather than about Sir Randall's unhappy fate. Josephine Marcus behaved with her usual acerbic wit. Teddy Wharton imposed a distance between himself and the others, including his wife. Monsieur Baptiste and Vasili Pavlenko had appeared less than devastated, and the Frenchman's mention of New York hotels held a hint of yearning, as if he longed to be away from here.

And my parents . . . once again, they left me with a certainty they were being less than straightforward. In fact, I had asked Mother point blank what she meant earlier in the dining room when she said I shouldn't be there, and she had shown me a wide look of surprise.

"I merely meant these are hardly circumstances for a young girl like you."

"I've already explained to Father that I'm no longer a child. And you mustn't blame Mrs. Wharton for my being here."

"I certainly do not blame Edith." But the hiss of her breath told me differently.

I decided it was time to seek out Mrs. Wharton and ask her some pointed questions. Leaving Mother to her own devices in the second-floor sitting room, Patch and I went below. I'd last seen Mrs. Wharton on the covered veranda outside the billiard room. I headed there now, but in the Stair Hall, I was stopped by the estate manager, Mr. Dunn.

"Miss Cross, a word if you please." The beginnings of a

disapproving frown appeared as he glanced down at Patch, but he made no comment.

"Certainly, Mr. Dunn." I hid my surprise that he would wish to speak to me. "What may I do for you? If it has something to do with Mr. Vanderbilt or the house, you should really speak with my father. I defer all decisions concerning the property to him, now that he's here."

"No, Miss Cross, it's you I mean to speak with. It's about your article. Is there any way you might leave out this unfortunate business when you write about the retreat?"

I balked for the briefest instant. "Mr. Dunn . . . you mean pretend nothing happened? How can I? Once the police have finished their investigation and the body has been released, this will all be a matter of public record."

He sighed. "Yes, but the average citizen doesn't always concern himself with public record, and newspapers are quite well known for exaggerating details. We all know it is the sensational story and the sordid details that sell copies—that can even propel a small-town paper to national prominence."

The insinuation reminded me of my rival, Ed Billings, and made my hackles rise. "Are you accusing me of unethical journalism? I would never—"

"No, Miss Cross. I apologize if that seemed to be the case. But do understand that Mr. Vanderbilt has my every loyalty. You know he wishes to sell the property. Think of the potential damage of a story like this. How many people will be willing to purchase the site of a man's death? And a suicide at that. The property will be all but cursed. Its value will plummet."

"Really, sir, this is 1896, not 1698. No one believes in curses anymore."

"Don't they? Do you believe our society to be free of superstition? I'm only asking you to think of Mr. Vanderbilt—

of all your Vanderbilt relatives, and of yourself. This story will surely send your name, along with those of all your relatives, catapulting across the country." He raised his eyebrows and gazed down at me from his superior height. Rather than recoiling from his scrutiny, I in turn studied him closely. Something in his tone challenged me to envision the consequences of attaching my name to such a scandal, but rather than a warning, his very posture and the animation with which he spoke seemed to *en*courage rather than discourage. An appeal to my journalistic ambitions?

I couldn't fathom why he would tempt me to write an article he believed might injure his employer. Did he fear losing his position should the house sell? But no, I remembered that he administered Uncle Frederick's other estates as well as this one. If the property were to sell, he would not be out of a job.

Puzzling . . . Perhaps I'd read him incorrectly.

"I'll think about what you've said, Mr. Dunn. Come, Patch." I started to turn away but the man spoke my name again. I waited.

"If there is anything I can do for you, please let me know."

"Thank you. I'm sure we'll be fine. You, Irene, Carl, and Mrs. Harris are doing a splendid job so far."

He stepped closer to me, crowding me and making me want to retreat up the stairs. "I meant you personally, Miss Cross. You and I should stick together. We are rather two of a kind."

Indignation traveled through me. Was this a romantic overture? Whatever it was, it felt intrusive. "What do you mean?"

"Only that you and I are here for professional reasons. We are not guests, but neither are we servants. It can be a tenuous balancing act, no?"

My ire disappeared as quickly as it had come. "I see. Yes, you're right, I suppose. Thank you, Mr. Dunn. Patch?"

My dog no longer stood at my side. I heard his steps pattering across the dining room. His sensitive nose must have sniffed out something savory cooking in the kitchen, and since he and Mrs. Harris were already fast friends, I decided to let him enjoy his visit. I went in search of Mrs. Wharton.

Chapter 6

"Mrs. Wharton, why did you really ask me to stay here? And please tell me the truth."

I'd found the woman outside, where the lawns rose to a rocky crest smothered in late-season wildflowers before falling away to the Cliff Walk. She sat on a garden bench gazing out at the ocean. She held one hand anchored at the crown of her hat, while the other held her dress against her knees in defiance of a brisk wind determined to reveal silk stockings and a pair of tasseled, low-heeled boots.

With a wounded expression she turned to me where I had settled on the bench beside her. "Whatever has led you to find insincerity in my words and actions, Miss Cross?"

I hesitated over that, at a loss for words. "I'm sorry," I said at length. I, too, held my skirts against the wind. "It's just that nothing here is as it seems, is it?"

"What a cryptic thing to say. Randall's death has left us all distraught, to be sure, but you talk as if there is some plot afoot."

"Isn't there? If you tell me your reasons for wanting me to

stay at Rough Point have not changed from yesterday, I'll believe you. But what I do not believe is that my parents are happy to see me here. And I wondered if perhaps . . ."

"If perhaps I had engineered your reunion with your parents?" She pursed her lips. "Why would I do that? I'm not one to meddle in the affairs of other people's families."

The wind plucked tendrils from the braid hanging down my back. I had come out without my hat, as I often did at home, and shaded my eyes from the afternoon sun with my hand. My aunt Alice Vanderbilt would have been mortified by my failure to heed precautions against freckling. "Why would my parents plan to come to Newport, tell neither me nor my brother, and not seem pleased to learn I'm staying in the same house as they?"

"I cannot speak for your parents' reasons, but I can tell you how this retreat came to be." She was momentarily distracted by the drone of a bumblebee hovering in a patch of black-eyed Susans and snowy sweet alyssum. I remained silent, waiting for her to gather her thoughts. She turned back to me. "In Paris, your parents often spoke of Newport, of the old days before people like your relatives and yes, my own parents, drove the intelligentsia away. One could see the affection they felt for this place, hear it in their voices. So, when both Niccolo and Claude found reasons to come to America, they decided to arrive early and see Newport for themselves. Vasili planned to come with them."

"Why Vasili? Did he also have business here?"

"No, not exactly, although should Claude direct *Carmen* in New York, he will of course choose Vasili as his choreographer."

"You say 'of course' as if it's a given. Do they always work together? I thought Mr. Pavlenko is employed by the Imperial Russian Ballet."

"He is, but the ballet season doesn't begin again till spring.

In answer to your question, no, they didn't always work together, not until . . ."

"The accident that prevents Mr. Pavlenko from ever dancing again?"

She nodded and changed the subject. "Once Josephine heard of their plans, she decided it was time to see America again, too. I don't think anyone minded really, although Claude refused to be railroaded into casting her as his Carmen."

"Why is that?"

"You'll have to ask Claude. Perhaps after the misfortune of our failed collaboration, he simply doesn't wish to work with members of our little set anymore. Vasili excepted, of course. But then they're the very best of friends."

"I find that rather odd." I toed the grass curling around my feet. "I'd sooner expect Vasili and Niccolo to be close companions—they're so close in age. But Vasili and Monsieur Baptiste . . ." I shrugged. "How did you and your husband come to be involved in the retreat?"

"Ah. I thought of offering Land's End, but as I believe I mentioned to you, I knew my family would close in on us immediately." She breathed in the sea air, sweetly fragranced by the flowers. Beyond our tranquil scene, out beyond the cliffs, the ocean foamed with the restless force I'd sensed last night, coiled energy waiting to trounce our shores. "The thought of seeing Newport from an artist's singular perspective proved too much of an enticement to be ignored. I wished to experience those distant, idyllic times, before greed and extravagance and social competition put their taint on this place. And I could not do that at Land's End."

"So your family still doesn't know you're back?" When she shook her head, I felt a burst of indignation on the part of her kin. Being the last to learn of my parents' return still chafed. Had they also believed including me would taint their singular perspective upon coming home? "I take it my parents decided to travel with the others, and arranged to lease the house."

Mrs. Wharton's answer surprised me. "No, I arranged for the house, actually. At that time, it didn't seem that your parents had any intention of coming home. It was very sudden, their change of heart. Only days before we set sail. And then Randall came along as well. I suppose he didn't want to be left behind all alone, especially with the disappointments he'd recently suffered. And he had been toying with the notion of buying property in 'the colonies,' as he called this country. I told him Rough Point was for sale." She fell silent a moment and then said, "One cannot help but wonder, if we had all remained in France . . . ."

I placed my hand over hers. "Don't. You'll only torture yourself with thoughts like that."

When I left her, I was no less perplexed about my parents' behavior, nor any more enlightened about the dynamics that drove this group.

That evening after dinner, Niccolo retreated to his bedroom, and to his cello. I sat at the half landing, soaking in the sweet perfection of each note, allowing the melody to envelop me and squeeze tears into my eyes. At the same time, my thoughts went hurtling over time and place and circumstance. My mind replayed my last and only conversation with Sir Randall, then flashed the image of his body broken against the rocks. I went further back in time, and relived the moment my mother had chosen a younger Mrs. Wharton over the child I had been. I saw my parents as they were now, distant and secretive. And I considered all that Edith Wharton had imparted to me as we sat on the bench with the wide, restless ocean stretched before us.

Whatever answers I sought seemed as ungraspable as the tide. At one point, as Niccolo's playing continued to wash over me, I considered taking Patch and going home to Gull Manor. Why stay? A man had died, had taken his own life, and I could do nothing to change that. My parents were being somehow deceitful, and once again I could do nothing about it. If Mrs. Wharton wanted my advice concerning her manuscript, she would know where to find me. This was no longer a retreat, but a study in tragedy and clashing egos.

But it was growing late, and dark, and there had been that final, silent request from Jesse, who seemed less than satisfied with the conclusions reached concerning Sir Randall's death. I wasn't sure what he hoped I would discover, but he had set me a challenge knowing full well I couldn't resist. With a new resolve I went up to bed, though I slept fitfully and woke often. Fatigue dragged at my limbs the next morning, but with my mind fully awake I quit my bed just after sunup, hoping I might enjoy a solitary breakfast before the others made their appearance.

It turned out I was not the earliest riser. Sobs—my mother's—came from the housekeeper's bedroom across the hall, where my parents were staying. I stopped at their threshold. I shouldn't have, but I couldn't bring myself to walk away. Before I put my ear to the door, I listened for signs of anyone else nearby. Voices echoed from downstairs, and I wondered if anyone had slept at all last night. Quickly I traversed the corridor to the gallery that looked down onto the Great Hall. From there I could see out the towering hall windows onto the lawns, dappled with the shadows of a cloudy sky. A steel gray ocean sent whitecaps to lather the cliff face. Closer in, I spotted the youthful Vasili and the older Claude walking together along the rise in the lawn, the former practically bouncing on his feet and the latter seeming pressed to keep up.

I also heard voices from inside, probably in the drawing room, perhaps the billiard room as well. I darted back to my parents' door, determined to discover not only why my mother was crying, but why they had been so evasive since their arrival. I held my skirts aside to keep them from brushing against the door and leaned in close, my ear to the wood. If a pang of guilt struck my conscience, I reasoned that circumstances warranted my breach of propriety.

"This will solve nothing," I heard my father say. "What's done is done, Beatrice. We can't change it."

"But it's our fault."

"We don't know that for sure. He might have done what he did for any number of reasons. Speculating won't bring him back."

"Oh, stop denying it." My mother's voice, choked with tears, rose in volume and pitch. "I warned you at the outset no good could come of your ridiculous little game. You should have left well enough alone. And now . . . now our friend's blood is on your hands. *Our* hands. I should have stopped you."

I gasped and whisked a hand to my mouth to stifle it. They had caused Sir Randall's death? My pulse thundered in my ears, drowning out any reply my father made. In the next instant, my mother cried out and a crash sounded from inside. My circumspection forgotten, I instinctively gripped the doorknob and pushed my way into the room.

My father stood at the foot of the bed, his face a mask of alarm. My mother sat at the dressing table, hands framing her face, the mirror reflecting a shock-ridden expression. Water dripped down the wall beside the table, and a mixture of sodden blossoms and shards of green glass littered the floor beneath.

I stood immobile, taking this all in. What a threesome we made, our gazes darting back and forth, each of us waiting for someone else to speak.

Mother's gaze met mine through the mirror. "I . . . uh . . .

had an accident, darling." Her hands slid from her cheeks and fell to her lap. She attempted a laugh, a weak and unconvincing effort. "Silly me, I tried to turn too fast and struck it with my elbow. It's quite all right. I don't believe the vase was anything of great value."

"You're up early," my father said. An accusation? He attempted to relax his stance and only succeeded in looking more ill at ease.

I saw no reason to maintain a charade. "Me, you, and everyone else, it would appear. What was going on in here? Mother, why were you crying? And please don't deny it, I heard you from the hallway. And your eyes are red and swollen."

She began to stammer in response, and my father crossed the room and placed a hand on her shoulder—one meant more to silence than to reassure, I thought. "Our good friend has just died, Emmaline. Surely you can understand our grief."

"I do understand, perhaps more than you realize. But that isn't why Mother was crying, is it? At least, not the simple fact of his death." I was about to continue, but Mother interrupted.

"Please, Arthur, let's just tell her."

"Beatrice." His fingers tightened on her shoulder, and a vein stood out on his temple. Then he breathed out a long sigh. "Very well. Emmaline, sit down."

I sat at the edge of the bed, near the footboard. Mother remained where she was at the dressing table, and Father dragged a side chair away from the wall.

He sat staring down at his shoes for some moments, then at length said, "You're aware Randall's recent sculptures hadn't been well received in the art world."

I nodded.

"There was one critic who took it upon himself to be particularly cruel, Henri Leclair. He was one of the first to publicly ridicule Randall, saying he should return to his hounds and horses."

"That was the man's way of saying Randall had no place in the art world," my mother explained. "Not only did his criticisms hurt Randall excessively, but paved the way for others to follow suit. I believe if not for that early assessment, other critics might have been more willing to give Randall's new abstracts a chance."

"I understand." I found myself gripping the brass finial on the corner of the footboard as my apprehensions slowly grew. "Sir Randall spoke to me of his disappointments. But what does this all have to do with the two of you?"

"This Leclair also had the most inelegant things to say about some of your father's work," my mother said, as if that explained everything. I frowned, and made a circular motion with my free hand, gesturing for my father to continue.

"Randall and I decided to teach Leclair a lesson," he said. "The man's a buffoon, with no more art expertise than a duck. Good grief, he hardly knows a Pissarro from a Monet. So we devised a plan . . ." He trailed off and glanced over at my mother, who closed her eyes and nodded. He turned back to me with a pained expression. "Randall publicly laughed off the criticism, and he invited Leclair to his Paris town house to show he harbored no hard feelings. Leclair went, and after a leisurely dinner Randall showed him a painting he had recently acquired. He said he trusted Leclair's discretion as well as his expertise to validate his purchase."

Father fell silent, swallowing. A sheen of perspiration gleamed across his forehead. My mother prompted, "Go on, Arthur. You can't stop now."

"Just say it, Father," I added. "What was this painting, and why would Randall want the opinion of a man he obviously disdained, and who disdained him?"

"Because Leclair was the most pompous ass you could ever meet—"

"Arthur, you shouldn't speak so in front of Emma."

"Mother, please." I couldn't help rolling my eyes. "Father, go on."

"We contrived for Randall to tell Leclair the painting was a lost work by Édouard Manet, an earlier version of his *Luncheon on the Grass*. Randall claimed he'd made the purchase from an anonymous seller, and that he was trusting Leclair to remain silent on the matter. Of course we knew he wouldn't."

I held up a hand. "Stop. I hear what you're saying. 'Contrived' and 'Randall claimed.' What was the truth about this painting?"

My parents traded glances. The silence grew heavy. As I was about to lose patience, Father said, "I painted it."

"What? Whatever do you mean, *you* painted it?"

"Darling, as your father said, he and Randall wanted to teach that awful man a lesson."

"And that lesson was what?" I tossed up my hands. "That Father is a competent art forger?"

"Well . . . yes, in a way," he said, far too calmly for my liking. "You see, we guessed Leclair would privately boast to his acquaintances and fellow art critics that he had verified a rare find, this so-called missing Manet. Once we let him brag a bit, we intended to admit our hoax, thus humiliating Leclair and exposing him for the ignorant fraud he is. Unfortunately . . ."

In the ensuing pause, Mother let out a moan that made me dread hearing the rest. I steeled myself, and demanded, "What happened next?"

"We never saw it coming, Emmaline. . . ."

"Indeed not, how could your father have anticipated such a thing?"

"What *thing*? If one of you doesn't finish this story, I

swear I'll . . ." I paused for lack of an appropriate consequence. What *would* I do? These were my parents, after all. I settled for an idle threat. "I'll run this story in the *Observer.*"

My mother gasped. "Emma, you wouldn't dare."

"Of course she wouldn't, Beatrice." Father raked his fingers through his hair. "What we hadn't realized was that Leclair was a criminal. Less than two weeks later, the painting was stolen right out of Randall's front parlor. Leclair had to have set it up, for he knew when the house would be empty. But that's not the worst of it. Whoever the thieves are, they apparently sold the painting on the black market. And whoever purchased it discovered the truth, albeit too late to cancel the transaction."

"If only they had consulted a competent expert beforehand, all this might have been avoided," Mother put in.

My father continued as if she hadn't interrupted. "The next thing we knew, Leclair disappeared, and threatening letters started showing up on Randall's doorstep. The buyer believed he and Leclair had worked together, and he wanted immediate recompense, one way or another, or he would expose Randall to the authorities as a fraud and a thief."

"But how could this person who deals in the black market expose Sir Randall without exposing himself?" I demanded to know.

"If he is someone of wealth and influence, as he most assuredly is, he need not fear the authorities," my father replied.

Yes, I understood that. My Vanderbilt relatives were not above dictating terms to police and lawmakers when they deemed it necessary. "What about this Leclair person? You said he disappeared. Do you know where he is now?"

Mother and Father traded ominous glances. Mother looked away, her bottom lip quivering. My father's shoulders bunched. "He's dead, Emmaline, in a so-called coaching accident."

An ill sensation gathered in the pit of my stomach. "Surely the buyer didn't . . . wouldn't have . . ."

"Emmaline, this is someone who deals in the black market. He's as much a criminal as the thieves who stole the painting. More so, in fact. He'll have resources and ways of exacting his revenge without ever dirtying his hands."

I let my head fall into my hands and curled my fingers into my hair. "You didn't think this was important enough to mention to Jesse yesterday?" I raised my face again. "Mother, Father, what were you thinking? Who else in your group knows about this?"

"No one," my mother said quickly. "I don't think anyone else knows."

"You don't *think*?" I raised my eyebrows at her, incredulous.

"None of the others here know," Father said with more conviction. "And no one outside the group knows we're here. We put out that Randall was returning to England and that your mother and I would be joining him there."

"It would be easy enough for someone to verify that," I pointed out. "Don't you realize you might have been followed here, and Sir Randall—"

"He jumped, Emmaline," my father said tersely. Tears gathered in my mother's eyes and her lips quivered. "The distress of everything that happened—his poor reviews, the hoax, Leclair's death—it all became too much for him. He—"

All pretense of calm forgotten, my father broke off and compressed his lips. A tear rolled down my mother's cheek. "We should have realized how distraught he'd become," she said. "We let our friend down, and now he's . . ." A sob slipped out. "Oh, Arthur, how could we?"

How could they indeed? Judging them would serve no purpose, yet suddenly my brother Brady's antics in recent years began to make sense, if this was the kind of example my parents had set early on. I was finding it harder and harder to believe Sir Randall's death had been self-inflicted, however much I wanted to believe it, considering the alternative.

"Do the art thieves or the individual who bought the painting know who painted it?"

My father shrugged, shook his head. "I wouldn't think so. Randall surely wouldn't have given me up like that."

"Let's hope not," I said wearily. "Wait one minute. You didn't want me staying here for a reason." I narrowed my eyes at both my parents. "You aren't any more convinced Sir Randall's death was a suicide than I am. Or than Jesse is."

"Jesse suspects . . . ?" My mother trailed off and looked away.

"What makes you say that?" My father raised his chin to me. "He didn't express any such suspicions yesterday."

"I know," I said simply, remembering the look Jesse had sent me right before he left the dining room. Speculation became rife in both my parents' gazes, but I offered no other explanation.

Finally, Father said, "He's wrong. And the reason we were opposed to you staying here—" He paused and addressed my mother. "We *were* opposed, and we might as well admit it. Our daughter is no dunce." He looked back at me. "We feared Randall would tell you too much, and you with your reporter's instinct for details would hound us until the whole truth came out."

I bit down against a sudden pang. Here I had thought perhaps my parents had feared for my welfare if the art buyer *had* followed them to Newport. But no, their concerns had been for themselves, for saving face in front of their daughter. Determined not to show my disappointment, I drew myself up and swallowed a sense of bitterness. "Well, for all your efforts, the whole truth has come out, hasn't it?" I scowled. "Or is there more?"

"No, that's the whole of it," my mother said quickly.

"I'm going down to telephone Jesse." I turned about and started for the door. My mother called out my name in a plea I didn't heed.

I put in my call, yet found myself somehow tongue-tied when Jesse came on the line. I knew I needed to inform him of this new information, but my father's prank, I found, smoldered like an ember of shame inside me. I told myself the telephone was not the proper forum by which to divulge such information, that Jesse, as a longtime family friend, deserved to hear of this matter in person and have the chance to question my father firsthand. It was an excuse, of course. I simply wasn't ready to speak the words out loud. So instead I asked Jesse if the coroner had discovered anything about Sir Randall's head wounds.

"I'm afraid the results are inconclusive and destined to remain that way," he replied. "There simply isn't any clear evidence that the injuries might have been caused by anything other than the cliff face."

"I feared that might be the case. But Jesse, do *you* believe Sir Randall committed suicide?"

"Do you?" he countered.

I shook my head, then said out loud, "Not entirely, no. I have a nagging sensation that won't go away. I'd spoken with Sir Randall that afternoon, and he didn't talk like a man intent on dying. In fact, the last time I saw him he seemed greatly encouraged. Of course, I didn't know him well enough to be certain of that."

"There is something about these artists that leaves me uneasy, Emma," he said at length.

My father's confession prodded again, and again I persuaded myself to wait until I saw Jesse in person to explain to him about the hoax. But I agreed with him—all was not right when it came to this incongruent group of friends.

"I'd prefer it if you'd let me handle this case from here on in," he said at length. "Go home. Please."

He was right. Home was the safest option. But when had I ever chosen the safest option? "I'm going to stay on for today at least and try to find out as much as I can about these people." Before he could argue, I said, "I promise to keep clear of the cliffs."

Jesse's groan of frustration tickled my ear. "I'll be back once the coroner makes his final report. And Emma . . ."

I waited, growing puzzled as his silence persisted. Had we lost the connection? I was about to give the hand crank a turn to summon back the operator, when Jesse spoke again. "Promise me you'll be careful."

It was nothing he hadn't said to me before, yet it was unlike anything he had ever said before. The slight tremor in his voice traveled through me, producing a quiver, a trill, before settling in my heart with a warm vibration. He had been plain enough in the past and I understood his affections for me—at least I thought I did. There was something more here, something unexpectedly poignant. Something I was not ready to hear—and might never be ready to hear.

I drew a breath that rasped in my throat. "I will. I promise. And if I learn anything I'll telephone you immediately."

I hung up before he could reply.

Chapter 7

After luncheon, I returned to the service wing to look for Patch. I found him in the porch, and rather than attacking my legs in his usual fashion, he walked sedately to me with his head sagging low. His tail gave a few halfhearted wags.

"What's wrong, boy?"

He sat, leaning his weight against my legs, and I crouched to pet him. A surge of affection prompted me to wrap my arms around him. "It left its mark on you, didn't it, finding Sir Randall like that?" Was that possible? Could an animal be so affected by human misfortune? Could he understand the significance of what he had discovered yesterday morning? "Goodness, you don't blame yourself, do you? You don't think, because you found Sir Randall, that his death was somehow your fault?"

At a noise in the doorway of the servants' hall, I glanced up to see Mrs. Harris holding her flour-coated arms out from her sides to spare her cotton dress, though a good measure of flour also dusted her apron. The savory fragrances of roasting meat and baking pastry crust filled the air around me, making me momentarily homesick for my kitchen at home and Nanny's flavorful cooking.

Mrs. Harris regarded me keenly, and I laughed halfheartedly beneath her scrutiny. "You must think I'm daft, talking to a dog this way."

"I don't think anything of the sort, miss. A dog's got his sensibilities, same as a person. He barely touched the veal trimmings I set out for his breakfast. My guess is, he needs a good romp to put yesterday out of his mind."

I stood up, which brought Patch immediately onto four legs as well. "You're right. Come on, Patch, let's have a run, shall we?"

Once beyond the porch and the service courtyard, Patch took a sharp left turn, toward the cliffs. True, quite a lot of lawn lay between us and the precipice, but if indeed yesterday continued to haunt my little friend, a change of scenery would do him good.

"This way," I called to him.

He continued to run eastward. I beckoned again and quickened my steps, but instead of continuing to the edge of the property, he headed southward and stopped at the gate of the kitchen garden. I raised my hems and bolted forward, regretting not having found some rope to fashion a leash.

The pungency of loam and growing things greeted me from over the high privet hedges as I approached the garden. Though winter dormancy would come within a few weeks, the cultivated rows still teemed with life.

I soon discovered what had lured Patch to this spot, as voices and laughter sounded within. I peeked through the gate. A good dozen or so yards down the lengthy enclosure, two men walked side by side away from me, their hands playfully skimming the tops of the taller plants—tomatoes, okra, chard, and basil. A few accented words drifted my way, and I identified the pair as Vasili Pavlenko, the Russian, and Claude Baptiste, the Frenchman. The latter wore a dark cutaway and light gray trousers; the former wore a matching suit in beige with thin brown stripes. Both sported boaters.

As I watched, they came to a halt and faced each other. They spoke more quietly now, whereupon the elder Claude pressed a hand to his chest, eliciting a burst of laughter from the former dancer. Though I considered this an odd place for a stroll, I dismissed their presence and was about to guide Patch away when he let out a bark.

And then another. With his nose pressed between the bars of the wrought iron gate, he began a serenade of howling. His first outburst had resulted in the two men lurching apart, and now they turned their perplexed faces in our direction. My own face flamed, and I began to stammer.

"Sorry. Dogs, you know. He took off. I tried to stop him. Didn't mean to interrupt . . . uh . . . that is, disturb you . . ." I left off, feeling inexplicably nonplussed. I hadn't done anything wrong, really. Anyone might enter the kitchen garden—it wasn't off limits, and in fact at any time Mrs. Harris or Irene might have entered to pluck herbs or vegetables for tonight's dinner. So why did I feel like a trespasser, intruding where I had no right to be?

Then again, why had they suddenly put several feet between them, each now standing on one of the two outer walkways that ran the garden's perimeters, when, before Patch's interruption, they had stood together on one of the smaller paths that connected the two main ones? Their startled expressions lingered as if they were two rabbits caught marauding the carrot patch, until Vasili murmured something and the two men visibly relaxed. They started toward me.

"I'm so sorry," I continued to apologize.

"Not at all, Miss Cross." The handsome young Russian grinned, all hints of unease vanishing. "Your dog, he likes to play, yes?"

With a sniff that might have expressed the tiniest bit of disdain, Claude unlatched the gate and they both stepped through. Patch backed away and sat, something he rarely did when presented with a new potential playmate. I frowned down at him in concern.

"He's been acting strangely this morning."

"Are not we all?" Vasili murmured.

"Perhaps he misses his home." Claude brushed his palms against the sides of his coat as if to dislodge bits of foliage or dust. "Have you considered returning him to familiar surroundings?"

"He'd likely only follow me back here. He knows the way now."

The Frenchman cast me a significant look, one whose meaning didn't elude me. *Go home as well, Miss Cross.* Both men seemed coiled on the balls of their feet in apparent eagerness to be away. On a journalist's instinct, I employed a lady's prerogative to impose on their good breeding.

"I've been wondering about the work you came here to accomplish," I said, forestalling their departure. "The work you'll now dedicate to Sir Randall. I'm fascinated to learn more about both of you."

"We were discussing just that when you appeared." Vasili cast a pointed glance at Patch. "We have decided to collaborate."

"On *Carmen*?" I pressed my hands together, not altogether insincerely. True, I wanted to keep them talking, but the notion of these men bringing such life to the stage truly did thrill me.

"Shh." Claude darted a glance up at the house. "We spoke in the garden for a reason, Miss Cross. Can you be discreet?"

"I most certainly can."

"I do not wish Miss Marcus to learn of our plans. Not yet."

Vasili nodded his agreement.

"Then you won't cast her as Carmen," I said. The Frenchman shook his head. "But why not? She's one of the best in the world, isn't she?"

"She was," Vasili said.

"She is losing her talents," Claude added. "Her voice—it is not what it was, though she will not admit to it. Either she does not hear, or she cannot accept."

In the past two days I had found ample reason to reassess my opinion of Josephine Marcus and no longer admired her as I once had. Still, my stomach sank at the thought of the music world losing such a talent. A brush against my skirts signaled that Patch had come to my side, and I took comfort in his warm body once more pressed against my legs. "Perhaps she needs to rest her voice."

"I suggested as much to her," the Frenchman said. "She took offense and told me to mind my business."

I considered a moment, still reluctant to accept that a renowned soprano could be silenced and summarily dismissed. "Do you think it has to do with her smoking cigarettes?"

Vasili let out a laugh. Again, Claude shrugged. "If anything, the smoking is said to help."

I wrinkled my nose. "I realize some people believe in the health benefits of tobacco, but I know how I feel in a room full of smoke—as though I cannot breathe."

"Perhaps she has taken up her cigarettes as an excuse, to blame for her fading voice." Vasili kicked at blades of grass, and again I felt his eagerness to be gone.

"But the two of you have decided to collaborate," I said brightly—and relentlessly, refusing to allow them to slip away. I was not a reporter for nothing, and I knew how to force my way into a story. "Mr. Pavlenko, I assume you will choreograph the opera. Do you intend something new for the production? Perhaps a full departure from the traditional step design?"

"Yes, and in fact . . ."

Slowly we strolled while they talked and I listened. I managed to steer us back around to the front of the house, where Patch lingered at my side for a time, but finally took off, bounding and leaping in his usual way. It came as a tremendous relief to watch his ears, one white and the other brown, flapping with each playful stride. He held my gaze while Vasili and Claude had my ear. What they described sounded uncannily similar to Sir Randall's ideas about sculpture—a kind of trimmed-down, modernized rendering of the traditional production. Even their notions of set design dispensed with fussy details to create a backdrop reminiscent of a bullfighting ring. The audience's attention, they maintained, would be held by the performance of the libretto, rather than on ornate visual minutiae.

It occurred to me that theater encompassed the senses of both sight and hearing, and robbing the audience of one or the other might lead to disappointment. I held my tongue. I also considered questioning Monsieur Baptiste about his failed partnership with Mrs. Wharton, but thought better of it. Rather, I carefully observed the pair. Had they recognized the similarities between their philosophy and Sir Randall's? Had they collaborated with him? Or had they simply borrowed his ideas, possibly without his blessing?

To my surprise the two men began demonstrating the "Chorus of Soldiers" from act one of *Carmen*. Claude hummed the melody, a bit nasally but in tune. With their arms held wide they indicated how the soldiers would enter the stage and where they would be positioned. I watched, amazed, as the pair filled my imagination with images of the performance. They themselves moved in a choreographed dance that delighted me . . . and Patch as well, who trotted over to inspect the goings-on. His former reticence at the garden had vanished in his eagerness to join what he apparently interpreted as a frolicsome game, and he added his own yips and barks to create a harmonious ruckus. Rather than humming now, Claude Baptiste bellowed the melody, while Vasili pirouetted and executed a stunning *jeté entrelacé.*

Ballet was not part of this particular opera, but that didn't stop Vasili. My hand flew to my mouth as he leaped away from us across the lawn in a *saut de basque*, jumping and turning again and again with his legs outstretched until he propelled himself straight up in a thrilling twist several feet in the air. His hair flashed in the sunlight, and his toned and well-proportioned figure seemed lighter than the scuttling clouds overhead.

He landed on his feet and paused, breathing heavily, his head bowed. One hand went to his hip. He pressed it there a moment before slowly turning around and making his way back to us. His expression turned sad, his smile apologetic.

"Well," was all he said, and he looked away.

I had not fully understood previously, but now my heart physically hurt as I realized how very much he had lost due to his injury. For brief seconds his face had been filled with utter joy, and that joy had filled me as well as I beheld even those small traces of his talent. Only because of that joy could I even slightly fathom the depths of despair he experienced each time he remembered his former life.

His friend clapped him on the shoulder. His hand remained there as Claude Baptiste turned to me. "Miss Cross, if you will excuse us now."

"Of course, I . . . Thank you so much for sharing your plans with me."

They walked off together, talking and laughing as they had been when Patch and I first found them. They seemed an odd pair of friends, mismatched in age and physical appearance. I supposed their artistic natures provided common ground enough, and I was glad the Frenchman was able to prevent his younger friend from falling hopelessly into melancholy.

It struck me how many calamities this group of artists had endured—Sir Randall's failing career, depression, and subsequent death; the injury that prevented Vasili from ever dancing professionally again; Josephine Marcus's fading voice. Were there other hidden misfortunes waiting to be discovered?

That evening before dinner I retired to my room to complete the notes I'd taken during the day. I attempted to describe the impromptu performance by Vasili Pavlenko, with admittedly little true success. I had also spent time with Niccolo Lionetti, who had played his cello for me. He'd explained how he allowed his instrument to guide his playing, rather than merely following the sheet music. I could not say I entirely understood him, but I did conclude that he achieved something extraordinary.

A knock at my door stilled my thoughts and my pencil. "Come in."

My mother poked her head into the room. "Are you terribly busy?"

Part of me wished to tell her yes, I was. Why did this reluctance to speak privately with either of my parents continue to linger? I'd more than come to terms with the old bitterness once directed at Mrs. Wharton, so why my hesitation with Mother and Father? What was I truly avoiding?

"No," I said, "not terribly." I smiled and gestured for her to come in. When she sat on the edge of my bed, I pivoted on my chair before the dressing table, which I'd been using as a desk. A heavy silence fell between us, as obvious as it was awkward. Mother stared down at her hands, resting in her lap.

"You're angry with us," she said at length. I winced, not having expected such directness.

"Shouldn't I be? Father committed fraud in Paris—"

"It was only meant to be a prank. We never intended for it to become so out of hand."

"And then you concealed your actions from everyone, including me." Suddenly I found myself falling into the maternal role I often assumed with Brady. How odd to take such a stance with my own mother. "Not only might you have endangered yourselves and your friends, but you came home under false pretenses."

"Yes, all that is true, and I apologize for it. Again." She added emphasis to that last word, as if to suggest I might accept her contrition with an ounce of graciousness. "There is something more here, isn't there? Something that began long ago."

Her perceptiveness rendered me at a momentary loss. I needed a moment to gather my thoughts, and so I stalled for time. "Why do you say that?"

She smiled and released a breathy little laugh. "You've been avoiding us since our arrival. Since before you knew about the hoax."

"I've been doing my job, Mother." I kept my voice light, amiable. But she was correct. I *had* been avoiding them. "It's my task to interview everyone here and learn about the course their careers have taken. I can't spend all my time with you and Father."

"You've spent precious little time with your father and me. I'd say as little as you can manage. Your father is as much an artist as anyone else here, yet you haven't asked him a single question about his career."

"I thought I'd familiarize myself with the others first."

She studied me, her brow furrowing. "Is it because we went away to Paris? We never would have gone if we thought you'd be alone. But you weren't, were you? You had Aunt Sadie and Nanny. And your cousins, of course."

Again, she was right, on both counts. When they first left the country, I had already taken up residence at Gull Manor. Great-Aunt Sadie had been alive then and had wanted me to learn the nuances of the house and property she intended leaving me when she passed. Nanny had come with me as well, so essentially I'd had two strong female influences and, with my Vanderbilt cousins here part of the year, a stable family around me.

But Aunt Sadie hadn't been as strong as I'd believed, and had left this world less than two years later. And Nanny . . . I'd never realized just how much she had aged since my childhood. She had always seemed timeless to me—never young, never changing, always the same stolid, stoic support she had always been. Then one day I truly looked at her and knew she needed taking care of as much as I did, that I could no longer lean so wholly against her but must be as obliging to her as she had always been to me.

"And you had Brady," Mother added, unaware of my thoughts.

It was my turn to laugh. "Brady had *me*, you mean. My goodness, until last summer he was a child. I can't tell you how often I had to intervene with Jesse to have charges of drunk and disorderly conduct dismissed."

"It can't have been as bad as all that." She flashed a grin, but guilt flickered behind her eyes. Was she remembering her first husband, Brady's father? Stuart Braden Gale III had been a dashing sportsman with charisma that lit up any room—or so I'd been told. But accompanying that affability had been ribald behavior, a reckless disregard for his own welfare and that of others, and a propensity for spending far more money than he could ever make. Thus had been my brother's path as well until life taught him a painful lesson that forced him into sobriety and responsibility. He was still my lighthearted half brother, but the devil-may-care attitude had, one might say, been relinquished to the devil.

But perhaps Mother had touched upon the heart of what troubled me. "Brady needed you last summer," I said. "Yes, he had me, Nanny, Jesse . . ." I'd been about to mention another name but I trailed off lest Mother ask questions. I had no desire to talk about Derrick Andrews, not with her, not with anyone. I felt his absence too keenly. For the foreseeable future he remained beyond my reach, and it simply hurt too much to contemplate him as anything more than a fond but distant memory.

A lie perhaps, but one that helped me live through each day without him.

"Brady had us, but your presence would have meant the world to him," I finished rather feebly.

"Brady and I corresponded following those awful events of last summer. Any animosity that might have existed on his part has been resolved." She reached out across the narrow distance between us. "Why then should you hold grudges on his behalf?" Another question I couldn't answer. She continued to beckon with her outstretched hand. "Emma, come sit with me. Please," she added, as if already anticipating my refusal.

With my attention on the scene outside my window, I rose. A misting rain was falling and the treetops swayed back and forth in a sensual dance. I searched for remnants of the afternoon sun behind the pewter-edged clouds crouching low in the sky. My earlier prophesy of an approaching storm seemed about to be fulfilled.

I sat on the bed beside my mother, at first perching rigidly, then forcing myself to relax as the mattress sank beneath me.

"Thank you," she said, aware, perhaps even more than I,

of how difficult that had been for me. I only wished I could explain the reasons. She hadn't been a poor mother, quite the contrary. Through both my parents I had learned about art and self-expression and been exposed to a multitude of ideas unheard of in most children's lives. I couldn't but credit them with setting early examples that readied me for the independence Aunt Sadie would later foster in me, and that had ultimately allowed me, as an adult, to stride into the offices of the Newport *Observer* with several articles in hand and a request for employment.

There *had* been times in recent years when my burdens had become overwhelming, and I had wished nothing more than to have my parents here to relieve my anxieties. This had garnered my resentment, yet I couldn't but admit I persevered and eventually triumphed. My confidence in my own abilities had grown accordingly—but would it have, if my parents had been here?

Perhaps I had more to be grateful for than I thought.

I slipped my hand into hers and immediately sensed the relief that washed over her. I gave her fingers a little squeeze. "Perhaps we must become reacquainted. It's been several years, and I've changed since we met last."

"Of that I have no doubt, darling. Your father and I are very proud of you. You've achieved a lot, and we believe you'll achieve more." She leaned a little away as if to view me from a distance. "I wonder, would you have accomplished as much had we been here?"

Goodness, had she read my mind? Perhaps, but the matter was far from simple, and our relationship was far from entirely mended. It was, however, a beginning. Arching my eyebrows, I said, "I suppose we'll never know, will we?"

That produced a rueful chuckle, but Mother sobered quickly. "If you're wondering why I came alone to speak with you, it's because your father is rather hurt, Emma, by how you've ignored him so far. He would never admit it, but there it is. Perhaps you might . . ."

"Perhaps I'll ask him for an interview after dinner, and suggest again that I sit for a portrait," I finished for her.

Mother replied by embracing me, and with only an instant's hesitation I returned the hug. We had made a stride, but there would need to be more.

That evening I again donned Cousin Gertrude's champagne Rouff gown, this time without the jacket. Instead I draped an embroidered shawl of Aunt Sadie's over my shoulders and wondered why we were bothering to dress for dinner. Jesse hadn't returned with more questions about Sir Randall, which meant the coroner hadn't yet finalized his report about the head injury.

I patted my hair in place, adjusted my shawl, and was just opening my bedroom door when a muffled but distinct caterwauling made its way down the main second-floor hallway. My parents' door swung open and they stepped out, apparently ready for dinner. They, too, stopped short to listen.

"What on earth?" they chorused. Then my mother said, "That sounds like Josephine."

Shrieks set us in motion. The three of us hurried to the main landing of the upper story, where more doors were opening. Teddy and Edith Wharton joined us. My parents and I didn't stop, but followed the shrieks across the gallery to the northern wing of bedrooms. Others peeked out of their rooms, inquiring what the matter was. I came to a halt outside Miss Marcus's bedroom. Mother had been correct. It was from behind the opera singer's door that the shrieking emanated, accompanied by an odd whooshing sound as well.

"Miss Marcus," I called out, my hand on the knob.

"Josephine!" My mother stood behind me, craning over my shoulder. "Emma, quickly, open the door."

I swung it open. Miss Marcus was nowhere to be seen, but her cries continued, along with the now identifiable sound of gushing water.

"The bathroom." Mrs. Wharton pushed past me. At the open bathroom door she gripped the lintel with both hands in an attempt to stop herself. She didn't quite, and raised a splash when her feet hit the bathroom floor. "Good gracious!"

Mother and I came up behind her to discover a pond spreading across the marble tiles. Miss Marcus stood several feet back from the pedestal sink, her head down and her arms held out in front of her like a shield against the plume arcing from a pipe that ran up the wall. Water streamed from her hair and clothes and she appeared frozen in shock, except for her formidable shouts. I had wished to hear her sing. Now I was learning just how powerful a trained soprano's voice could be.

For a moment astonishment held us all immobile. Then my father's hand came down on my shoulder, nudging me out of the way. Mrs. Wharton stepped aside, too, and Father and Mr. Wharton proceeded into the bathroom. Their feet slid on the tiles, and they grabbed each other's shoulders in an attempt to avoid falling. By some miracle they remained upright, raising splashes that sent the water eddying into the marble baseboards, around the feet of the claw foot tub, and the base of the pedestal sink.

Fighting through the spray, my father made his way to the offending pipe. He wrapped his hands around it in a futile attempt to stem the flow. He became instantly soaked. At Miss Marcus's side, Mr. Wharton struggled out of his evening coat and tossed it around her shoulders, not that the dripping coat was any better than her sodden gown. With an arm around her waist he guided her to the bathroom door, where Mrs. Wharton took over.

"Come, Josephine, dearest, it's all right. Just a broken pipe. We'll soon have you set to rights."

Several male voices filled the bedroom behind me as I continued to monitor my father's efforts to stop the water, now with Mr. Wharton's help. Countless times their feet seemed about to slide out from under them. They clutched the sink to keep from sprawling.

I was nudged again, and Niccolo Lionetti, Carl, and Mr. Dunn streamed around me. I couldn't help thinking the efforts of five men would be no more effective than those of one. The bathroom fell to chaos: water and shouts and dripping figures until Mr. Dunn shooed the other three away and Carl helped them maneuver over the wet floor back into the bedroom. Mr. Dunn sank to his knees, instantly drenching his trousers, reached under the sink, and found the main valve. The thing squeaked in protest as he twisted and twisted, but gradually the spray diminished and finally ebbed to a feeble *drip, drip, drip*.

In the bedroom, Mrs. Wharton and my mother attempted to comfort Miss Marcus.

"All right?" The soprano's voice shot to high C. "Does this look *all right* to you?" She held her arms up and away from her plum silk gown. "This dress is from Madame Paquin—*Paquin* I tell you—and it's ruined. And my hair, my *shoes.*" She gave a fierce tug on her hems, displaying the watermarks on a pair of exquisite, yellow satin evening slippers adorned with purple beading. "And the shock of it all. I thought I was being attacked. I didn't know what was happening—I had no idea! I thought I was about die, truly I did."

My mother let out a breath of relief. "I didn't know what to think with all that screaming. Thank goodness it's only a broken water pipe and nothing more serious than that. Josephine will be fine. Gentlemen, thank you, but I suggest you leave us now to help her to dry off and change."

At the bathroom sink, Mr. Dunn straightened, running his hands over his hair, which had been forced from its usual slicked-back style to something resembling the spiky vegetation I'd spied in the kitchen garden. He tugged to straighten his coat for good measure. With his dignity thusly reassembled as far as was possible, he walked like a condemned man across the flooded floor into the bedroom.

"You!" Miss Marcus's finger shot out. She would grant no quarter, it seemed. "How could you let his happen?"

"I . . . uh . . . I'm so very sorry . . . I can't imagine . . . the handyman . . . it should have been inspected . . . may I . . . get you something?"

"No, indeed," Miss Marcus shouted, "unless it is to undo all this damage your incompetence has inflicted upon me."

Glancing around at the others, I could have attested that Miss Marcus was not the sole recipient of those damages. Water verily dripped from Father, Mr. Wharton, Niccolo, and even Mrs. Wharton. My own hems showed dark stains where the water had lapped them, and the moisture was spreading to my stockings and felt cold against my ankles. I held my tongue and decided that with my mother and Mrs. Wharton there to attend to our indignant victim, I had no reason to remain. I followed the men out into the corridor, where I heard Mr. Dunn promising to have the handyman remedy the broken pipe immediately.

I met Vasili Pavlenko outside his bedroom on my way back to my room. "What was that about?" He was in vest and shirtsleeves, and seemed to be fumbling to secure a cuff link.

I took hold of the jeweled piece and snapped the backing into place, remembering with a start that I used to do so for my father. "Everything is all right. Just a broken water pipe in Miss Marcus's bathroom. It was quite a mess and rather traumatizing for her."

"That I do not doubt." He inspected my handiwork and gave the sapphire-studded link a slight turn. He jerked his chin in the direction of my hemline. "You are wet."

"A little, but not nearly as bad as some of the others. If you'll excuse me, I need to change again before dinner. Everyone does, so if I were you I wouldn't hurry down to the dining room."

"No, I should think not," he said with an amused chuckle.

Chapter 8

Some forty-five minutes later, eight of us, in dry clothes, gathered around the dining table. No one sat, but remained standing and trading wary looks. A horrible sinking sensation robbed me of my appetite.

The table had been set for nine. Like a nightmarish repetition of last night, someone was missing.

"I'll wager Claude couldn't decide which cravat to wear." Mrs. Wharton gave a weak laugh. "You all know how he can be."

"Was he there with the rest of us in Josephine's room?" My father gripped the back of his chair. "Does anyone remember seeing him?"

Heads shook in reply. Miss Marcus raised a hand to lightly touch a reset curl. "I certainly wouldn't remember if he'd been there or not. It's all a blur."

"He may have fallen asleep," Vasili Pavlenko said with an eagerness that hinted at desperation.

Apparently I wasn't the only one experiencing doubts coupled with a sense of dread. Last night, a man had gone missing at dinner, and the next morning we found Sir Randall at the bottom of the cliff. . . .

"Perhaps we should go check on him," Mother suggested.

No one moved. Rain splattered the windows, and gusts of wind sent sheets of water angling across the dusky rear lawns. In the distance, thunder rumbled, and Miss Marcus shivered. "How I hate this weather."

"I will check on him." Vasili stepped away from the table and, in a motion nearly as graceful as his earlier pirouettes, turned about and started for the doorway. A flurry of activity broke out behind him as first the Whartons and then the rest of the company abandoned the table and bustled to follow. I took up the rear. The stairs creaked beneath the weight of the small stampede. At the upper landing the group came to a halt and waited as Vasili approached Claude Baptiste's bedroom door. He knocked and called out the man's name.

"No answer," he said to us unnecessarily.

"Try the door," my father said.

Mother sidestepped toward the upper gallery. "Perhaps we ladies should wait farther along the hallway. He might have fallen asleep in a state of dishabille."

When neither Mrs. Wharton, Miss Marcus, nor I moved to join her, Mother moved back to my side and slipped her hand into mine. Vasili opened the bedroom door and called Claude's name again, and everyone craned their necks to see inside. Just as with Miss Marcus earlier, I saw no sign of him. The bedclothes lay perfectly unrumpled, just as Irene had left them this morning after cleaning the room. A suit of clothing draped the mahogany valet stand. Unlike the earlier scene, however, not a sound met our ears.

"He might have gone for a walk." Miss Marcus's voice quavered slightly.

"Claude? Are you here?" Vasili ventured farther into the room, and the rest of us filed through behind him. It was then I noticed the bathroom door stood ajar. Vasili reached it and pushed the door inward.

His cry echoed off the tiled walls. Russian words tore from his throat. The men—my father, Niccolo, and Teddy Wharton—scrambled into the bathroom. Miss Marcus trembled violently, and at another anguished cry from Vasili, she let out a scream. My mother and Mrs. Wharton immediately flanked her. With their faces filled with horror and their eyes wide with questions, they turned her about, tugging gently when her feet didn't move.

"Come away, Josephine." My mother glanced over her shoulder at me. "You too, Emma."

But I had already set my course. Mother called out to me again, but too late. I stepped into the bathroom, the marble seemingly alive with the echoes of Vasili's grief. He had sunk to his knees, moaning, his head resting on the rim of the ornate tub. Beside his own face lay that of Claude Baptiste—his eyes open but sightless, his skin as pale as the surrounding marble of the tub.

"He is cold . . . he is dead. . . ."

My father bent over Vasili and half coaxed, half hauled him to his feet. His body slack, Monsieur Baptiste's head and shoulders slid down into the water with a splash.

"Nyet—*nyet*!" Shouting in his native tongue, the former dancer broke away from my father and threw himself back onto the floor beside the tub. Pathetically, he reached in, soaking his sleeves to the elbows, and raised the Frenchman's torso until his shoulders and head again rested on the side of the tub. My father turned around, I presumed, to seek the help of the other men. He spotted me.

"Emmaline, go. You don't belong here." He closed his hands over Vasili's shaking shoulders even as he addressed me.

I ignored Father's command and inched closer. For reasons I would never understand, Fate had decreed this kind of tragedy to be exactly where I belonged. Claude Baptiste's body lay submerged in the spacious tub except for his head and shoulders, held upright by a shaking Vasili. From what I could see of the Frenchman, he appeared to be fully undressed. Out of respect I didn't confirm that myself.

"Is he wearing anything?" I asked my father.

His face stony, he shook his head. "He must have been taking a bath and dozed off. Someone needs to alert the police."

Wearily I nodded. "I'll telephone Jesse. Father, you and the others need to leave."

"Yes. After we carry him into the bedroom."

"No." I spoke sharply, and each man viewed me with varying degrees of perplexity. Except Vasili, who glared up at me from beneath his brows. His eyes were red and already swollen; he wiped his nose on his wet sleeve. "You cannot move him yet," I said more gently.

"We cannot leave him," Vasili shouted, his voice rough with tears. Father again closed his hands over the younger man's shoulders.

"We must. The police must be able to examine the . . ." I almost said *body* but caught myself in time. ". . . The scene, and we've already done enough damage."

"Are you saying . . ." Teddy Wharton stepped in front of me, essentially blocking my way into the bedroom. "Are you calling this a . . ."

"I'm not calling it anything, Mr. Wharton. Whatever happened here is for the police to determine, and the less we interfere the better. Now if you'll excuse me, I had better make that telephone call."

Jesse and two policemen arrived over three quarters of an hour later, citing the rain for the delay. He brought with him a waft of cold air when he stepped inside, for in the past hours our lovely late summer had abandoned us to the chill of an autumn storm. Jesse's shoes scattered droplets as he stamped them on the mat in the front vestibule, and his coat sleeves gleamed with moisture where the open sides of the police buggy had let the rain in. His red hair hung in a fringe of dark, sodden russet over his forehead and around his ears, and with one hand he swept it back.

"Upstairs?" he asked without preamble.

"Monsieur Baptiste's bedroom," I told him just as bluntly. "I'm afraid several of us traipsed into that bathroom. There's no telling what evidence we disturbed."

Jesse nodded to his men, who shuffled by and made their way to the stairs. "So you don't believe this could have been an accident . . . or a suicide, perhaps brought on by Sir Randall's death?"

"Do you?" It wasn't a question really, but a firm guess that Jesse and I shared the same view.

His hand rose, the backs of his fingers grazing my cheek. It was a gesture he'd repeated countless times in the past, beginning when I was a child and he my father's young friend, a rookie policeman, and our neighbor on the Point. I had grown up in the ensuing years and Jesse had come to see me differently, so that what had once been an offhand gesture of affection had taken on a great deal more meaning. Though instinct urged me to look away, I held his gaze, saw sentiments I wasn't sure I wished to see, and smiled sadly.

He met my smile with one that held equal melancholy. "I'm sorry this is happening again."

I merely nodded and helped him off with his overcoat. "Come," I said, "I'll lead the way."

When we reached the Stair Hall we were immediately surrounded by the others and the deafening jumble of their voices. It seemed no one viewed this second death as an accident and they demanded to know what Jesse intended to do about it. Loudest and most bitter among them, Vasili leaned like a broken man against the wide doorway of the Great Hall, his arms held tight around him, his handsome features almost feral.

Mrs. Wharton alone attempted to use reason to calm them, raising her voice above theirs to remind them we didn't yet know how Claude died. Miss Marcus turned to snap at her with impatient words that bordered on hysteria. Only my parents looked on silently, their gazes swimming with foreboding and speculation. The dealer in black market art—is that what they feared? Had that man—or men—traced my parents and Sir Randall all the way to Newport? But why then murder Claude Baptiste, who had nothing to do with the hoax, at least as far as my parents knew . . . or had admitted.

Jesse raised his hands for silence. The uproar dwindled and then ceased altogether. But it was a silence fraught with tension ready to reignite at any moment.

"Please don't panic," he said. "Leave this to my men and me."

"Much good you have done so far." Vasili spat the words and hugged himself tighter. "You leave us here to be picked off one by one."

"There can be no satisfaction for them at present," I whispered in Jesse's ear. He turned at my urging and we started up the stairs. The grumbling that broke out below followed us up to the second-floor landing. There I quickly led Jesse to Claude's bedroom door, but a sudden barking and the sound of Irene's voice stopped us from stepping through.

Patch came loping in from the servants' wing—he must have come up the back stairs—and trotted down the hall to me. He sniffed at my hand, gave a lick, and then bounced to Jesse to convey similar greetings.

Irene appeared a second or two later. "I'm so sorry, Miss Cross. I'd left the stairwell door open and he slipped past me." She stooped to seize his collar but he was too quick for her, circling Jesse's legs and squeezing between us.

"It's all right, Irene." I sighed ruefully down at him. "I'll look after him now, thank you."

Irene curtsied and retraced her steps. Jesse and I, with Patch trotting between us, entered the bedroom and went through to the bathroom. I admonished Patch in my firmest voice to stay in the bedroom. Now that he had apparently gotten his way he seemed content to obey me, although his eyes remained alert and his ears twitched with interest.

Without Vasili to hold him, Monsieur Baptiste lay submerged. Upon seeing me enter the room with Jesse, one of the uniformed policemen stretched a towel across the middle portion of the tub, effectively shielding the man's private parts from view. Jesse addressed one of the officers. "Have you found anything significant?"

A heavyset man with small blue eyes and a double chin, Officer Eubanks removed his domed cap and ran a hand through curly blond hair in need of a barber's skills. "As you can see, there's no mess to signify a struggle, other than these few small puddles around the tub. But they could have been the result of the victim reaching for the soap or his shaving kit."

"Where's the razor?" Jesse scanned the room, taking in details I had missed earlier in my initial shock and in my haste to clear the room. A shaving kit occupied a stool pulled close to the tub. Jesse went to it and lifted the embossed leather case in his hands. He ran a finger lightly down the flat surface of the straight razor. "Dry as a bone. So is the velvet lining." He examined the glass shelf along the wall above the tub. "Here are his shaving soap and brush, but neither looks as if it had been used." He studied the items with a frown that steadily deepened. "This seems to rule out suicide, doesn't it?"

"Sir?" another of the policemen said, but I deduced Jesse's meaning and replied for him.

"A man intent on suicide doesn't bother to ready his shaving kit. What happened, then?" I found myself hoping for another possibility than the one currently prodding my insides until I felt vaguely nauseated. "An accident? Perhaps he fell asleep and slid under. With large tubs like this, it's altogether possible." Not like my tub at home, whose short length made it necessary for the bather to sit with bent knees.

"Hmm . . ." Jesse didn't look up as he absently acknowledged my question, but stared fixedly down at the body. He placed himself between me and the victim, essentially blocking my view, and used his thumb and forefinger to lift the towel. He peered beneath and then let the towel drop back into place. Then he dipped a hand into the water and lifted his wet fingers close to his nose. "Appears he used the seawater taps for a salt bath."

I glanced at the double faucets. I had of course seen this before, as most of the summer cottages lining Bellevue Avenue contained baths equipped for both freshwater and the therapeutic benefits of salt.

Jesse next moved to the far end of the tub and peered down into the water at Claude's feet, or so I thought. I grew puzzled but remained silent, waiting for him to complete his examination. Finally, he straightened. "I can't be sure, but there appears to be slight redness around both ankles."

"Could he have been resting his feet on the rim of the tub?" I asked.

Jesse and Officer Eubanks exchanged ominous looks that provided a very different answer.

"You mean, he was yanked under . . . by his ankles?" The brutality of such an act drew a gasp from me.

"It would have been a quick death," Officer Eubanks said.

"What makes you say that?" I demanded, taken aback by the almost nonchalant pronouncement.

Jesse turned away from the body. Taking my arm, he drew me away from the tub. "If someone entered the room, perhaps while Monsieur Baptiste was relaxing with his eyes closed, that person might have reached into the water, grabbed his ankles, and pulled. That would have forced the victim's head under with such force the water would have gushed into his nose and mouth. Drowning is almost instantaneous. He wouldn't even have had time to struggle."

I whisked a hand to my mouth, my reply tumbling breathlessly into my palm. "How utterly savage."

"Or," Jesse went on, "as you said, he'd propped his feet up on the rim, or he was in the habit of wearing his garters too tight. We'll need confirmation from the coroner." He turned and nodded to the men behind him. "Go ahead and drain the tub, but we'll leave the body where it is until the coroner arrives." He slowly walked to the bathroom door, face bent toward the floor as he went. When he reached the threshold, he stopped and turned back around. "How many towels are in the room? Have you counted?"

A young rookie with sloping shoulders and a bumpy complexion shook his head. "Is it important?"

"Everything is important," Jesse snapped. In a calmer voice he added, "We'll need to ask the maid how many she left. I'm wondering if someone didn't use one to mop up any water he tracked as he made his exit."

"That's brilliant," I said with a surge of admiration. "I wouldn't have thought of that."

He smiled grimly. "Let's you and I take a look around the bedroom, see if anything seems disturbed."

As Jesse and I each took a side of the bedroom and began opening drawers and cabinets, Patch wove zigzags back and forth to see what we were up to. To him of course this was all a game, enhanced by his newfound freedom to explore beyond the kitchen and service areas. We did not share in his enjoyment. It was a somber task, rifling through a dead man's belongings, and one we abandoned almost eagerly when the coroner made his appearance some half hour later, along with two men bearing a stretcher.

"Wicked night," he said in greeting, and trudged past us. A pair of spectacles sat low on a wide nose, the lenses slightly fogged from the rain. A stocky man approaching fifty, his shuffling gait drew my attention to his large feet.

"Jesse, the rug. We need to see if it's wet or not. I hope we haven't contaminated potential evidence."

He turned away from the drawer he had just opened in the writing desk. "What do you mean?"

"You, your men, the coroner . . . you've all walked on the rug with your damp shoes. We should have checked for moisture first."

His gaze darted from the bedroom door to the bathroom door and back. "What were we thinking?"

"Maybe it isn't too late." I sat in the desk chair and slipped off my house shoes. "You did wipe your feet on the mat downstairs. Perhaps your men did as well. Besides, the act of walking through the house would have dried their shoes considerably."

I began a slow walk to the bathroom door, letting the slightly worn path in the Persian rug guide me. Dampness seeped into my stockings. "Someone who passed through this room left a considerably wet trail."

"Yes, but who?"

"Perhaps someone who slipped in after the incident with Miss Marcus."

"What incident?"

"Oh, yes, that's right. I haven't had time to explain." I

took the time now, reviewing the events that had left us all with soaked feet at the least, in dripping clothing at the worst. "We've been waiting for the handyman to examine the pipe and determine the reason for the leak."

Jesse remained silent as he took this in. Then he said, "Come, let's see what the coroner has to say."

Barking echoed loudly against the bathroom walls, causing Jesse to frown.

"Emma, please . . ."

"I'm sorry. Patch, come here," I called out, but my mischievous pup paid no heed. Jesse and I entered the bathroom to discover Patch standing on his hind legs with his front paws propped on the rim of the tub. One floppy ear cocked higher than the other, he leaned down into the tub, working his nose as if Nanny had just removed a savory roast from the oven. A low whine in his throat became a whimper. The coroner and the policemen made no attempt to intervene, but their scowls conveyed their annoyance.

"Patch, come away. Stop that." Horrified to find my dog enthralled by a dead man, I hurried over to him and grasped his collar. A wash of relief surged as I saw that Claude Baptiste's body had been draped with a sheet. "Naughty boy. Get down from there this instant."

The coroner shook his head. "Perhaps he senses something we humans can't perceive."

"Such as what?" Jesse came up behind me.

The coroner didn't reply, but I thought of how Patch had found Sir Randall. Was he telling us now that Monsieur Baptiste's death was no accident? Could Patch somehow know that? I stared into his endlessly dark eyes in an attempt to glean whatever knowledge lay behind them. He gazed back with a loving earnestness that made me believe he would comply if he could.

Jesse's hands closed over my shoulders, breaking the spell. "You'd better go, Emma, and take Patch with you. They'll be moving the body out now."

"There is no way that pipe could have sprung a leak, sir. I checked all the plumbing the week before the guests arrived, as Mr. Vanderbilt instructed. Everything was sound."

Jim Royston, part-time handyman to Rough Point and several other estates along Bellevue Avenue, simmered in defiance of Mr. Dunn's accusations that he had neglected his duties. He was about Jesse's age, a lifelong Newporter, and as well liked as he was well known among the locals. He had just come downstairs after mending the faulty plumbing in Miss Marcus's bathroom, and now, as I watched from the Great Hall, the two men were held in a kind of standoff in the vestibule.

"That doesn't change the fact that the pipe did in fact burst." Mr. Dunn raised his eyebrows and stared down the length of his aquiline nose at the handyman. His mustache twitched disdainfully. "Had you taken the time to check more thoroughly, you surely would have found the defect. I have no choice but to let Mr. Vanderbilt know you have been derelict in your duties. I'm sure he'll wish to employ another handyman."

"I didn't come out in this foul weather to be insulted *or* threatened." Mr. Royston's grip tightened around the handle of his toolbox. "I know my business, sir. If I tell you the pipes were sound, the pipes were sound. Someone must have tampered with the fitting."

"Any why would someone wish to do that?"

Why indeed. I could think of only one reason.

"I believe the pipe in Miss Marcus's room was a diversion," I told Jesse some minutes later when we found ourselves alone in the library. To make certain we remained alone, I closed the pocket doors that separated the library from the drawing room. Outside in the growing dusk, the rain hammered the roof of the adjoining piazza, while the wind sent sticks and old leaves scuttling across its marble floor. Although the windows in the library had been shut against the weather, the scents of damp earth and foliage permeated the room to mingle with the pungency of leather and stale tobacco. My gaze immediately found the silver ashtray I had left on the sofa table. I flipped the lid open to find it littered with stubs, ash, and bits of tobacco. The porcelain Capodimonte vase hadn't been returned to the room.

"It very well might have been," Jesse replied. "But again, until the coroner makes his report, we can't call this a murder. All we know is that Monsieur Baptiste's lungs were filled with water, and the fact of it being saltwater had brought his death on that much quicker. But as for the red smudges on his ankles . . ." He shook his head.

"If those marks turn out to be bruises, we might be able to match them to the size and grip of an individual."

"We might." Jesse sank onto the silk brocade sofa and pressed back against the cushions. He let his head fall back until he stared up at the ceiling.

"Oh dear." I abruptly sat down beside him.

"What?"

I felt his gaze boring into me even as I stared down at the mythical creatures woven into the area rug. I had all but forgotten to convey a possibly vital piece of information. Could I blame the commotion and upset of the past hours for having caused me to forget? Perhaps, yet even now I hesitated to explain my father's artistic hoax—partly out of loyalty and the desire to respect my parents' confidence, but also, I must admit, out of a sense of chagrin that my own father would perpetrate such a childish prank.

"Emma, if there is something you need to tell me—"

"There is," I interrupted. Trying to ignore the heat that climbed into my cheeks and loath to look Jesse in the eye, I repeated what my parents told me about the painting hoax.

He listened in silence, but I sensed him growing rigid and saw the tension building in the opening and closing of his fists. He was angry with me and rightfully so.

"You might have told me this right away."

"I'm sorry. It was thoughtless of me to wait."

"Yes, it was, Emma." His tone cut in a way it never had before, and I was shocked at the sting of moisture behind my eyes. "Withholding information from me puts you in danger, and that is intolerable. I've come to rely on your instincts and your deductive reasoning—you're as clever as any man, perhaps more so. No, not *perhaps*, most certainly. But if you can't trust me enough to be honest, and if I can't trust you enough to know you're being honest in turn, then I'll no longer seek out your investigative skills as I have in the past. And that would be a great loss to me, and to Newport."

His voice softened at those last words, yet that stabbed at me even more acutely than his anger. "I'm sorry," I said in a small voice but he silenced me by placing a hand over both of mine where I clutched them in my lap.

"No, I'm sorry." He offered me a conciliatory smile. "I can't endure the idea of you putting yourself in danger. Promise you'll tell me anything you learn, as soon as you learn it."

"Yes, I promise."

That fondness from which I so often hid blossomed in his eyes, and this time I couldn't look away, couldn't pretend his feelings for me didn't exist. Nor could I deny his vulnerability when it came to me. An understanding passed between us and I let it. I acknowledged it with the slightest of nods, for I couldn't be so cruel at that moment as to feign ignorance or indifference. Yet what I also could not do was reply in kind, for that too would have been the height of cruelty, unless it had been possible for me to return his feelings wholeheartedly.

My heart was not whole, however, and not entirely mine to give, not then. I had been granted the esteem of two men: one whom I could happily accept, were we not entirely mismatched socially, not to mention his mother would never welcome me into her family, and marriage between us would force me to make difficult, even painful changes to my life; the other, Jesse, was a Newporter, an old friend, and suitable in every way except one—he didn't spark my passion, not as Derrick Andrews did.

My only solution thus far was to make no decision at all. Cowardly? Yes, although I preferred the term *prudent*.

Jesse nodded once as if he'd reached a decision, or perhaps an acceptance. With a slap to the arm of the sofa he pushed to his feet. "It's time we had a frank talk with your uncle Frederick's tenants. All of them, including your parents."

Chapter 9

As if parting a pair of stage curtains, Jesse slid the library's pocket doors open to find an assembled audience seated and waiting. Seven faces turned in our direction, all of them filled with questions. Jesse and I had precious few answers to offer.

But we did have questions of our own, and Jesse didn't waste a moment prevaricating. He forged a path to my father, who stood with his arms folded in front of the rear-facing French doors. Storm clouds and driving sheets of rain framed him while the electric lamps tossed an eerie contrast of light and shadow across his features.

"Who is this art buyer you've managed to enrage?"

My father's face twitched as his gaze swerved over Jesse's shoulder to me.

"I'm sorry, Father. I should have told Jesse sooner. At this point there can be no secrets."

"An enraged art buyer? Whatever are you talking about?" Miss Marcus was seated on the sofa beside Mrs. Wharton, the two women creating a striking contrast with each other.

The latter was lean, dressed in clean, classic lines, and sat primly upright. The former was full-figured, her ample bosom half-spilling from her bodice, and she lounged back against the cushions in a way my aunt Alice would have declared slovenly.

Mrs. Wharton placed a hand over Miss Marcus's, not in comfort, I surmised, but in an attempt to curb the woman's tongue. Her next words seemed to confirm this. "We agreed to let Detective Whyte do his job, Josephine. And you promised to remain calm."

Miss Marcus responded by eyeing the brandy cart beside the fireplace. Vasili Pavlenko hunched in an armchair near it. From one hand dangled a crystal tumbler half filled with clear liquid I guessed wasn't water. He looked dreadful, as if he had awakened only seconds earlier from a particularly harrowing nightmare. His gaze darted about the room from beneath the now ragged fringe of his wavy golden hair, his eyes glazed with suspicion.

My father sighed heavily and shoved a hand in his coat pocket. "The trouble is, Jesse, I don't know who they are. Thieves and black market dealers don't ordinarily leave calling cards, do they?"

"Father, sarcasm isn't helping."

Jesse turned to address the others. "Do the rest of you know anything about this?"

Heads shook in denial, all except one. Niccolo Lionetti sat motionless in his chair, silently chewing his bottom lip. Jesse went to stand in front of him with a wide-legged stance. "Signore?"

"Randall . . . he may have said . . . something . . . to me . . ."

"*Might* have?" My father lurched away from the French doors.

Without turning around Jesse held out a hand in an obvious demand for silence. He ruminated down at the musician. "Explain."

Niccolo shrugged. "He was most agitated—back in Paris—and when I asked him why, he said some things. Eh, something about a painting, and how he would be made to pay. I did not fully comprehend at the time." He raised an accusing gaze to my father. "Randall said it was *your* fault, Arturo."

"*My* fault?" Father's voice boomed with indignation. "I didn't force Randall into our scheme, and I certainly never meant things to become so out of hand. It was to have been a prank, nothing more."

My mother rose and went to his side, and lightly touched his forearm. "Arthur, I'm sure Randall understood that."

"Did he?" He flinched, taking his arm out of her reach. "And now Niccolo is practically accusing me of . . ."

Jesse whirled to face him. "Of what?"

Father's mouth hung open. He closed it and shook his head. His brow furrowed as he regarded Jesse with a pained, baffled look, as if he believed Jesse's suspicions had turned in his direction.

Had they? Queasiness roiled deep in my stomach.

"If you wish to put blame where it is deserved, look to *him*." Vasili Pavlenko pointed directly at the cello player. "Niccolo."

The name all but slithered from the Russian's tongue. The man in question lunged to his feet so violently his chair rocked, nearly tipping over backward before righting itself. "Liar! I was nowhere near the cliffs when Randall died."

"Never mind Randall," Vasili volleyed back. "I speak of tonight. Of Claude. Where were you when *he* died only hours ago?"

Niccolo shouted something back in Italian, and though the exact meaning was lost on me, I understood the sentiment well enough—so well I took an involuntary step backward, away from the scene fast becoming volatile. Miss Marcus, too, had come to her feet and began shouting protests at Vasili's implied accusation. Mrs. Wharton once again tried to calm her, but Miss Marcus shook off the other woman's efforts. Her high-pitched utterances created a staccato disharmony with the deeper male voices.

Jesse raised his hands. "Quiet—*now*—or I'll have you all arrested."

I compressed my lips against a smile. Jesse would not have dared speak that way to my Vanderbilt relatives or any other member of the Four Hundred. Had he forgotten the Whartons were among those lofty individuals? The threat, however, had its immediate result. The room grew silent, until Teddy Wharton raised his chin defiantly.

"On what grounds?"

I realized the man had said little else thus far. A recollection came rolling back. The night Sir Randall went missing, I noticed grass stuck to Mr. Wharton's boots. He had gone outside and returned without bothering to change into house shoes. Why? Had he been in too much of a hurry to join the others in the Great Hall for Niccolo's performance? Or had his haste been for another reason? And there had been that incident when he rudely broke up a conversation between his wife and Sir Randall.

But while he might have taken issue with Sir Randall concerning Mrs. Wharton, I could conceive of no reason he might have harbored ill will toward Monsieur Baptiste.

In answer to Teddy Wharton's question, Jesse retorted, "Obstructing justice. Now then, Mr. Pavlenko, explain why you would question the whereabouts of Signore Lionetti tonight."

Niccolo, about to retake his seat, straightened to full

height again. "I was with everyone else, in Josephine's room. You all saw me. Everyone who was there. *You* were not there, Vasili. Why?"

"I was with Claude. We were downstairs in the billiard room until we went to our separate suites to change for dinner. Anyone might have gained entrance into Claude's room *after* the bursting pipe."

Vasili was correct. If indeed the faulty pipe had been a diversion necessitating that everyone change clothes yet again, anyone might have slipped into Claude Baptiste's room to murder him. But as Vasili himself admitted, he hadn't been with the rest of us in Miss Marcus's bathroom. I had met him in the hallway on my own way back to change. He claimed to have been in the billiard room with Monsieur Baptiste, but who would have seen them?

After witnessing Vasili's friendship with the Frenchman, I found it nearly impossible to imagine him murdering the man. Jesse calmly repeated his question to Vasili. Why would he question Niccolo's whereabouts earlier?

The young man scowled. "He had cause to want Claude dead."

"Liar! You know that is not true!"

"Signore Lionetti," Jesse said calmly, "I will have you removed if you cannot control your outbursts. Now then . . ."

"He wanted Claude dead for Josephine," Vasili said. The woman yelped a protest, but fell silent when Jesse turned a warning look in her direction. The Russian choreographer continued. "Her career is fading, and she was depending on Claude to help her rise again. When he would not, she became enraged. But what can a woman do? A woman is weak. She needed a man to avenge her, so she asked her lover. Niccolo did it for her."

Niccolo sneered. "That is absurd."

Miss Marcus added her vehement concurrence. "We are not lovers."

But I wondered, for not only did a rancorous link exist between Miss Marcus and Claude Baptiste, but also between that same lady and Sir Randall. Their mutual acrimony had been palpable, although the reasons for it remained unclear. And it was no secret that she and Niccolo had forged some kind of relationship. Lovers? Perhaps. Conspiring killers? It was possible.

If that were true, then my father's art hoax had nothing to do with events at Rough Point. Unless . . .

Niccolo had admitted to knowing at least vague details about the hoax. Could he and Josephine have used this to their advantage, perhaps by initiating the theft and subsequent threats themselves? I conjectured about none of this out loud, but determined to discuss these possibilities with Jesse at the first opportunity.

"I think it's time for all of us to leave Rough Point. To leave Newport." My father brushed a hand over his pomaded hair. "It's been a disaster of a visit."

Through the murmurs of agreement Jesse's voice rang out. "No one is going anywhere until we discover what happened and who, if anyone, is at fault."

"You suspect one of us?" Beneath Mrs. Wharton's question ran a frisson of excitement, or so I thought.

"That's putting the cart before the horse," Jesse replied. "We still haven't determined for certain if either death was accidental or suicide. At the same time, I can't rule any of you out either. You are free to leave Rough Point, but none of you may leave Newport until this investigation is complete."

"Then I suggest you and I go home, Edith." Teddy Wharton gazed in dismay out the French doors, where the rain continued to pound the landscape. "As soon as we may."

"And what are we supposed to do until then? Sit here waiting for another of us to die in some gruesome way?" The beginnings of hysteria again edged Miss Marcus's tone and peeked out from the whites of her eyes. "Niccolo is innocent, of that I have no doubt. But how do we know one of these art thieves isn't in the house right now? Or that one among us hasn't become unhinged?" Her eyes narrowed as she looked directly at Vasili. "So I ask again. What are we to do? How can we be safe trapped here in this horrid house?"

"We stay together," my mother said. "No one must be alone. And . . ." She perused the room, her gaze landing on the brass fireplace tools beside the hearth. "Perhaps we should arm ourselves."

Jesse went to confer with his men, leaving the artists in the drawing room to bicker to their hearts' content. I followed him, passing Mr. Dunn on my way to the Stair Hall. He carried a tray of covered platters, and behind him trailed Irene and Carl, each carrying a similar burden.

"Food helps in situations such as these," he said, and kept going. The comment took me aback, for I wondered what other similar situation he might have witnessed. Though last summer brought deadly circumstances to the homes of my other Vanderbilt relatives here in Newport, neither Frederick nor Louise, nor, by extension, Mr. Dunn, had been involved. Perhaps he merely meant stressful times in general.

I caught up with Jesse on the half landing. I begged his patience a moment and bade him sit with me on the little velvet settee beneath the stained glass windows.

"I remembered something else," I said, and he grimaced.

"I thought you were going to tell me everything from now on, and not keep anything to yourself."

"I certainly didn't intend to keep this from you," I hastened to defend myself. "I'd forgotten, honestly. But last night when

Randall went missing, but before any of us feared he had come to any harm, I noticed grass on Teddy Wharton's shoes." I sat back, waiting for Jesse's reaction. I was to be disappointed, for he looked at me askance.

"He took a walk. If you're insinuating Mr. Wharton met Sir Randall along the Cliff Walk and pushed him, a few blades of grass on his shoes is not enough to prove it. Or even to give it serious consideration."

"Don't you understand, guests in a house such as this always bring two complete sets of footwear—boots to wear outdoors, and shoes reserved exclusively for indoors. No well-bred gentleman would ever think to track remnants of the gardens into the house. So why didn't Teddy Wharton change his shoes?"

His incredulity eased from his features. "I wouldn't have thought of that."

"No, I don't suppose I would have either if I hadn't grown up with relatives such as mine." Indeed, most Newporters were lucky if they owned two pairs of shoes, one for every day and one for church. "And not only that, but I happen to have witnessed ill will toward Sir Randall on Mr. Wharton's part." I lowered my voice. "It had to do with Mrs. Wharton."

"You mean, Mrs. Wharton and Sir Randall . . . ?"

"No, I don't believe so, not at all. But Mr. Wharton may have believed it." I glanced at the upper steps, where rain streaming down the stained-glass windows cast odd moving shadows against the stair runner. "It's a motive, isn't it?"

"But what about Monsieur Baptiste? Have you ever seen any hostilities between him and Mr. Wharton?"

"No, but that doesn't mean there weren't any. Perhaps Mr. Wharton is an insanely jealous husband, always out to avenge his wife's honor." Even to me, that sounded melodramatic and hollow, like a scene from a deplorably written play.

Jesse obviously agreed with that assessment, for he summarily dismissed the possibility. "Anything else?"

I stared at those shifting shadows on the stairs again. "Well, there is Niccolo Lionetti knowing about my father's and Sir Randall's painting hoax, not to mention the animosity that existed between Miss Marcus and Sir Randall."

"Which brings us back to your father again."

My gaze snapped to his. "Surely you don't think my father had anything to do with this."

He shook his head, but he didn't answer me.

Before Jesse made his way back to town that night, he spoke to Irene about the number of towels she delivered to the bathrooms each morning. The number, six, was exactly what we found on the shelves in Monsieur Baptiste's bathroom.

This led to several conclusions. First, it seemed unlikely that anyone who had been caught in the spray in Miss Marcus's room could have then entered Claude Baptiste's bathroom without leaving a wet trail across the tiled floor, yet the culprit hadn't needed to mop the floor with a towel. Yet the bedroom rug *had* been damp, suggesting it had been the police after all who tracked in rain from outside. The only people in the house who hadn't been soaked in Miss Marcus's deluge, other than myself, Mother, and Mrs. Wharton, had been Irene . . . and Vasili.

Irene could have no reason to kill anyone, and I refused to believe my mother or Mrs. Wharton could be guilty. That left Vasili, but only an accomplished actor could have feigned the grief displayed by the young Russian at his friend's death.

An actor. . .

As a ballet *dancer*, Vasili would have been trained in drama and theatrics. Jesse would call that a stretch, however, so I tucked the thought away but did not entirely dismiss it.

I worried about Jesse and the other officials driving through the storm, but he let me know they arrived safely in town with a brief telephone call I could barely hear over the crackling lines. Those of us who remained behind, disturbed by the notion of murderous art thieves and black market dealers, spent a sleepless night in the drawing room and library, where none of us would be alone.

Patch lay by my feet all night as I slumbered fitfully, sitting up in a wing chair. The occasional snore drifted through the two rooms, only to break off with a snort as the individual caught him- or herself dozing and awoke with a start. By dawn everyone began to stir in earnest, standing and stretching sore limbs and necks, groaning, and even muttering oaths. The downpour continued with little promise of respite, while an ashen mist robbed the landscape of dimension, rendering the lawns and sky and the distant sea flat and lifeless. It was unlikely any of us would be leaving Rough Point today.

Mr. Dunn announced a simple breakfast would be served in the dining room. Simple, perhaps, but Mrs. Harris outdid herself in quantity. Sitting down to fluffy scrambled eggs, bacon, muffins, and porridge reminded me of Nanny's plain but hearty cooking at home. Though I arrived at the table believing I had little appetite, I nonetheless tucked in with surprising vigor, as did the others. On a day where nerves were already strained to breaking, I immediately saw the wisdom of foregoing fancier delicacies in favor of a fortifying New England breakfast.

We did not, however, arrive at the table wielding andirons

or other similar weaponry, as my mother had suggested. Still, the meal was a tense affair that included little conversation but a good many flashes of suspicion from one end of the table to the other. The rain that ceaselessly pelted the windows didn't help, nor did the wind that howled off the ocean to batter the outer walls and whine beneath the eaves of the covered verandas.

"How I wish that would stop," Miss Marcus said. Her fork slipped from her fingers to clatter against her plate.

"Are you going to start complaining again, Josephine? Perhaps make another scene?" A threat echoed behind Vasili's question, and Miss Marcus flinched and compressed her lips as if she *had* been about to go on but thought better of it. Vasili's hands shook this morning, and after a few bites he began pushing his food around on his plate. Instead of coffee or tea, a tumbler of the same clear liquid as last night sat by his elbow, and once again I suspected the contents were something other than water.

That startled me, for a man who imbibed at breakfast enjoyed few if any rational moments the rest of the day. Is that what he wished, to obliterate thoughts of his friend? I understood what grief could do to a person, but I also knew the dangers of giving oneself over to spirits in an effort to silence one's demons. My half brother Brady had often indulged to excess in the past, but he had done so out of youthful exuberance and an underdeveloped sense of responsibility. Much to my relief he had since discovered the merits of moderation, at least for the most part. No, it was my cousin Reggie, the youngest of Cornelius Vanderbilt's sons, who came to mind.

The advantages his older brothers, Neily and Alfred, enjoyed due to their family connections, seemed to have become, for Reggie, unbearable burdens, ones he couldn't face with a sober mind. I'm not altogether sure I understood, except that whenever I considered trading places with any of my Vanderbilt relatives, a certainty welled up inside me that I couldn't bear the artifice of such an existence. Though my own life could be challenging at times, both financially and personally, my perseverance and triumphs were a source of immeasurable pride.

Could that be what Reggie missed, perhaps without even realizing it? At the age of seventeen he seemed infinitely older, not in maturity but in how quickly life had already begun to beat him down. And now with his father ill and his mother's attention completely focused on her husband's well-being, Reggie had no one to correct him or curb his undisciplined ways.

I stole another glance at Vasili, sitting on the other side of Mrs. Wharton two seats down from me. Little more than his trembling hands, framing his plate, were visible to me, but that alone told a self-destructive narrative. I didn't have to ponder long to understand what he missed in his life. His friend, yes, but also his talent, his rare ability to perform. Beyond a doubt choreography came as a distant second to his life's passion. Perhaps Claude Baptiste had been able to help his young friend cope. Who would serve that function now? I found myself sincerely hoping the answer wouldn't lie permanently within that crystal tumbler.

"Mr. Pavlenko," I ventured, leaning over the table to speak to him. "Would it comfort you to speak of your friend?"

As if by reflex he reached out and snatched his glass between unsteady fingers, prompting me to hold my breath lest the thing drop and shatter against the tabletop. He managed to hold on to it long enough to bring it to his lips for a swig. He then banged it beside his plate but didn't release his hold on it. His next words rang sharp with bitterness. "What can one say, Miss Cross, about a man who lay dead?"

"I thought we might honor Monsieur Baptiste by talking about his accomplishments, and . . ." I trailed off as the young man laughed harshly.

"Accomplishments that are all in the past now. There will be no more of them. No *Carmen*, nothing." He aimed a scowl at Miss Marcus.

She dropped her fork again and pushed her plate away from her. "You are correct, Vasili, there will be no *Carmen*. Do you think I take pleasure in that?"

"I think yes, you are glad. If you could not have the role, you are happy no one will."

"Now see here, Vasili." Signore Lionetti thumped a fist against the table, so hard his fork rattled against his plate. "You have no right to say such things. No reason to take this out on Josephine."

"But he blames us," Miss Marcus said in a nasty tone. "He said as much last night. He has no cause, no evidence, but he blames us all the same because he needs to lash out at someone. But then, he blames us—all of us—for so much. Don't you, Vasili?"

Again, that reference to Vasili Pavlenko blaming his fellow artists—for what? I considered his injury. Had some or all of them somehow caused it? With two men dead and these so-called friends nearly at one another's throats, I abandoned all former resolve to mind my business. It was time for answers. But not here, where these clever people might suddenly decide to work together and cover up the facts I sought. I would need to approach them separately. Only then could I sift through their various responses and glean something of the truth.

"Josephine, please," Mrs. Wharton murmured over Miss Marcus's continued complaints. "This isn't helping matters."

"I'm only speaking the truth, Edith. This is Vasili's way of avoiding any responsibility for his own life," the opera singer nearly shouted. "Besides, he began this. I'm merely responding in kind."

"He isn't himself." My father speared a forkful of eggs. "Of all of us, he was closest to Claude, and this has been a terrible shock to him."

"Will you speak of me as if I am not in the room?" Vasili raised his glass again, this time in a mock toast. He smirked. "I speak for myself. I do not need any of you to be my tongue."

"Vasili, please. My daughter's idea is a lovely one." My mother cast a fond look in my direction, but misgivings and guardedness peeked out from her eyes as well. "She is no stranger to tragedy, you see. She understands."

Perhaps my mother knew more about the past two summers than I had believed. I would have to inquire with Brady about just how much he had included in his letters to our parents during the previous year.

"Do you, Miss Cross?" Mr. Pavlenko looked over at me, his expression both skeptical and cynical. "You have experienced great loss in your young life?"

I almost quipped back that I wasn't many years his junior. But I refused to be dragged into the general discord. "Quite a bit of loss, yes. And I have found that speaking openly of the departed has healing effects. However if you don't wish to—"

"I do not." He pushed out of his chair, snatched the tumbler, and walked none too steadily from the room.

The others fell silent and I felt their stares on me, brimming with a range of emotions from chagrin to anger, though whether at me for pressing the issue or Vasili for his overreaction spurred by drink, I couldn't say.

"Never mind, dearest." Mother rose from her chair and came round the table to me. She placed a hand on my shoulder. "You meant well, and beneath his pain Vasili knows that. Look—" Her hand left my shoulder to point out the windows. "The rain seems to be tapering off. Wouldn't it be wonderful if we could all quit this place?"

"None of us may go far," I reminded her. "Jesse's orders."

"At least we wouldn't have to remain here waiting to see who will be the next to . . ." With a shudder that shook her bosom, Miss Marcus let the thought go unfinished.

My father paled. "I do wish you'd cease your role as harbinger of doom, Josephine. There is no proof yet of foul play. Randall was melancholic enough to have jumped from that cliff. And Claude—who knows how much he and Vasili had to drink before he took his bath? It isn't inconceivable that he simply fell asleep." But rather than reassuring, Father's tone conveyed a desperate need to convince himself.

"Then again, we don't want to split up either." Mrs. Wharton lifted the porcelain teapot from the table and refilled her cup. "If someone *is* targeting our little group, splitting up will make their task easier, won't it?"

Niccolo Lionetti let his head sag into his hands, his fingers tangling in his dark curls. "To go separate ways would make it more difficult to find us, no?"

"In a town the size of Newport?" Mrs. Wharton laughed lightly. "I'm afraid there is nowhere to hide, Niccolo."

"Perhaps not," her husband blurted, "but I see no reason for you and me to remain here, Edith. We should seize the opportunity the moment the rain lets up and make our way to Land's End, where we should have gone all along."

She offered him a haughty tilt of her chin. "And if Ledge Road is flooded?"

"How bad could it be?" he murmured moodily.

"Bad enough to sweep us off the road, Teddy."

"Then we'll get out and walk."

"I will *not* wade through a river of rainwater simply to humor you."

Mr. and Mrs. Wharton continued their heated debate over the merits of returning to Land's End or remaining at Rough Point, with Mr. Wharton becoming more and more petulant with each hostile volley. My own nerves were stretched thin, not only due to the shock of two deaths in two days' time, but because of the web of animosity that defined this group. Not for the first time I marveled that they were friends at all. I wished to shake sense into them all and insist they learn better manners.

Instead I left the table and drifted to the window. To say the rain had abated would be a gross overstatement. The headland continued to take a sound pummeling, the drops splattering upwards from the lagoon that had formed in the depression between the terrace and the rocky rise closer to the cliffs. But the precipitation had eased enough to allow a clearer view across the landscape.

The autumn flowers carpeting the rise only yesterday now lay in tatters, flattened by the deluge. My gaze traveled farther, and I realized something. Due to those dips and hillocks in the land, I couldn't see the footbridge from here, nor could we have seen the bridge from the Great Hall the night we gathered to hear Niccolo play. From the second floor, yes, but from nowhere on the ground floor would anyone have seen what occurred on the bridge.

We could, however, have seen anyone crossing the lawn from the house to the Cliff Walk, which made it doubtful someone among this group had murdered Sir Randall. From the recital onward we were all accounted for, except perhaps for the brief interlude when everyone had dressed for dinner. But most of the bedrooms looked out over the back of the house. Again, anyone heading to the footbridge would have run a great risk of being seen. Those facts alone might lead one to believe either Sir Randall had taken his own life, had fallen accidentally, or his attacker came along the Cliff Walk from somewhere beyond Rough Point. Father's art thieves?

But if that were so, how had that same person then crossed the lawns in the opposite direction and gained entrance to the house to murder Monsieur Baptiste without attracting the notice of the guests and servants?

I shook my head. All my instincts insisted the threat, if there was one, came from within, rather than without. But how . . . ?

As I again scanned the rear of the property, one landmark in particular drew my notice: the kitchen garden. Stretching from just beyond the service courtyard, the rectangular plot continued some two hundred feet along the southern edge of the property, ending in another gate closer to the Cliff Walk. Privet hedges formed tall, nearly solid walls around the garden, the intention being to shelter the cultivated plants from the winds, but also, I realized now, providing a private walkway across the property. I hadn't seen Claude and Vasili among the herbs and vegetables yesterday until I walked right up to the gate and peered in.

I remembered, too, that Patch had led me to the garden yesterday. I had wanted to keep him to the front of the house but he had insisted on leading me on a chase to the garden gate. Why? Had Patch seen something occur in the garden the evening Sir Randall died? On the surface it seemed a silly question and Jesse would have told me I was stretching facts to suit my hunches again. But Jesse wasn't here, and experience had taught me never to discount a possibility, no matter how far-fetched.

My senses abuzz, I longed for a break in the weather so I could inspect the garden. Perhaps I would find nothing, but I could at least walk the length from one end to another and judge whether my theory held plausibility. I glanced back to the rock-strewn ridge with its desolate bench and shredded flowers. And I realized I shouldn't wait, for should the weather deteriorate before it improved, every blast of rain and wind could potentially destroy any clues the garden might harbor. Even now it might be too late, but I had to try and I mustn't waste another minute.

Chapter 10

"Thank you for coming with me, Mrs. Wharton." I spoke loudly to be heard over the rain. Though no longer torrential, a steady shower continued while intermittent gusts had us angling our umbrellas to prevent them from being shoved inside out. In the servants' porch we had borrowed ill-fitting mackintoshes, buttoning them to our chins and tying the hoods tight around our faces, and we each found a pair of tolerably fitting galoshes.

Sensing an adventure, Patch had begged to come along, but after taking him out to the service courtyard to accomplish his business, I returned him to Mrs. Harris's watchful eye in the kitchen. He would only ramble about and bring attention to Mrs. Wharton and myself as we went about our task.

"I'm willing to endure a dousing for you, Miss Cross," she said in response to my thanks, putting emphasis on *you.*

I knew she referred to the argument she'd had at breakfast with her husband, concerning the wisdom of attempting to drive home on potentially flooded Ledge Road. Living on Ocean Avenue as I did, I fully understood the dangers of deluged roads and had seen firsthand that what appeared to be a shallow puddle could in fact be a rushing stream waiting to drag an unsuspecting traveler into the thrashing tide. Yet while I had sided with Mrs. Wharton at the time, I had no desire to revisit the awkwardness of the rift between husband and wife.

When I gave no answer she walked ahead of me to open the garden gate. She placed a hand on my arm to still me before I could walk through. "I know you found Teddy's and my behavior abominable this morning. I apologize for that."

"It is none of my business." And yet curiosity rose up inside me. This morning wasn't the first time I'd found Teddy Wharton's behavior bordering on abominable.

"We had the bad taste to make it everyone's business, unfortunately. I regret that. But you see, he often drives me to my wits' end, and you've seen only a small bit of it. It isn't his fault, really. My husband suffers from acute melancholia, as his physician calls it, and I try to be tolerant. If only I'd been blessed with a more patient nature."

I bit my tongue to keep from questioning her. If this melancholy caused her husband to lash out verbally, what about physically? Was he prone to sudden acts of violence? I needed to learn more about this, but not here in the rain, when we had other matters to attend to. "You don't need to apologize, Mrs. Wharton."

"Perhaps not, but I wished you to understand. Now then . . ." She followed me into the garden and latched the gate behind us. "What are we looking for?"

"First, whether or not we would be visible from the house as we traverse the main garden paths." I scrubbed droplets from my eyes and held my umbrella to shield me as much as possible. Head down, I moved to the outer path on the right side. "And also anything someone might have dropped or disturbed as they made their way from one end to the other. You take the left-hand path, and we'll simply study the ground at each step."

"Sounds rather tedious."

I straightened to regard her. "It's all right if you'd prefer to return to the house. I wouldn't mind, truly."

She was already shaking her head and grinning, even as she moved to the path I had indicated. "Not a bit of it, Miss Cross. We all agreed none of us should be alone and I must admit I'm rather flattered you thought to include me in your intrigue. Do you do this sort of thing often?"

I briefly wondered about the earnestness of her question, or whether Brady informed my parents of my activities these past two summers, and they in turn had regaled their friends with my exploits. Would they have done such a thing—used the dangers I'd faced as a source of amusement?

"What is it, Miss Cross? You look perturbed. Did I say something?"

"No, I'm sorry, it's nothing. And yes, I seem to do this more often than one would wish."

She nodded as if only now realizing the gravity of the situation, that this was not a game but an attempt to discover who might have pushed Sir Randall to his death. "Then let's get on with it, shall we?"

With rows of vegetation separating us, we painstakingly made our way along the garden's length. I paid particular attention to the first of the stepping-stones that connected the two walkways, where Claude and Vasili had stood talking yesterday. The rain had washed away all signs of their having been there. Not a footprint had survived the onslaught, and one could no longer distinguish whether either man had trod on the foliage, or if the rain had flattened the plants.

Mrs. Wharton appeared at my shoulder. "Did you find something?"

"Only the suggestion that our efforts will be in vain." I shook my head. "I already knew Monsieur Baptiste and Mr. Pavlenko were out here yesterday, but today's rain has washed away all signs of their presence. I can only surmise evidence of anyone else who passed this way to have met with a similar fate."

"What on earth would Claude and Vasili be doing out here? I hardly think either of them has an interest in horticulture, nor are they the sort to find pleasure in plucking vegetables like a kitchen hand."

"I suspect they wished for privacy, and where better on the estate? I have to admit, their friendship puzzled me."

She made her way back to the left-hand path, saying as she went, "They were an odd match, I'll give you that. But it was Claude who coaxed Vasili to begin caring about his life again after the accident. . . ."

"Can you tell me what happened?"

"A train derailment. Teddy and I weren't in Europe at the time. We were in New York. The others don't like to talk about it, and Vasili won't speak of it at all."

Her words triggered the memory of Miss Marcus's accusation that Claude refused to cast her as Carmen because he and Vasili blamed them all for what happened. "Does Mr. Pavlenko blame the others for the accident?"

"I don't see why he would. None of the others were on the train with him that night, so it isn't as if anyone could have helped him when the train derailed."

We continued our visual sweep of the garden paths, every so often turning and assessing whether we could be seen from the house. The garden's tall hedges even shielded much of the view from the upper story, proving my theory correct: that someone could have made his or her way down to the Cliff Walk from the house without being spotted.

By the time we reached the far gate we had discovered nothing of interest in our inspection, nor did I expect to find anything once we stepped back out onto the lawn. The gate creaked and then clanged shut behind us. Mrs. Wharton and I stood side by side staring down at nothing but gleaming spikes of grass. I let out a sigh.

Mrs. Wharton was not to be deterred, however, and took several strides before coming to a halt. Then she turned about and gazed up at the house. "Only someone on the third floor could see us from here. I believe you are correct in your assumption that this would have been the route taken by someone intent on harming Randall."

"Yes, I see that. But I still have no proof of that having occurred."

Suddenly my companion leaned over, holding her umbrella, not over her head, but over whatever had caught her attention on the ground. "Miss Cross, come here."

I closed the distance in several steps and followed the line of Mrs. Wharton's pointing finger. "Is this something?" she asked.

Balancing my umbrella against my shoulder, I sank to a crouch and reached out, carefully grasping the item in question between my thumb and forefinger. It immediately threatened to dissolve at my touch, so I let it fall into my palm and cupped it gently. Mrs. Wharton took hold of my elbow to help me up, and then we both stood beneath our umbrellas squinting down at the sodden roll of brown paper stuffed with shreds of partially charred tobacco.

"A cigarette," she said.

"Indeed." My pulse jumped. Had I found my clue? I whirled about to judge the distance between us and the garden. For a more accurate measure, I walked back to the gate and counted my paces.

"Someone may have tossed it over the gate," Mrs. Wharton suggested.

I had immediately thought of that, too. "It's not impossible," I hated to admit, "though it would have been a far toss."

"Perhaps Vasili or Claude."

"Possibly . . ."

"Or the last time the gardener was here."

"No, definitely not the gardener," I said quickly.

"How do you know?"

"Because no one who works for my uncle Frederick would dare litter his lawn, not even with a morsel as small as this."

Mrs. Wharton nodded in understanding. "I don't suppose they would at that."

"It's possible whoever pushed Sir Randall crept through the garden to avoid being seen on his way to the footbridge, and to calm his nerves he smoked a cigarette along the way, dropping it here before continuing on." I slipped the morsel into the pocket of my mackintosh.

"You believe it was one of us, then." She didn't pose this as a question, but rather a calm statement of fact.

"Or one of the servants," I murmured, but without much conviction. With the group only recently arrived from Europe, I could not imagine Mrs. Harris, Irene, Carl, or even surly Mr. Dunn having had the time to develop a grudge against any of the guests.

Which left the guests themselves, among whom grudges seemed to flourish like barnacles on a hull. As to which member of the group, I couldn't begin to guess. Most of them smoked these vile cigarettes, even Miss Marcus. And considering the temperamental nature of these artists and the tangle of rancor that existed between them, who could say which of them finally snapped. There was Vasili with his mysterious resentments concerning his accident; Miss Marcus with her bitterness over her fading career; Niccolo Lionetti, perhaps in love with Josephine Marcus and acting on her behalf; Teddy Wharton and his acute melancholia, seeming always to find fault in his wife and obviously jealous of other men; my own father, who had angered a black market art dealer and put the entire group of his friends at risk. As for my mother and Mrs. Wharton, I could not find enough reason to suspect either of them.

"If the same person killed both men," I said to Mrs. Wharton, "he must have had access to the house."

"*Has* access."

"Yes."

"And your thoughts concerning the staff?"

I frowned. "What motive could a member of the staff have to murder someone they've never met before? Their lives depend on their positions, as they would have little recourse if they were to be dismissed. Servants may grumble, but most are grateful for their employment, and I cannot see any of them doing anything to risk that."

I half expected Mrs. Wharton to resolve then and there to quit Rough Point, flooded roads or no. She did not, but as the raindrops became plumper, making loud, plop-plop sounds on our umbrellas, she increased my admiration of her by stoically saying, "Come, the storm is picking up again. We'd best get back."

Mr. Dunn had intercepted me in the Stair Hall as Mrs. Wharton and I were about to return to our rooms to change into dry clothing. "Miss Cross, a telephone call for you. You may use Mr. Vanderbilt's office. The connection is most tenuous so I suggest you hurry."

I could hear quiet murmurs and the clicking of ivory balls coming from the billiard room. Other voices drifted down the staircase from the sitting room upstairs. Mrs. Wharton scampered up the steps ahead of me, eager to be dry. I felt the same eagerness, as well as wishing to stash away the bit of evidence I had found outside. I held it now in a small tea leaf tin Mrs. Harris found for me in a cupboard.

"Who is it, Mr. Dunn?"

He eyed my wet hems but only said, "A Mrs. O'Neal."

I hurried past him. In my uncle's office I came to an abrupt halt, my shoes skidding slightly on the polished wood floor. I hadn't expected to find my father standing before the desk, with the receiver in hand. "Father—Mr. Dunn said Nanny called. Is that her you're speaking to?"

Nodding, he held the handset of the brass and ebony desk phone to his ear and spoke into the receiver. "Emma's here, Nanny, so I'll pass you over to her. Good speaking to you." To me he said, "I was just attempting to contact the Western Union office in town to send a wire to your brother in New York. The operator interrupted with Nanny's call. Here you are."

As he passed by me he paused and reached his arms around me. He said nothing, just squeezed me a moment before smiling down at me, then let go and strode away.

A glow spread inside me the likes of which I hadn't felt in a good many years. Tears misted my eyes as I recalled what it had been like, upon occasion, to be the absolute center of someone else's world—my father's world. For there *had* been times when he had set aside his artistic endeavors and made time for me. As I grew older and his career began to flourish, those times became fewer and farther between, until I'd learned to live without his attentions. But I realized now I had never stopped missing them.

Blinking and even wiping a damp sleeve across my eyes, I set down the tea tin and snatched up the telephone receiver. "Hello, Nanny? Is everything all right? Are *you* all right?"

"We're fine here, sweetie." Her voice crackled and popped across the wire. "We've plenty of stores in the larder and canned goods in the cupboards. I'm calling to say you mustn't even think of attempting . . ." Here static enveloped her words, and I called her name into the mouthpiece. After a moment, I heard her again. "Did you hear?"

"We were cut off for a moment."

"I said you mustn't try to come home until the storm is over. The waves are engulfing parts of Ocean Avenue. Almy Pond is overflowing. You'll never make it."

"All right, Nanny, I'll stay put."

"Good. And one other thing—"

The line went dead. I tapped the switch hook several times and was rewarded by another burst of static followed by dead air. Whatever else Nanny wished to tell me would have to wait. At least I knew she and Katie were safe.

Thus assured, I began the climb to the second story. I saw no sign of either of my parents, but I met Miss Marcus and Niccolo on their way down. At the landing I hesitated, still clutching my tea tin in one hand. The dampness from outside clung to my clothing, but the warmth of my father's embrace lingered. I remembered what my mother had said about Father being hurt by my aloofness, and a burning guilt spread from my heart outward. Mother had also mentioned Aunt Sadie as part of the reason they felt confident I would be all right when they left for Paris. Had I, in my desire to prove myself as independent as my great-aunt, led my parents to believe I simply hadn't needed them anymore . . . in effect, pushed them away?

No one could lay claim to a perfect life. I certainly couldn't. Whatever their faults, whatever misdeeds drove them from Paris back to America, they were still my parents. They loved me in their way, and I loved them in return. Perhaps it was time I ceased judging and learned to forgive and accept them as they were. I crossed the landing and knocked at their door. Although I heard their voices inside, muffled through the door, I received no answer. I knocked again, louder, and this time distinctly heard a bustle of shuffling feet, the thump of a heavy object, and a door closing. From inside, the key turned in the lock, and my mother cracked the bedroom door a few inches.

"Oh, it's you, Emma. Uh . . . do you need something, darling?" It didn't escape my notice that she didn't widen the door, or that my father hovered several feet behind her, looking rather like a thief who had been interrupted on his nightly prowl. He didn't greet me or invite me in. What happened to the affectionate father I'd met in Uncle Frederick's office? My suspicions emerged to all but obliterate my daughterly resolve of moments ago.

"What are you doing?" I asked bluntly.

"Nothing. We merely wanted a few moments away from the others. You understand, darling. It's been so stressful."

Yes, it had, but stress didn't explain my mother's wide-eyed, nervous look or my father's continued impersonation of a thief confronted by the night watchman.

"May I come in?" I didn't wait for an answer, but thrust my arm into the gap and elbowed the door wider. Mother hesitated an instant, but apparently when she saw I would not be deterred she stepped aside so I could enter. "What was all that noise I heard before you came to the door?"

Father still hadn't moved from his startled stance. "Emmaline, I don't believe I like your tone. Are you accusing your mother and me of something?"

"Should I be?" With that I went to the wardrobe and flung the doors open. Not a stitch hung from the rod, but two valises occupied the floor of the piece. That had been the thump I'd heard. I pivoted on my heel. "Going somewhere?"

Neither of them said anything. Color suffused Mother's cheeks, and Father's lips flattened.

"Jesse said no one may leave Newport," I reminded them.

"Now, Emma, we have no intention of leaving Newport," my mother assured me.

"That's right, Emmaline." His features tight, Father slipped his cigarette case from his breast pocket, opened it, and then closed it with a snap without having removed one of its contents. "There are plenty of places to stay right here in Newport." His expression softened. "If what has happened has anything to do with that . . . you know, that painting . . . then your mother and I might be better off somewhere else rather than staying here and endangering another of our friends."

"We all agreed, Father, that remaining here together was safer than splitting up. Besides, Nanny tells me Ocean Avenue is flooded. There is no saying what condition other roads are in. Bellevue might very well be reduced to a sea of mud. It would be dangerous to go anywhere at present."

"We don't plan to go very far," Mother said.

I narrowed my eyes at her, and then at my father. "Just where *were* you planning to go, then?" Did this have anything to do with my father's attempted telephone call?

They traded a look, and Father said, "The Breakers, where else? Your mother and I are always welcome."

"You can't go there. You know you can't. The house has been shut down for the winter. Even the chandeliers and wall sconces will be wrapped in linen. What will you do, stumble around in the dark, sit on covered furniture, and sleep on stripped beds? Not to mention the kitchen larders will be bare, with only enough stores for a skeleton staff."

"I'm sure with one wire to New York—"

"You cannot!" My voice rose and I took a moment to collect my composure. More calmly I said, "You cannot bother Aunt Alice about anything, not with Uncle Cornelius still so ill."

My uncle, the recognized head of the Vanderbilt family, had suffered a stroke of apoplexy in July. The circumstances had been deplorable and it still made me cringe inwardly to remember the awful scene moments before he collapsed. The attack had left him considerably weakened and partially paralyzed. The thought of disturbing my aunt and uncle with any matter, great or small, raised my protective hackles. I would not allow it.

"He's as bad as that, darling? We thought after all this time . . ."

I swung around to face my mother so abruptly she flinched and trailed off. "He is *very* bad. His physicians have forbidden him to work, which they needn't have bothered doing since he is in no condition to walk up and down stairs, much less manage his railroads. Uncle William and Alfred have taken charge."

"Alfred? Not Neily?" Father frowned in puzzlement.

I shook my head sadly. Father was correct. Ordinarily Neily, as firstborn son, should have stepped in for his father. But in this case, it was his younger brother, Alfred, whom his parents had chosen for the task. "Not Neily," I said, "not after his elopement with Grace Wilson. News of Neily's engagement is what brought on the stroke in the first place, and now that they're married Uncle Cornelius has cast him off and written him out of his will."

"I was so sure Cornelius would relent about that. Grace is a lovely girl and her father is as rich as Midas." Father pursed his lips around a low whistle. "Poor Neily. I suppose you don't cross a Vanderbilt, not even your own father, and expect to get away with it."

"Yes, well, I'm sure you can see this rules out The Breakers as any sort of haven for the time being."

"You're right, of course, darling." With an innocent expression, Mother capitulated much too easily. "We'll stay. Won't we, Arthur?"

My father conceded with a nod. Then his gaze dropped to my hems. "Why are you wet? Surely you haven't been traipsing outside in this weather?"

"Goodness, Emma, your father is right. You look like you've gone wading at the beach." Mother looked distinctly satisfied at having found a way to turn the questioning back around to me. Her eyebrows rose to meet the fringe of her curled bangs. "What *have* you been doing?"

I could trust them with the truth, or I could make up an excuse. I hesitated for a split second before deciding on a partial truth. "Patch needed to go out, so I brought him into the service courtyard."

I left their room feeling unsettled and not a little skeptical. If I had learned anything from being a journalist, and from the events of the past two summers, it was that when backed into a corner people will say anything, true or not. I didn't like myself one bit for mistrusting my parents or for lying to them, but my instincts told me they weren't being entirely honest.

In my room I searched about for a secure hiding place for my tea tin and settled on the bottom of my own valise, placed at the back of the wardrobe closet. As Mrs. Wharton and I had verified, no one from the house would have seen me retrieve the cigarette stub, and I therefore saw no good reason why anyone would search my room. I would pass this evidence to Jesse at the first opportunity.

Quickly I changed my clothes for dry stockings and a fresh skirt and shirtwaist. With Aunt Sadie's embroidered shawl tied around my shoulders to ward off the chill that pervaded the house, I returned downstairs with my damp things with the intention of hanging them in the cellar laundry room. My encounter with my parents continued to trouble me. Their unexpected arrival in Newport had raised my suspicions, and nothing in their behavior since justified lowering my guard. Was I being a disloyal daughter? Part of me believed so, saw myself as having become so jaded due to my recent experiences with crime and murder that I could no longer look upon the very people who raised me without assuming there must be some guilt. I wanted to escape such thinking, to return to the Emma who trusted unconditionally until proven wrong—as I had trusted Brady last summer, believing in his innocence even when evidence pointed to the contrary.

But if I believed my parents were guilty, what exactly had I thought they'd done? Murdered Sir Randall and Claude Baptiste? No, I could honestly state that I didn't believe that. Perhaps some of my old self remained after all. Still, that nagging sensation wouldn't quite leave me.

As I passed the doorway to Uncle Frederick's office, I detoured in, albeit partially against my will. Father said he had been attempting to wire Brady when the operator interrupted with Nanny's call. It would be simple enough to verify that—if I could get through to town.

I set my damp clothing down and picked up the telephone. I heard nothing at first and, disappointed, was about to give up, but after tapping repeatedly at the switch hook I heard a voice.

"Operator. How may I direct your call?"

"Gayla, is that you?"

"Is this Emma?" asked the familiar voice on the other end. My old schoolmate launched into numerous inquiries, as she was apt to do. "How is everything? Is your uncle Cornelius still feeling poorly? Have you heard from your cousin since he eloped? What a pickle that was. Oh, I heard Ocean Avenue is flooded. Oh, dear, are you calling for help? Is anyone hurt . . . ?"

In a town as tightly knit as Newport, rumor and gossip spread like wildfire, so I wasn't at all surprised that our main operator knew the intimate details of my relatives' lives. I knew her to be a good-natured young woman at heart, and I appreciated her concern, truly I did, but Gayla was wasting precious time. The line could go dead again at any moment. Her chatter did reassure me on one matter, however. Word of the two deaths at Rough Point had not yet gotten around town, or Gayla would have insisted I tell her everything I knew.

I called her name to silence her, even as part of me yearned to tell her I'd made a mistake and hang up. "Gayla, I understand my father tried to wire Brady in New York a little while ago."

I held my breath, waiting for her to verify that my father had, indeed, tried to place a call to the Western Union office in town.

"How is Brady faring in the big city?" she asked instead.

"He's fine, Gayla. The point is, Nanny interrupted the call, and then the line went dead. Is it possible for him to try again now?" An ember of guilt seared beneath my breastbone. This constituted deceit on my part, even if ultimately my hunch proved correct.

"Yes, when Mrs. O'Neal came on the line wanting to speak to you over at Rough Point, it sounded important enough to break in on your father. I've been a bit worried, I don't mind telling you. That place is too isolated for my comfort, stuck out there on that promontory and all exposed to the worst of the weather. Funny, though, you must have misunderstood what your father said. You can't send a wire from Lo—"

Scratchy static replaced Gayla's voice, followed once more by dead air. From *where*? I practically screamed the question into the ineffectual gadget. Good grief, a little rain and suddenly we were thrust back decades in time. What had she been about to say? *Lo*—with the *o* pronounced with an *au* sound. What logically came after that?

I seized on a possibility. Long Wharf? Had my father been placing a call down to the wharf to book passage on a steamer?

My hands trembled slightly as I replaced the receiver onto the switch hook. I stood motionless for several seconds, lost somewhere between having my suspicions confirmed and disbelieving my father would have lied to me. My mother too, for she went along with this story of wishing to move over to The Breakers.

So I had caught them in the act of attempting to flee Aquidneck Island. The question remained as to their motive. To avoid endangering more of their friends, as they claimed? To remove *themselves* from danger? If so, how cowardly of them. Or had they wished to escape becoming suspects themselves?

These were questions I couldn't answer, nor did I believe I'd gain any satisfaction from confronting them. If they had lied once they'd lie again. I raised my hands and let my forehead sink into them. What was I going to do?

Another question I couldn't answer.

After leaving my rain-dampened outfit with Irene, I found myself walking aimlessly back into the main portion of the house. Thoughts and suspicions clashed in my mind, as turbulent as the weather outside. Those shadows that so disturbed my cousin Consuelo descended heavily over me, making me shiver from both the chill and the foreboding I couldn't shake.

I didn't know where to go, whom to talk to. If I could have gotten through on the telephone, I would have called Jesse. With the storm showing little sign of abating, who knew how soon he would return to Rough Point, or what he might reveal when he arrived.

In any case, I needed time to calm down and think over what I had learned—*possibly* learned. Perhaps Gayla hadn't been about to say "Long Wharf." Perhaps my father had first telephoned a friend in town. Goodness knew my parents still had countless acquaintances despite their lengthy absence.

Passing through the Stair Hall on my way to the drawing room, I nearly collided with Niccolo, who came charging blindly out of the billiard room. I jumped out of the way, receding into the alcove beneath the half landing. He continued into the Great Hall, where his footsteps bombarded the marble floor and echoed against the ceiling two stories high. A moment later Miss Marcus exited the billiard room in a flurry of skirts and the clatter of her high-heeled mules. Her bosom straining to escape her bodice, she looked furious and augmented that impression by shouting Niccolo's name with a demand he return. It was a demand he evidently ignored, for he could not but have heard her. Even Mrs. Harris in the kitchen would have heard her command. Like Niccolo, Miss Marcus didn't see me as she breezed by and followed his path into the Great Hall.

I hesitated for several seconds before I, too, crossed the Great Hall, but at a slower pace than my predecessors and with lighter footfalls. Though a fire cracked in the drawing room hearth, I found the room empty, and a glance out the

French doors confirmed they hadn't gone out onto the covered veranda. The library?

Perhaps I sank to a new low, but asking questions of any of these people—including my own parents—had yet to yield forthright answers. The only person I felt I could trust was Mrs. Wharton, and for all I knew I could be entirely wrong about her. After all, she did harbor her own resentment toward Claude Baptiste due to his ending their collaboration on their play. But whereas Miss Marcus's disappointment over the role of Carmen stemmed from desperation over a fading career, Mrs. Wharton's career as a writer was only just beginning. It made no sense for her to have become enraged enough to kill the Frenchman.

In one matter I had no doubts. Miss Marcus and Niccolo Lionetti were somehow involved with each other, whether as intimates, coconspirators, or merely friends, I could not say, but now they appeared incensed with each other and I wanted to know why. In light of events and my unspoken promise to be Jesse's eyes and ears in his absence, I felt it my duty to learn more.

I turned to proceed into the library but a gasp escaped my lips. The sight of Teddy Wharton sitting with his back to me in one of the wing chairs stopped me in my tracks. I hadn't noticed him upon entering the room and now I saw my subterfuge foiled. Except . . . as I slowly came around his chair I realized his eyes were closed, his head propped against the carved frame, and his mouth slightly parted. Without wasting another moment I tiptoed past him, ready to pretend to be in search of a book as I neared the library doors.

To my bewilderment, no voices emanated from the library either. After seeing Niccolo and Miss Marcus in such a state only moments ago, I could not believe they had fallen into so abrupt a silence. I peeked in to discover the room vacant, the lights doused, the fireplace cold.

Then movement caught my eye. Another set of French doors led out to the covered piazza, often used for outdoor dining and evening entertainments in the summer months. The pair stood with their backs to me, as if Niccolo had turned away from Miss Marcus and started to walk off. She stood poised with her hands on her hips, and the jerky movements of her shoulders suggested she was speaking sharply to him. Surrounding them on three sides beyond the piazza, the storm seethed, sending gusts beneath the roof to ruffle Niccolo's hair and Miss Marcus's skirts.

Two dead men and a host of mysteries hovering over this baffling group of friends sent me into the library. Thanks to the lack of hearth fire or lamplight, the shadows would cloak me should one of my quarry happen to glance inside. I positioned myself to the right of the doors and leaned toward the closer of the two just enough to press my ear to the miniscule gap between the door and the lintel. This seemed to have become quite a habit of late, me listening in with my ear pressed to doors. I refused to allow a nagging sense of shame to deter me.

Their words were muffled and garbled by wind and rain, but Niccolo apparently turned, perhaps moved closer to Miss Marcus, and raised his voice. I heard him well enough now, the words crystal clear despite his accent. "Perhaps you wish I died rather than Randall or Claude. That would make you happy, yes, Josephine?"

I dared to peer with one eye through the closest pane of glass. Miss Marcus had raised both hands in a gesture that seemed to beseech him to be quiet. His features contorted in anger, and once again he ignored her command.

"I have been more than patient while you play me for a fool. Do you enjoy laughing at me, Josephine?"

Voices in the drawing room startled me out of my concentration. I backed away from the doors and snatched a book off a shelf—any book—ready to pretend this was my reason for entering the library. Suddenly one of the French doors opened. I retreated into the gloom of the closest corner and pressed myself to the bookcases behind me. I held the book I'd seized in front of me like a shield. Niccolo stomped past without seeing me, partly due to the shadows and partly to his never raising his eyes from the floor. A glimpse of his profile made me wince and shrink deeper against the shelves. Miss Marcus followed him inside and shut the door behind her hard enough to rattle the glass. With tangled wisps of hair floating about her face and her dress windblown into wrinkles, she looked almost slovenly. She, too, crossed the library into the drawing room without seeing me.

I breathed a sigh of relief, until I heard Miss Marcus's voice and the sound of her skirts rustling against the brocade upholstery of a drawing room chair.

"I'm sorry about Niccolo," she said to whomever else occupied the room. "He has the manners of a goat sometimes."

"I'm sure he didn't mean any insult. He is terribly upset. We all are." I recognized my mother's voice. Was Father there as well? Would I have to hide in the library all afternoon? I glanced outside, weighing the prospect of exiting through the piazza and making my way around to the service entrance. The continuing downpour quickly dissuaded me of that option.

Teddy Wharton must have been startled awake, for I heard his voice after a throaty snort. "What? What is it? Has something happened?"

"Nothing, Teddy," his wife said with a note of impatience.

After a hesitation he asked, "Did you leave me alone in here? We're not supposed to be alone."

"No, of course not," Mrs. Wharton lied smoothly. "Go back to sleep."

Chapter 11

I stood pressed into the corner of the library for another ten minutes. I know that because the bronze figurine mantel clock ticked away each eternal second with maddening precision. The voices in the other room droned on. They spoke of Sir Randall and Monsieur Baptiste, of the likelihood of having to remain at Rough Point indefinitely, or whether Jesse and his men would complete their investigation quickly. Then silence fell. Perhaps they were wondering if one among them in that very room had committed murder. I could only imagine the suspicions springing to life as these friends regarded one another. My father, absent previously, arrived and he added his opinions to theirs. I stiffened at his mention of my name. Had anyone seen me lately, he inquired. My mother expressed concern, but Mrs. Wharton reassured her.

"I saw her only a little while ago. I believe she's spending time with that adorable dog of hers."

Another lie. She seemed to do it both readily and well. Before I could contemplate the significance of that, Father spoke again.

"On the contrary, I wish we would all wake up." Miss Marcus let out a dramatic sigh. "I wish nothing more than to open my eyes and find myself transported back to Paris. I wish I'd never set foot on American soil, let alone come to Newport. Surely this is all nothing but a nightmare."

"She already spent time with that animal this morning. She told us she took him outside. Silly thing to do in this weather. Isn't that what the maid is for?" He paused, and when no one commented he added in a rumbling monotone, "Seems just another ploy to avoid her mother and me."

"Arthur, really," Mother scolded. I mentally visualized the disapproving glare she no doubt sent him from beneath her lashes, and the blush of embarrassment that stained her complexion to hear my father air family matters in front of others. "It's obvious she loves that dog. Besides, he wasn't supposed to be here, and I'm sure Emma doesn't wish to overburden our tiny staff."

"Yes, that's very true," Mrs. Wharton said eagerly. "Your daughter is a most considerate young woman. I like and admire her very much. You've done a splendid job raising her."

Again, Mrs. Wharton came to my rescue and deflected questions away from my evidence-hunting activities that morning. I silently applauded her. Whoever dropped that cigarette stub had been careless, and I didn't wish to inspire our culprit into being more careful.

"Such a fuss some people make over animals." Miss Marcus sounded bored as well as drained. Her confrontation with Niccolo must have depleted her energy. "I'll never understand why any sane person would invite a beast to share their home. Barns and the wilderness are for animals. That and coat collars."

I believe gasps followed her pronouncement, followed by protests, but the blood roared so loudly in my ears I couldn't be sure. My pulse points throbbed, and I wanted nothing so much as to charge out of my corner and give the woman a thorough scolding. Only knowing I would receive one in return for eavesdropping held me in place. But I vowed never to leave Patch alone with that woman. Coat collars, indeed.

"Emma?"

At the sound of my name, I gasped and dropped the book

I held. It landed on the carpet with a heavy thud, the cover flipping open and the pages riffling. My heart pounded and I was about to stammer out an excuse when I both recognized the voice and saw the speaker step into the library.

"You may come out now," Mrs. Wharton calmly said, her hands clasped at her waist. "The others have left the drawing room."

Slowly I vacated my corner, only now realizing I'd pressed so hard against the shelves I'd likely left indentations on my back. "How did you know I was here?"

She grinned. "I followed you from the Stair Hall. I was on the half landing when Niccolo burst out of the billiard room, followed by Josephine. I saw you hasten after them, and I thought perhaps you might need . . ." She shrugged, her grin widening. "I don't know. Reinforcements? I surmised that you intended spying on them."

Indignation forced my mouth open, until I couldn't but concede, both to myself and her, that she was correct. "Regrettably, I've been doing quite a lot of that lately."

"Am I included on your list of suspects?"

"No," I said immediately, but then remembered that I had eavesdropped on her conversation with Sir Randall right before her husband rudely interrupted them. She must have seen the truth written in the lines of my face, for she laughed ruefully.

"Well, I assume I must have passed muster for you to include me in your evidence gathering."

"Most certainly. And I didn't mean to eavesdrop that time." No, that wasn't entirely true. I amended my own statement. "I didn't *set out* to eavesdrop. It was the afternoon before Sir Randall died. You all perplexed me to such lengths, I merely wished to gain some understanding of why . . ."

"Why such mismatched characters could possibly become friends?"

"I'm sorry, but you are a rather contrary group."

"And cantankerous," she added with a tilt of her chin.

I couldn't deny it. "So, when I heard you and Sir Randall talking together, especially when your voices seemed to be coming from the dining room, where no one really should have been at that time of day . . . yes, I decided to listen—but only for a moment."

Her brows converged. "Was that when Teddy found Randall and me in the office and practically dragged me out by the arm?"

"Yes, and it was also when I realized you're a very kind person. You encouraged Sir Randall when others of your group showed him little patience."

"Josephine."

"She certainly didn't seem to like him much, and neither did—" I broke off, having been about to speak Teddy Wharton's name.

"My husband," she finished for me. "No, he didn't. But he doesn't particularly like any man I show an interest in, even though my interest has never been anything but professional. Teddy simply won't understand. Or perhaps he cannot."

His melancholy, as she had explained to me earlier. If he perceived his wife's creative endeavors as flirting, as he apparently had that time, would his melancholy magnify his anger enough to drive him to revenge? To murder?

Once again, I was left with conflicting evidence and motives. And once again Mrs. Wharton accurately read my mood, for she took my hand and brought me to sit beside her on the sofa beneath the front window. She perched on the edge of the cushion with her perfect, finishing school posture. I attempted to emulate her, but with questionable success.

"And now you're doing more—much more—than simply trying to understand us, Miss Cross. You're looking for a murderer among us. How can I help? And I mean *truly* be of help, to you and Detective Whyte."

I met her gaze in the half-light and held it several long, steady moments. Like me, she had literary aspirations, which meant human nature was of acute interest to her. One could not endeavor to take up the pen without that inherent fascination. With her skills and her travels, she could very well provide the extra insight needed to ultimately reveal the motive, from among myriad motives, that led to the deaths of two men.

Even if the guilty party turned out to be her husband? Perhaps. Did I trust her? Every instinct told me I could as she returned my gaze with barely a blink. At that instant her less-than-beautiful face held only kindness, intelligence, and patience—ample patience to allow me whatever time I needed to reach a decision.

I laid my hand over hers. "Can you do that, Mrs. Wharton? Can you put yourself in relative danger to help expose one of your friends, if indeed it is one of them, as a cold-blooded murderer and hand them over to the police?"

"Yes, Miss Cross, I believe I can do just that," she replied without the slightest prevarication. I smiled, for she reminded me of the friend I had made over the summer, Grace Wilson, who was now my cousin Neily's wife. She, too, had been eager to lend me her assistance, but where I believed a portion of Grace's courage stemmed from her sheltered upbringing and an inability to envision just how perilous the world could be, I detected none of the same naïveté in Mrs. Wharton, despite the similarities in their privileged lifestyles.

I rose to slide the pocket doors closed, and then resumed my seat beside her. "Very good, then. What can you tell me about Miss Marcus and Niccolo Lionetti? I witnessed more than a friendly spat. Are they . . ." I drew a breath and blurted the word. "Lovers?"

To my chagrin she laughed, but then quickly apologized. "I'm sorry. It's just that you are so young, Miss Cross, but seem to hold such knowledge of people and the world. It's rather sad, in a way, for I see it as a sign the world is fast changing. When I was your age . . . well. But I don't mean to criticize. I applaud your pluck, Miss Cross. Now then, as for Niccolo and Josephine, I believe you are correct. Naturally the two were drawn to each other from the start of their acquaintance, for they share a common passion for music. Did you know Niccolo has played many times in the orchestras accompanying the operas Josephine has performed in?"

"I didn't know that, but it makes sense."

"That is how Niccolo found his way into our little circle. To her credit, Josephine has always appreciated singular talent in others, and when she discovered what magic he creates on his cello, she spoke of him to anyone involved in the theater who would listen. And whenever she was invited into society, she brought Niccolo along. That is how he gained his patron."

"The owner of the Montagnana."

"Correct, an Italian *visconte*, and due to the man's resources and connections, Niccolo now has a recognized name in Europe. He owes that to Josephine. But as to your question, the pair began spending more and more time together, especially over the past year, much to Sir Randall's displeasure."

"He didn't approve?"

She sent a gaze skyward and shook her head. "Poor Randall, I believe he was quite smitten with Josephine. He tried to pretend otherwise, but it was plain to all who saw them together."

I thought about that a moment. "I'm going to guess that Josephine is closer in age to Sir Randall than to Signore Lionetti."

"I wouldn't quite say that. I believe her age to fall somewhere in between. But yes, she is a good ten years older than Niccolo. Does that shock you, Miss Cross? A woman involved with a much younger man?"

"Ten years seems a wide gap, but is it really?" I was thinking of Jesse and his affections for me. No one would think twice were we to court and ultimately marry. In fact, people would call it a fine and sensible match. Yet part of the Vanderbilts' objections to Grace Wilson had been the age difference between Neily and her, even though she was only a couple of years older than he.

But if Sir Randall had intentions toward Miss Marcus. . . . "No wonder he took Miss Marcus's derision so much to heart," I said. "Her snide comments about his artwork truly wounded him. I witnessed as much. Now I see her criticisms weren't merely an affront to his talents, but to him as a man. How sad, and how unfeeling of her to treat him so unkindly. Unless . . . did she know of his regard?"

"As I said, it was there for all to see, and I don't believe Josephine is as blind as that." Mrs. Wharton compressed her lips in a disparaging moue. "I'm afraid our prima donna is not the most considerate of individuals."

"To say the least," I agreed. "I heard what she said about animals and coat collars." My dislike of the woman grew exponentially, but I shoved aside my personal judgment and tried to think objectively. I did so out loud, for Mrs. Wharton's benefit. "Vasili Pavlenko blamed Niccolo for Monseiur Baptiste's death. He said Niccolo did it for Josephine. Then there is the painting hoax propagated by my father and Sir Randall. Niccolo admitted to knowing about it, that Sir Randall had confided in him, although Niccolo claimed he didn't fully understand the circumstances at the time. But I wonder . . ."

With a slight frown she waited for me to continue.

"What if Sir Randall told Niccolo everything, and Niccolo used the information to his advantage? He claimed Sir Randall confided in him *after* the painting was stolen, but what if he lied? Perhaps Niccolo knew about the hoax and he himself arranged for the painting to be stolen and the threatening messages delivered to Sir Randall's doorstep?"

"But why would he do such a thing?"

"For the same reason he might have murdered Claude Baptiste—for Josephine. Perhaps he viewed Sir Randall as a rival."

"An older, wealthier man vying for Josephine's affections," Mrs. Wharton murmured as if weighing the possibility in her mind. She nodded.

"And goodness knows, Miss Marcus and Niccolo have not exactly exhibited the most amorous of sentiments toward each other lately. Perhaps Miss Marcus had begun to tire of him back in Paris."

"All this speculation, and so much of it pointing to either Josephine or Niccolo or both." For the first time since I'd met her, Mrs. Wharton's shoulders sagged.

"So far they are the only two in your circle with possible motives against both Sir Randall and Monsieur Baptiste."

She slunk down farther still, until her back rested uncharacteristically against the pillows behind her. "My dear Miss Cross, perhaps I am not capable of assisting you after all. I cannot conceive of a young man like Niccolo Lionetti, who creates such heaven-sent beauty on his instrument, being capable of stubbing out the life of another human being. I am afraid I cannot think as you do, however much I might try." She regarded me with obvious regret. "I am very sorry to have to let you down."

"But there you are wrong, Mrs. Wharton. It is exactly because you know these people so well that your insight is invaluable. With possible motives and clues, Jesse and I can find links between individuals, but we cannot with any accuracy predict which of your friends might actually commit a violent act. I need your instincts and your honesty." I smiled as kindly as I knew how. "Surely you didn't believe I would have you directly accuse or confront any of your friends, or put you in harm's way."

"Then I am to be a consultant of sorts."

"Exactly."

She brightened considerably and sat up straighter. "And if we can prove that none of us is guilty . . ."

"I will be as overjoyed as you. But that won't mean we are in any less danger."

Chapter 12

It was decided we would not change for dinner that evening. In fact, the group almost forewent dinner altogether. With two men discovered missing, and then deceased, after failing to turn up in the dining room, a kind of superstition concerning the evening meal had settled over the group. Mrs. Wharton and my mother managed to convince the others of the uselessness of going hungry. The compromise involved staying together in the public rooms of the house until it was time to retire, whereupon each room would be searched, declared safe, and locked by its occupant from the inside. We also kept our bedroom doors locked when we were elsewhere.

However, that didn't stop me from running upstairs when my father discovered he had left his cigarette case in the upper salon. The task provided an opportunity, and I hastened to say I would retrieve it for him.

I found it where he said he had left it, on the side table next to the sofa. I flipped the case open to discover it about three-quarters full. Would he notice one missing? If so, he might merely believe one of his friends had helped themselves. I detoured into my bedroom and stashed the cigarette in my dressing table. Later I would compare it, if possible, to the stub I had found outside.

I didn't know why I hadn't thought of this sooner, but would I be able to steal one from each of Rough Point's guests who indulged in tobacco? And would a comparison to the soggy specimen I found yield any significant results? It was worth a try, no matter how unlikely.

With Father's cigarette case in hand I left the servants' wing and stepped back into the main corridor. Voices from below blended to a dull murmur, but a sudden and much closer click echoed loudly in the stillness. I froze in place when pcrhaps I should have immediately fled down the stairs, except that the noise had seemed to come from my aunt's bedroom, presently being used by the Whartons, directly opposite the landing.

I hadn't heard anyone coming up the stairs. With everyone still below, then, who could be in the Whartons' suite? A jiggle followed another click, and then the knob turned. My heart reached up and squeezed my throat, and simultaneously I measured the distance both to the main stairs and those at the far end of the servants' wing. Which way to run?

The door opened and a scream rose up inside me, ready to burst forth. It never did. The tall young man who shouldered his way out of the room with a circle of keys dangling in his hand nodded in recognition and deference.

"Good evening, Miss Cross, may I do anything for you?"

I pressed my hand to my bosom and spoke breathlessly. "Carl, you gave me a fright."

"I'm very sorry about that, miss. I didn't think anyone would be up here now. I was told no one would come up until later."

That gave me an uneasy feeling and made me study him more closely. "Just what are you doing up here? Why were you in the Whartons' suite?"

If he took offense at my obvious suspicion, he showed no outward sign. "Mr. Dunn sent me up to test all the locks, and to mark each key according to room." I noticed then he also carried what appeared to be an old quill sharpener. He held it up. "You see, I'm putting notches in the shaft of each key so we can easily tell them apart. With everyone locking their doors constantly, we don't want anyone to become accidentally locked out. Or in, for that matter. But not to worry, Miss Cross, these keys will be kept in the safe in the butler's pantry and only removed if absolutely necessary. And only Mr. Dunn has the combination."

"A good precaution." I continued my scrutiny. He seemed thoroughly at ease and unperturbed by my presence. "I hope the staff is taking safety precautions as well."

"We are indeed, Miss Cross." He paused, though he obviously wished to say more.

"Yes, Carl?"

"Do you really think those men were murdered? It is possible, isn't it, that both deaths were an accident? I mean, the baronet was unfamiliar with our cliffs, and maybe the French gentleman fell asleep."

"Maybe, Carl. I wish it were so. Better these were accidents than crimes. But still, it's awfully coincidental." I didn't add that I no longer believed in coincidences.

"I suppose. Well, if you'll excuse me, I should get back to testing the locks."

He moved on, but I remained where I was, staring at his back until he disappeared from view at the other end of the gallery. I had wanted to ask him who decided Mr. Dunn would be trusted with the master keys, but the answer was obvious. As estate manager, Mr. Dunn was not only the senior staff member, but my uncle's most trusted employee. I certainly had no reason to mistrust him. . . .

That conversation we had days ago, when he had termed us two of a kind and suggested we should "stick together," ran through my mind. I had taken offense and he had been quick to explain his meaning, which should have mollified me. Except that it hadn't. Something about the man continued to bother me, though his behavior had been impeccable ever since. And as I had pointed out to Mrs. Wharton, none of the staff had previously known the guests, or had any reason to harm them.

Perhaps my aversion to Mr. Dunn stemmed from nothing more sinister than his pencil mustache. Were I the man's wife or mother or even his sister, I would have insisted he grow it thicker or shave it off.

I managed to pilfer a cigarette from Niccolo Lionetti's case after dinner. When I compared this, and the one from my father's case, with the remnant I'd found outside, the results were thoroughly inconclusive. The rain had robbed the tiny stub of most of its odor, so that I couldn't discern if it was ordinary tobacco or one of the flavored varieties the group sometimes smoked. Nor did the outer wrapping appear much different from the other two. It didn't look as though my find would yield any more insight than that someone had walked the length of the garden and tossed the end of his or her cigarette into the grass. I returned the stub to the tea tin and prepared for bed.

Hours into a restless night, a sound shivered its way through the house. Though far off and muted through the walls, Patch's mournful wails had me sitting upright immediately. He had been left to roam downstairs, and now he frantically fulfilled his duty as guard dog. At the same time I noticed the storm hadn't abated, but continued to lash my windows.

With little forethought I hopped out of bed and unlocked my bedroom door. Through the gap I created I heard my parents' door opening, and spied my father stepping out, a fire poker in hand.

"What the devil is that dog going on about?" He had dressed hastily in trousers and a shirt he hadn't bothered to tuck in.

Mother crept out behind him. "What is it, Arthur? Dear heavens, has someone broken in?"

I opened my door wider. From the main corridor we heard the Whartons' voices, and then those of Niccolo and Miss Marcus.

"Where is Vasili?" I heard Mrs. Wharton ask.

Below, Patch's howling became strained and hoarse. A crash interrupted, startling my poor dog into silence. He quickly took up the alarm again. I followed my parents to the top of the main stairs.

"What do we do?" The whites of Niccolo's eyes glowed with fear. He, too, had improvised a weapon on his way out of his room in the form of a silver ewer, which he clutched in one hand like a pistol. Teddy Wharton noticed it and about-faced into the bedroom he shared with his wife. He returned seconds later wielding a spiked candlestick in trembling hands.

Miss Marcus backed away from the landing. "You can't mean to go down there."

"You women wait up here," Father ordered, and started down. The other men allowed him several stairs' head start before trading glances and following. When Father paused in the eerie glow of the half landing, the others froze where they were. "Mr. Dunn," he called out. "Are you down there?"

I stood on the top step and leaned over to see into the hall below. The lamp in the alcove went on, a sudden burst of light that sent spots dancing before my eyes. A figure moved to the base of the steps.

"It's me, Carl, Mr. Cross. Mr. Dunn is on his way."

"What in hell is taking him so long?" Teddy Wharton muttered. "And what's got that damn dog so riled up?"

"Teddy," Mrs. Wharton said with a caution in her voice, but she said nothing else. Carl spoke again.

"I only just came up from my room below. I haven't found Miss Cross's dog yet, but it sounds as though he's in the north wing."

"The drawing room?" Father continued down, trailed by the other two men. Vasili still hadn't appeared, and a sense of dread spread through me.

"Father, be careful, please." Before I could say more Mr. Dunn emerged from the dining room in his dressing gown. From his hand dangled a cast iron frying pan. Father and Niccolo flanked him, with Mr. Wharton and Carl right behind them, and together, armed with fire poker, ewer, candlestick, and frying pan, they moved as a small force through the Great Hall.

Patch let out a cry so sorrowful I couldn't stop myself from scurrying down the steps. Had someone harmed my dog? Regret at having agreed to let him guard the downstairs rose up and prompted me to ignore my mother's plea.

"Emma, come back here. It's not safe."

When I reached the bottom I realized I was not alone, for Mrs. Wharton had followed me down. She stilled me with a hand on my shoulder. "Don't go off blindly, Miss Cross, or you might make matters worse."

"But Patch . . . and Vasili. Where is he?" I turned my face up to my mother and Miss Marcus, hovering at the top of the stairs. "Bang on Vasili's door, go in if you have to. But see if he's safe."

Mother turned and hurried away while Miss Marcus stood

on the top step with her back pressed to the wall and her arms tight around her. Mother's voice rang out from across the gallery.

"Vasili, are you there? Vasili!" Sharp rapping at his door became a pounding of fists. "Vasili!"

"Go in," I shouted up at her.

Moments later she reappeared at the top of the stairs, her loose hair falling around her shoulders. "He's not there." She looked over her shoulder at Miss Marcus before grasping the banister and starting down. Only when she'd begun the descent from the half landing did Miss Marcus seem to awaken from her stupor.

"I'm not staying up here alone." With her colorful robe sweeping like a ball gown behind her, she rushed down to join us. "The men told us to stay put," she reminded us when she reached the Stair Hall, but none of us, Miss Marcus included, showed any inclination to go back upstairs.

"I don't hear him," I said as a fresh wave of anxiety struck me. In the preceding moments, Patch had fallen silent but I only now realized it. Replacing his barking came the shouts of the men calling Vasili's name. I grasped both my mother's and Mrs. Wharton's hands and set us all running through the Great Hall into the drawing room. Miss Marcus's slippers pattered behind us.

In the drawing room we were engulfed in blasts of damp wind blowing in through the open French doors. A lamp had been switched on, the light spilling a few feet into the covered portion of the veranda where Teddy Wharton crouched beside Patch, an arm securely hooked around the dog. The others were nowhere to be seen, but farther out on the lawn their voices competed with the slanting rain and battering gusts. Their makeshift weapons littered the wrought iron garden table.

"What's happening?" I called out to Mr. Wharton. My

mother slipped an arm around my waist, partly in comfort and partly, I guessed, to prevent me from hastening outside. "Is Patch all right?"

I needn't have asked. At the sound of my voice Patch slid his wet body from beneath Mr. Wharton's hold. He stopped just before reaching the threshold and gave a vigorous shake, spraying a cascade of droplets into the air. Then he continued to me, practically throwing himself into my arms as I sank to the floor.

"What happened out there, boy?" The desire to answer me shone in his glistening eyes. His weight sagging against me, he trembled from wet and cold and yes, fear or whatever it is a dog feels when he knows all is not right. "There's a good boy, don't worry now."

Even as I spoke the soothing words I strained to see out into the darkness and rain. "Mr. Wharton, what is happening?" I repeated. Not knowing was maddening.

Mrs. Wharton stepped past me and went to her husband's side. She said something I couldn't hear, and Teddy pressed to his feet and pointed to somewhere beyond the veranda. The cliffs again? My stomach sickened at the thought of the precipice having taken another life.

"Vasili's out there," Mrs. Wharton called back to us, at the same time Irene and Mrs. Harris entered the drawing room carrying piles of towels. They'd secured their dressing gowns beneath their chins and each had tied a shawl around her shoulders.

The cook dropped her burden on a nearby chair and stooped to wrap a towel around Patch. "Poor dear. Always watching out for everyone, isn't he?"

"Do you know what's happening here?" I asked her.

"No, miss, but Irene and I heard the commotion outside and figured people would need drying off."

"And you weren't afraid to come?" Miss Marcus demanded in a harsh tone. "Fools, how could you know if it were safe or not? There could have been a madman loose in the house intent on killing everyone."

"It's all right, Josephine." Mother attempted to draw Miss Marcus to her side but the opera singer shirked away.

"*You're* all here, aren't you?" the cook asked calmly. "Irene and I aren't about to cower in our rooms if Mr. Vanderbilt's guests need our services. Are we, Irene?"

The young woman shook her head but didn't appear nearly as confident as her superior.

"They're coming back," Mrs. Wharton called in again. "I believe they have him."

My father and Niccolo stumbled up the veranda steps, their hair and clothing streaming. Behind them, Mr. Dunn and Carl struggled to climb the steps, each with an arm slung around a seemingly unconscious Vasili. Father took Carl's place, helping Mr. Dunn seat Vasili on one of the wrought iron benches while the footman all but collapsed against the half wall of the porch. Mrs. Harris and Irene ran out to distribute towels among them. Irene tossed one over Vasili's shoulders, disturbing his tenuous balance where he sat. He started to topple, but Mr. Dunn reached out to hold him upright. Mrs. Wharton sat beside him, supporting his limp form against her side. She fanned at the air with her hand.

"Good heavens." She turned her face away from him.

Miss Marcus moved into the doorway. "What is going on? What was he doing outside like that? Scaring us all out of our wits. He must be mad."

"Perhaps," Father said. "We found him staggering close to the cliffs. God only knows what might have happened. He's dead drunk and beyond knowing or caring."

* * *

I awoke the next morning to find Mr. Dunn and Carl lighting kerosene lamps throughout the house, as the electricity had failed sometime after we all returned to bed. Meanwhile the rain continued to fall in dense sheets, like prison walls trapping us in a house of shadows and gloom.

Whatever atmosphere had once attracted me to Rough Point, whatever kinship of spirit I had felt here, had dissipated entirely and I longed to be away, longed to seek the homey comfort of Gull Manor's shabby but familiar interiors. But I knew the dangers of Ocean Avenue during one of these September storms. A wave had once arced over the road to envelop Barney and my carriage, and the terror of that moment, of the force of the water engulfing us in a blinding, strangling hold, lived inside me still. By some miracle, when the wave receded we remained on the road, drenched but breathing. I had climbed down to grasp Barney's halter and lead him the rest of the way home, praying with each step that we would live to hear Nanny's scolding and feel her welcoming embrace.

I went first to Uncle Frederick's office to test the telephone. Nothing. So we were cut off as well as having to make due with flame and whatever little light made its way through the fogged windows. Luckily Mrs. Harris's kitchen did not depend on electricity, and she provided us with another satisfying breakfast. The men had taken turns sitting in Vasili's room while he drifted in and out of semi-consciousness during the remaining hours of last night. Father said he had cried out often in Russian and once tried to rise from the bed, though he had laid back down readily enough when Father pressed his hands against his shoulders. Carl went up to watch over him while the rest of us ate our breakfast.

We were just finishing up when the door knocker sent its disturbing clanks echoing from the entrance hall. Pale faces, frozen in startlement, looked up from the table. No one moved. Even Patch, lying beneath the table at my feet, only lifted his head and sniffed at the air. It was as if no one remembered what that clanking could signify, and then decided it could signify nothing good. Who on earth could be out in such weather? How had they negotiated the flooded roads? What did they want?

Our visitor must have pulled the bell as well, for Carl strode from the butler's pantry to open the front door. His action roused us, and we all sprang to our feet and gathered in a tight group before following the footman through the Stair Hall. Patch pushed to the front of our little crush, his tail down and his ears pricked as a hooded figure all but stumbled across the threshold, literally shoved inside by a gust of wind.

Jesse stood dripping on the vestibule rug, bedraggled and looking as though he had fought his way through a monsoon. I hurried over to help Carl relieve him of his outerwear, although his suit was in little better condition and his shoes squelched at the slightest step.

"How in heaven did you get here?" I demanded in none too gentle a tone. I wanted to scold him as Nanny would have, but only just managed to bite back my admonitions.

"I had one of the men drive me down Bellevue as far as we could go. It's a swamp out there. The carriage kept sliding and shimmying over the muck. By Ruggles I got out and sent the carriage back."

"You walked all the way from Ruggles Avenue in this weather? Jesse, are you mad?"

As my voice rose, Carl made a discreet exit, backing out of the vestibule and into the cloakroom with Jesse's gleaming wet mackintosh, overcoat, and hat.

From the little knot of onlookers, Teddy Wharton demanded, "Well, have you discovered something?"

Jesse hesitated before shaking his head. "Not yet. The storm is slowing things down."

"Are you still calling Claude's death an accident?" my father asked.

"For now," Jesse confirmed. "I only came out to make certain the place was secure and you were all well."

"All the way out here in this weather for that? Emma is right, you're quite mad." For a moment my mother sounded just like Nanny. "I'll see that Carl brings in another place setting."

She retreated through the doorway. The others looked on another moment or two, then, obviously disappointed at Jesse's lack of news, turned around and followed her. Only Patch remained, watching us intently.

Jesse's manner changed immediately, became brisk and urgent. "I had to come, Emma. The weather didn't matter." He moved as if to draw me away from the front door, then regarded his sloshing shoes and remained on the rug. "I have news to tell you. And I couldn't leave you here all alone anymore."

"I'm not alone," I pointed out. "There are the others."

His expression hardened, turning the boyish features into those more resembling a soldier. "I don't trust them—any of them."

I forewent reminding him that two of the group were my parents. The agitation that lingered in his manner were not the results of his harrowing trek along Bellevue Avenue, I now understood, but something deeper that could not be cured by a cup of tea and a change of clothing, though he badly needed both.

"Tell me," I said. "Tell me quickly, and then we'll find you something dry to wear."

"The coroner discovered two things that rule out all possibility of Claude Baptiste's death being an accident. Those marks were definitely bruises around his ankles, making it a certainty someone stole into that bathroom while the man was relaxing in the tub, gripped his ankles, and pulled him under."

I shuddered at the horrific nature of such a death. Had it occurred quickly enough to spare Monsieur Baptiste the terror of feeling the water rush into his lungs? Had his last seconds been a harrowing eternity of knowing he was about to die?

Jesse had more to tell. "Remember how Patch barked and sniffed at the body as if trying to tell us something?"

At the sound of his name, my dog looked up and made a growling noise of acknowledgment, as if trying to join the conversation.

I nodded. "He can be a nuisance."

"Not a nuisance. He sensed something and he was right. The coroner discovered something lodged in Monsieur Baptiste's throat. A pebble."

"What?"

Jesse nodded. "Yes. I don't understand it, but there it is."

"Oh, Jesse . . . This is monstrous." Another bout of shivers racked me. "What are we dealing with here?"

He answered my question with another. "Do you see why I had to come? I can't take you away from here—that would be as dangerous as staying—but I couldn't let you stay here alone. Damn this storm."

The oath as much as his roughened voice penetrated the shield I always raised in the face of his sentiments toward me. My throat tightened and stung, and tears pricked the backs of my eyes. I struggled for a response, but he spoke again.

"I understand it's Derrick Andrews you would most want here with you. If I could bring him here for you I would, but that's impossible. I can at least keep you safe, if you'll let me."

That simple avowal broke my heart even while it swelled

with a newfound admiration for my friend. My eyes brimmed, and I blinked madly to no avail. "Oh, Jesse . . ."

He shook his head with the sad smile I'd come to know all too well. "No, Emma, don't say it. Don't say anything. Let's just get to work and find our culprit."

I swallowed my tears. "We make a good team." The steady *drip-drip* of water hitting the rug brought me back to my sensible self. "What a fool I am. Before anything else you need dry clothes." I turned to call into the main part of the house, "Father, find Jesse a suit of clothes, please."

Chapter 13

With Jesse dry and well fed, he and I, along with Patch, retired to Uncle Frederick's office, where we shut the door so we wouldn't have to worry about interruptions. I apprised him of the latest developments, including the cigarette stub Mrs. Wharton and I had found on the lawn. We both agreed any of the guests might have tossed it there. It would serve us little in finding our culprit. Then we turned to the matter of Vasili.

"Whether his behavior last night stemmed from grief or guilt," I said, "remains to be determined. But I've never seen a man in such a state."

"Why guilt? Is it likely he murdered his good friend?"

"My instincts say no, but my instincts have occasionally been wrong." I ignored the lift of his eyebrow. "There might be a dynamic to their relationship we don't yet understand, perhaps stemming from Vasili's accident. As a performer, he would naturally be something of an actor, skilled at creating illusions."

"Hmm." Despite the brevity of his response, Jesse gave my scenario serious consideration. I saw this in how he crossed his arms and narrowed his eyes as he regarded me.

"And from what I've been able to gather so far," I went on, "he blames some or all of his friends for the end of his career."

"Do you know why?"

I shook my head. "Mrs. Wharton tells me none of the others were on that train with him. I'd like to try talking to him and see if I can get him to confide in me. But then there is Miss Marcus."

"The opera singer," Jesse mused, "with numerous disputes between herself and several members of this group."

"She seems at odds with everyone. She is not a nice person, Jesse." I scowled, remembering her comments about where animals belong. I crouched beside Patch and treated him to a hug and a good scratch behind his ears. "She even fought with Niccolo, and I had believed the two to be especially close. Even lovers."

Jesse winced at the word *lovers* and blushed slightly. He was no innocent, but hearing the term from my lips had obviously taken him aback. Well, after my experiences over the past year, I was no innocent either.

Still, he managed to shock me with his next bit of information. "We were successful in reaching Sir Randall's son, James Clifford, in England. He wired back, asking if we found his father's diary."

"Diary? Your men went through his things. They didn't find a diary, did they?"

"No, which means either he hadn't brought it with him—"

"Unlikely," I interrupted. "People who keep diaries rarely if ever travel without them."

"Exactly. That means he either hid it well somewhere in his room—"

"Or someone stole it." My pulse raced. "Are you going to search the house?"

"We'll start in Sir Randall's room, in case it's still there. But no one must know we're searching. If someone else has the diary I don't want to frighten them into disposing of it."

"If they haven't already." I stood and leaned against the desk, my fingers playing along the grain of the mahogany surface. "What if he had it with him when he was pushed off the footbridge?"

"Then it's long gone, for it certainly wasn't found on him. Let's hope no one knew about this diary, that it's still in his room and will give us some insight into what happened to him."

"And to Claude Baptiste. You look through the room. You can explain it easily enough as routine. I'll speak with Vasili."

"I don't like that, Emma. You might accidentally strike a nerve. Even if he isn't our guilty party, in his state of mind there's no telling how he might react. I'll do it."

"He won't speak with you, I'm sure of it." I gazed out the window, where scattered debris of leaves and branches littered the lawn and the drive. "I'll bring Mrs. Wharton with me. We can use the excuse of bringing Vasili something to eat."

I turned back into the room to find Jesse studying me closely. "Are you sure you can trust her?"

I didn't hesitate. "Yes."

He looked at me askance, and I easily read his thoughts.

"I'm not wrong about this, Jesse, not this time. If you spent any time with her at all you'd understand."

He skewed his lips before nodding. "Be careful. Leave the door open so you have an avenue of escape."

We set off on our individual errands. I went first to the kitchen to ask Mrs. Harris to warm a bowl of soup, and to keep Patch with her for a while. She readily agreed to both. Then I found Mrs. Wharton in the drawing room with my mother, the two of them side by side on the settee that faced the French doors. Neither appeared to be enjoying the watery view outside, or to be in any state of relaxation. Both sat stiffly, their eyes wide but unseeing, their whispered words like the quivering leaves of a shaken tree limb. From the library came other voices, mostly male, although punctuated by Josephine Marcus's soft-spoken—for once—comments.

Upon seeing my mother I almost backed out of the room, for I wished to engage Mrs. Wharton's assistance privately. Too late, as my mother spotted me and called me in.

"Emma, you look as though you're on some urgent errand. Was Jesse neglecting to tell us something?"

How had she guessed? Despite years on my own and the subsequent rift between my parents and me, I still felt like a sneaking child who had just been apprehended, red-handed. Perhaps mothers possessed a second sight into their children's minds that never faded no matter the circumstances. I began to stutter an answer and found myself unable to lie.

"I wish to speak with Vasili, and I hoped Mrs. Wharton would accompany me."

Mother tilted her head. "Speak to him about what? About why he showed such lack of restraint last night? Darling, he is grieving the loss of his very close friend."

I ventured farther into the room and sat opposite them. "I wish to ask him about his accident."

"Oh, Emma, no." Mother gripped the arm of the settee and leaned forward. "You mustn't. Not now. It will only upset him more. Besides, what has that to do with Claude's death?"

Mrs. Wharton said nothing, but watched me with obvious interest. If she objected to my plan, she didn't show it. I drew a breath. "Before I answer that, what can you tell me about Vasili's accident?"

The color drained from Mother's complexion in one sweep. "Nothing . . . I wasn't on the train. None of us was. And Vasili has spoken of it so little."

I craned forward a bit. "Why would he blame his friends for what happened?"

"Does he?" An astonished light entered my mother's eyes. "He's never said anything to me. We were all in Versailles, just after the New Year. Everyone except Vasili, of course. It was such a beautiful time in the city. There was snow everywhere, yet the skies were clear and the weather had warmed considerably. A January thaw."

I nodded, waiting for her to continue.

"Claude wrote to Vasili in Paris, where he had been performing, to coax him to join us."

"Only Claude?" I asked. "Did the others lend their persuasion?"

"Well, yes. The Countess Yelana Morekova was to hold a grand ball, and Vasili is a favorite of hers. They're related somehow, you see. Both Josephine and Niccolo were hoping for personal introductions, since the countess is a fervent patron of the arts."

"So Niccolo and Miss Marcus very much wanted Vasili to come to Versailles?"

"We all did. We were having such a splendid time." Mother took on a dreamy expression, which cleared abruptly to be replaced by obvious regret. "Until we heard about the train derailment. He broke numerous bones and came perilously close to dying. Directly afterward, once he was awake and could speak again, he said he wished he *had* died."

Mrs. Wharton slipped her hand on top of my mother's, and Mother glanced at her appreciatively and blinked away tears. "But I still don't understand what this has to do with now, or why you would dredge up such unhappy memories in a man who is clearly distraught."

I traded a glance with Mrs. Wharton, one Mother saw, for she said, "You mean to say . . . Emma, you cannot believe Vasili had anything to do with what happened to Claude or . . . or Randall?"

"I only wish to speak with him, Mother. His behavior last night was extreme, you must admit."

She looked down at Mrs. Wharton's hand, still covering her own. "Well . . . yes. I've never seen grief take such a form before. But we can't know what's inside a man's mind . . ."

"Precisely, Mother. We can't know unless we speak with him."

"Then I will do it," she said with a lift of her chin.

I shook my head. "I'm more qualified. I earn my keep by questioning people, and I've grown rather skilled in the task."

"Fine, but I'll go with you." A wounded note entered Mother's voice. "You wished to ask Edith to accompany you." Slowly she slid her hand from beneath the other woman's. "Is there some reason Edith is more qualified than your own mother?"

Poor Mrs. Wharton, hopelessly ensnared in our family discord, looked distinctly uncomfortable. In fact she implored me with her eyes to remedy the situation as quickly as possible. But the truth was that Mrs. Wharton *was* more qualified to help me question Vasili. She hadn't been in Versailles at the time and played no part in persuading Vasili to make the trip. He would therefore have no reason to resent her and might speak more freely in front of her.

But would Mother accept this reasoning?

An idea came to me. "Mrs. Wharton and I will question Vasili." Before Mother could protest, as she drew breath to do, I added, "And you'll take up position right outside the door, where you can listen in and not only be able to tell us later if Vasili's words ring true, but you can call for help should he become overly agitated. Will you assist us?"

Her posture visibly relaxed. "Since you put it that way. Yes, most certainly, darling."

"Mother, please put that fire poker down. I'm sure it won't be necessary."

My mother, Mrs. Wharton, and I climbed the back staircase together, having stopped in the kitchen first for a bowl of soup and some of Mrs. Harris's freshly baked bread. Mrs. Wharton carried the tray, while my mother wielded the brass fireplace tool from the drawing room. I carried a second tray with a teacup and a stout little pot that hovered beneath a tea cozy decorated with yellow flowers on a bright blue background. Too cheerful, surely, for our present destination, but I hadn't wished to bother the obliging cook with such a trifle.

"You yourself said my job was to protect you and Edith should Vasili become aggressive," Mother replied rather testily.

"No, I said your job was to call for help should he become *agitated*. There is a difference." I sighed. "Never mind, it doesn't matter."

Slightly muffled by Niccolo's closed bedroom door, sweet notes from his cello filled the upstairs corridor and led us across the gallery and into the north wing. Mother knocked on Vasili's door, then stepped aside so as not to be seen. We heard a grunt from inside, then footsteps, and the door opened. Carl calmly poked his head out. He had been standing guard over our patient—for lack of a better word—since before breakfast.

"Yes?" he whispered.

"We'll take over for a while," I said. He nodded, and with a glance over his shoulder, stepped into the hall. Mother had already taken her position beside the door, poker in hand. Carl saw this but after a blink of surprise he merely continued on his way. Mrs. Wharton and I went inside and closed the door but for an inch-wide gap.

Vasili lay on the four-poster on his back. His eyes were closed and he appeared to be asleep. But at the sound of Mrs. Wharton setting her tray on top of the long dresser, his eyes opened to stare up at the ceiling. He snapped in none too gentle a voice, "*Kto eto*?"

Still holding the tea things, I looked to Mrs. Wharton in puzzlement. She went to the bedside. "It's Edith and Miss Cross, Vasili."

Without shifting his gaze away from the ceiling, he said in the same guttural tone, "*Chto ty khochesh'*?"

She raised her head to address me in a whisper. "He wants to know what we want." To him she said, "We brought you tea and something to eat."

"*Ukhodit'*."

Mrs. Wharton leaned closer to him. "We will not go away, Vasili. You must eat. I have some lovely soup for you, and Miss Cross has brought tea."

"Tea." He spat the word. "What use is tea? Bring me vodka. That buffoon in livery refused even when I threw the box at him."

A glint of silver identified this object, a carved trinket box that lay on its side at a corner of the Aubusson rug. Poor Carl had had his task cut out for him. To my relief, the end table where the box likely originated, within Vasili's reach, had been swept clean of all other possible projectiles. Even the bedside lamp now occupied the top of the bureau on the wall opposite the bed.

"*Chert poberi*," Vasili mumbled, and closed his eyes. Mrs. Wharton winced.

"What did that mean?" I mouthed to her.

"I shan't repeat it." She reached for the pillow beneath Vasili's head and tugged. "You'll need to sit up. Come now, don't be stubborn. We will not leave until we've seen some honest sustenance go into you."

Somehow we did just that, managing to nearly empty the bowl of soup and get several cups of tea into him. Perhaps the young man secretly craved someone to take care of him. Perhaps he simply didn't have the strength to fight us. The meal seemed to mellow him. He stopped mumbling in Russian and no longer burst out with words that made Mrs. Wharton flinch. He complained of a headache. I went into the bathroom that adjoined the next bedroom and wet a washcloth in cold water. Behind the closed door that led into the next room, Niccolo's cello resonated gently.

I returned to Vasili's bedside and placed the cold washcloth across his forehead. Then I stepped back, for all purposes out of sight, and let Mrs. Wharton do the talking.

"You cannot continue on this self-destructive course," she said. "Whatever were you thinking last night? You might have been killed."

Her admonishment met with a grunt.

"Is this what Claude would have wanted?" she asked bluntly.

"What difference does it make?"

"Very much of a difference. If you are truly his friend, you'll continue as he would have wished."

Nothing moved but his eyes as he took her in. "And how is that?"

"As a man who lives to his potential."

He muttered in Russian, and I guessed this would be another comment Mrs. Wharton would not repeat. "My potential is dead. It died on a train between Paris and Versailles."

"That's not true—"

He sprang upright, prompting Mrs. Wharton to recoil. Yet to her credit she stood her ground as his features twisted and he began to rail. "A choreographer? I was a rising star of the ballet. By now I would have been the principal male lead—choreographers would have staged their work for me. Me! Now I am nothing." Like a sail abandoned by the wind, he fell back against the pillows, limp and pale. "I did not wish to go. I wished to remain in Paris. They would have been back soon enough. But they would not leave me alone. They insisted. How I hate them for that. All of them. They destroyed me, left me with nothing."

Mrs. Wharton, too, had paled, but she continued to speak calmly. "They could not have known what would happen, Vasili. They certainly never meant you harm. . . ." She trailed off at the adamant shaking of his head.

"No, they were selfish. They cared only about themselves. Josephine . . . Niccolo . . ." His voice became so low I almost didn't hear the last name he spoke. "Claude."

Mrs. Wharton darted a glance at me, one I hardly dared return lest Vasili notice my incredulity and refuse to say more. I barely breathed. He went on, his vehemence growing.

"Claude, he denied it, but he wished to meet her—Yelana—as much as the others did. She was all they cared about. Her money. Her connections. Claude, Niccolo . . ." He turned his head and pinned me with an accusing glare. "Your father."

"But Claude was your friend," I couldn't stop myself from saying. "You're grieving over him. . . ."

I'd made a mistake—make that two. The second was in

speaking, in challenging his assertions. But the first mistake I'd made was to leave the cup, saucer, and teapot on the end table beside him. He reached out and in one swift motion grabbed the handle of the pot and flung it in a spray of russet liquid across the room. It hit the front of the bureau with an explosion of shards and tea, splattering the drawers, the wall, the floor and rug. I barely managed to lurch out of harm's way.

At the same time the door burst open. Mother stood in the doorway, the fire poker raised like a sword. She took one step before a pair of hands gripped her shoulders from behind and moved her aside. Before she could react beyond her expression of surprise, Jesse strode into the room. He took in the scene—the shattered teapot, Mrs. Wharton's and my astonished faces, and Vasili, half on and half off the bed, looking enraged and ready to spring at the closest victim.

Jesse's appearance stopped us all cold, even Vasili. For a second or two no one moved, until Jesse somehow diffused the situation merely by asking, "Is everything all right in here?"

In his left hand he gripped a book bound in dark brown leather.

The broken teapot brought Niccolo and my father rushing into Vasili's room. Josephine and Teddy Wharton came hurrying in moments later as well. I let them all, my mother included, endeavor to soothe their young friend and used the opportunity to steal away. Jesse followed me and we made our way back downstairs to my uncle's office at the front of the house. It was only as I was closing the door that I realized Mrs. Wharton had trailed us as well.

"Don't shut me out, Miss Cross. You've asked for my help twice now. I am engaged in this matter and what is more, I believe I can be of further assistance."

My reply was to silently seek Jesse's concurrence. The room was dark and chilly, an extension of the continuing storm outside. I could make out little of his features but his nod conveyed his permission to allow Mrs. Wharton to join us. I locked the door behind her. Jesse attempted to switch on the electric desk lamp, to no avail.

"The power's been out all morning," I reminded him. I went to the corner cabinet and found a hurricane lamp and matches inside. "Uncle Frederick doesn't believe in putting one's faith entirely in electricity," I explained as I brought the lantern over to the desk.

Mrs. Wharton gestured to the hymnal-sized tome Jesse held. "That looks familiar. I recognize the red and gold ribbon place holder. That's Randall's, isn't it?"

"You knew he had a diary?" Jesse spoke sharply, and Mrs. Wharton, noticing, raised her chin.

"I would have mentioned it if I had remembered. I only saw him writing in it once, a couple of years ago. It surprised me, a man like Randall keeping a journal."

"How so?" Jesse asked.

"So few men do," she said, "unless they happen to be writers by profession. Men like Randall keep records, mostly lists of engagements, business dealings, estate improvements, that sort of thing, but I had the distinct impression at the time that this was quite different. You see, he snapped it closed rather quickly when I came upon him. We were all at Breighton Lodge at the time—that's Randall's estate in Suffolk. I haven't seen it or thought of it since."

"Have you looked through it yet?" I asked Jesse.

"I had only just discovered it tucked into a corner of the armoire, high on the top shelf. It was missed during the initial search due to the interior of the armoire and the leather being about the same color. At a glance it blended perfectly with the shelf, and lay beyond arm's reach."

He picked it up, but I placed a hand on the cover to keep him from opening it. "Before we get to this, Mrs. Wharton, can you explain what happened in Vasili's room? Why he accused Claude Baptiste as he did? Had you ever detected a hint of acrimony between them before? Because I certainly hadn't."

I took a moment to enlighten Jesse about Mrs. Wharton's conversation with Vasili, ending in the broken teapot. Her features grew taut as she considered my question. "They did argue, sometimes frequently. But none of us ever thought much of it. They were contentious in the way close friends often are, if you see what I mean."

I thought about that. Brady and I certainly argued on a regular basis, usually with me scolding him for ill-advised behavior while he defended his actions and insisted I mind my business. There had been heated episodes between us in the past, but that didn't mean we loved each other any less for it.

"What we saw minutes ago was not the habitual squabbling between friends," I pointed out.

"No," she agreed, "it seemed more the outburst of sentiments that had long been suppressed."

"Perhaps Mr. Pavlenko was conflicted in his friendship with Monsieur Baptiste," Jesse said. "Perhaps he blamed him as much as the others for his accident but didn't know how to set about expressing his anger."

"That makes sense." Mrs. Wharton steepled her fingers beneath her chin and paced a few steps. "Vasili was in a very bad way after the accident. Very depressed. It was Claude who convinced him he still had a life worth living. But perhaps beneath that optimism, Vasili continued to partly blame him for what happened." She stopped pacing and turned to us, her jaw hardening. "This is all but another way to say Vasili had a motive to murder Claude, isn't it?"

"It's merely a possibility," Jesse said. He didn't elaborate, but I knew he was also considering what I had told him about Josephine Marcus, how she had turned her enmity on both Sir Randall and Claude Baptiste. "Can you think of any motive Vasili might had had to kill Sir Randall?"

"None," Mrs. Wharton said without hesitation.

I remembered something. "Vasili never mentioned Sir Randall during his rant. He specifically named Niccolo, Miss Marcus, my father, and Claude . . . but not Sir Randall."

"Well, Randall had his own money and wouldn't have needed or cared about Countess Morekova's patronage, would he?" Mrs. Wharton gave a slight shrug. "He might have lent his voice to the others in persuading Vasili to join them in Versailles, but he wouldn't have had any other motive than wishing their friend to be present."

"So we might be able to link Vasili to Monsieur Baptiste's death, but not Sir Randall's, at least not presently." Jesse glanced down at the journal. "Perhaps this might shed some light."

He circled the desk to sit in Uncle Frederick's leather armchair. Mrs. Wharton and I stood on either side of him, leaning to read over his shoulder. He opened the book to where the ribbon marked Sir Randall's last entry.

> *Miss Cross gives me hope. A delightful young woman, she, and a true credit to Arthur and Beatrice. Now if Josephine would only find her amusement elsewhere rather than having it at my expense . . .*

The rest of the entry went on in a similar vein, ending with Sir Randall's intention of studying the cliffs for inspiration. A shiver went through me at the thought of him scribbling this entry only minutes before he returned to the Cliff Walk with his sketch pad.

Jesse flipped backward several entries to where Sir Randall and my parents had first arrived in New York. Though a distinctly gloomy tone pervaded, we read nothing to signify either an intention of suicide or an insufferable clash with any of his friends. Jesse flipped back another several entries. He leaned his chin on his hands and stared down at the pages.

"I might need to pore through the entire journal."

I gave a little groan of sympathy. "We could take turns going through it—wait. What is this?" Standing out against the uniform cut of the journal's pages about midway through, a single sheet protruded a hair's width beyond the rest. I opened to the place to discover a folded page that had been inserted. I unfolded it. "It's a letter . . . addressed to a solicitor in London."

Jesse was on his feet in an instant. He slid the paper closer to the lantern and all three of us craned our necks to read the words.

> *I, Sir Randall Clifford, being of sound mind and body, do herewith authorize a change to my last will and testament to exclude AC from all rights of inheritance . . .*

"Who is AC?" I mused. "Not his son, James. Did Sir Randall have a brother? Good heavens, *why* didn't he spell out the name?"

"This is only a draft," Mrs. Wharton said. "Leaving one to wonder if he ever sent the original, and if so, when."

Jesse turned to stare out the window at the thrashing foliage and driving sheets of rain. "This could be important. I need to wire his son again, and that solicitor." He breathed out heavily, in lieu, I guessed, of swearing.

I touched his shoulder. "You can't go out there again."

"I have to."

Chapter 14

As it turned out, Jesse didn't leave when he wished to, but it wasn't the storm that kept him at Rough Point.

As we exited Uncle Frederick's office a lovely melody drifted softly through the house. We met Miss Marcus in the Stair Hall.

Surprised to see her alone, I asked, "Where is everyone?"

She looked almost affronted by my question and for a moment I thought she would decline to answer or rebuff me in some way. Perhaps Mrs. Wharton's presence beside me caused her to relent. "Your parents are sitting with Vasili, and your mother suggested Niccolo return to his room to play, but that he leave his door open so Vasili would be soothed by the music."

No wonder I could hear his playing from so far away. "A good idea," I said to her, and then to Mrs. Wharton, "Perhaps we should join the others. Miss Marcus? Will you join us as well?"

"There *are* no others, Miss Cross," she said haughtily, "or had you forgotten? The only people downstairs at present are Teddy and myself, and the servants, of course." She sniffed disdainfully. "Teddy is in the drawing room, but he was being morose so I left him. As if matters aren't deplorable enough. Perhaps I'll practice my billiards."

"We shouldn't be alone. We all agreed about that," I reminded her.

"Yes, well, if you should hear my screams, please come running." With that, she swept past us into the billiard room, and a moment later I heard the strike of a match on friction. A wisp of smoke drifted through the doorway to tickle my nose. Mrs. Wharton and I traded shrugs, and as we headed to the drawing room, I heard the light clicking of the billiard balls being arranged in the triangular rack.

"She certainly marches to the beat of her own drum, doesn't she?" I commented as we passed through the Great Hall.

Mrs. Wharton chuckled. "Is that necessarily a bad thing?"

"No, it's one of the few things I admire about her."

"Admire about whom?" In the drawing room, Teddy Wharton occupied the settee beside the hearth, the one facing the French doors. He didn't look up as we entered the room, but continued staring out the doors. Water cascaded from the roof of the covered veranda, all but obscuring the view of the lawns.

"Josephine," his wife informed him. "We were noting how she skirts convention at every turn.

"Does she," he murmured back, "or does she simply pretend to?"

"Why, Teddy, what an odd thing to say. I don't see how there is a difference. Her behavior is what it is."

But Mr. Wharton's offhand observation produced its impact on me. The notion of pretending, not in a momentary situation, but constantly, as an act of simply being . . . could someone keep that up indefinitely? Show the world an outer self that bore little or no resemblance to the person within? I could almost point to examples of such individuals, but no, even with the most insincere personality, there had been signs, warnings. Whether or not others choose to heed those warnings was another matter. Was I failing to heed a warning now?

Was Miss Marcus pretending, and if so, to be what and for what purpose? What about the others? My parents had tried to pretend nothing was wrong but I saw through their charade quickly enough. Vasili seemed incapable of pretense, for he wore his heart on his sleeve. Niccolo, too, appeared genuine in the persona he presented the world. Even in his puzzling relationship with Miss Marcus, he wished for honesty, as the argument I had overheard between them in the piazza attested. It had been Miss Marcus who had insisted on secrecy.

My thoughts had distracted me from the conversation between the Whartons, but a sharp retort from Teddy reclaimed my attention.

"I don't see what business it is of yours, Edith."

"What business?" She made a sound of impatience in her throat. "Vasili is a friend. He is your friend, too."

"Ha. None of these people would give half a fig for me were they not all so utterly enamored of you, my dear. As it is, they merely tolerate me."

"Don't be ridiculous. I see now why Josephine chose to play billiards alone rather than remain here."

"Remain here *with me*?" Teddy's voice rose in challenge. "Is that what you mean to say, Edith?"

With a sigh Mrs. Wharton sat on the cushion beside him. "Oh, Teddy. I certainly do not *wish* to say such things. I do not like to. But please, can you not *try* to be more amiable?"

Her hand slid over his where it rested on his thigh. He flinched as though her touch burned him and abruptly stood. "I see I am not welcome here until I achieve a state of amiability deemed acceptable by the present company. If you will both excuse me. Miss Cross." He tipped his head without looking at me and marched away into the Great Hall.

My lips compressed against my sense of mortification, I darted a glance at Mrs. Wharton. If I could un-see and unhear what had just occurred and spare her the humiliation, I would have.

She met my gaze with a dismayed one of her own. "I'm terribly sorry about that."

"Please don't apologize." I left my own seat in the armchair and circled the sofa table to sit beside her. "Are you all right?"

Looking down at her lap, she nodded. "But you see what I mean about Teddy. His state of mind sometimes borders on irrational. And the worst part is that his surliness *is* driving the others away, along with others of our friends. They have tried to be understanding, but I fear their patience is reaching its limit."

We talked a while longer, with the rain and wind providing a backdrop as Mrs. Wharton recounted her courtship and early marriage. Mr. Wharton, she said, had seemed an entirely different kind of man then, and she had believed she found a kindred spirit, someone who loved traveling and the arts more than the accumulation of wealth, and with whom she might laugh at the vagaries of the Four Hundred.

The darkness, she explained, had crept in on their lives so gradually as to be imperceptible at first, but for a trying day here and there. But having once taken hold, there had been no banishing the melancholy, and while they did still experience happier moments, the current state of things at Rough Point was dragging heavily at Mr. Wharton's psyche. And perhaps we could not blame him for that.

Finally, she gave the cushion between us a firm pat. "That is quite enough of that. I fear I've fallen into my own state of melancholy."

I agreed that my companion could do with a change of focus. "Perhaps we should go up to check on how Vasili is faring," I suggested. "His outburst was my fault. I should have remained silent and allowed you to do the talking."

"You meant well," she replied. "There are many questions that still need answering and you were merely attempting to loosen his tongue."

Together we retraced our steps through the house. I heard no click of billiards as we entered the Stair Hall, but dismissed the absence as Mrs. Wharton and I started up. The stairs were dark, the upper hallway darker. As we entered the gallery with its wall of paintings on one side and the depths of the Great Hall on the other, a swath of ghostly white, thin and elongated, moved toward us from the opposite side. The two-story bay of windows in the Great Hall shed a gray, watery light over the image, making it seem to shimmy from side to side even as it approached. Mrs. Wharton and I halted abruptly and on instinct reached for each other's hands.

"What is it?" she whispered.

A deathly specter came to mind, and why wouldn't it in a house that had seen two deaths in so short a time? But my logical side wouldn't accept the fanciful notion, and I squinted to make out more of the figure in the dimness. It ceased moving at the center of the gallery, where the light from outside, however paltry, shined its strongest. A human form took shape. It proved not to be a rail-thin wraith cloaked in white, for now I clearly saw the outlines of the black dress beneath the starched pinafore.

"Irene?" I thought to chastise her for moving about the house in so mysterious a manner, but a hiccup of a sob burst from her lips just before her knees buckled and she sank to the floor.

Mrs. Wharton and I released our grip on each other and

hurried to the maid. By the time we reached her she had fallen onto her side, senseless. We crouched beside her.

I lifted her hand and held it to my cheek. "She's as cold as ice."

"Is she . . . is she . . ."

In reply to Mrs. Wharton's unspoken question I held my free hand in front of Irene's nose, while I also scrutinized the shallow rise and fall of her chest. "No, thank heavens." Still holding her hand, I patted it gently, then harder. "Irene? Irene, it's Miss Cross. Irene!"

"I'll get help." Mrs. Wharton pushed to her feet and scurried back the way we had come.

I continued patting the woman's hand and prodding her shoulder. She stirred but didn't awaken. I took my shawl from around my shoulders and laid it over her, even as I searched for signs of injury. None were apparent—no bruises and no blood—and her uniform, though rumpled from her fall, appeared sound enough. She suddenly drew in a trembling breath and her eyes fluttered.

"Irene. It's Miss Cross. You fainted, but you're safe, I'm here with you. Can you open your eyes, please?"

She struggled to do so, her eyelids continuing to flutter open and close. But her fingers closed tightly around my own, and with an effort she managed to lever an elbow beneath her and sit partially upright. Her eyes opened fully then, and she looked about dazedly, blinking as she took in her surroundings.

"What happened?"

"You fainted. Are you feeling ill?"

"No, I don't . . . don't think so . . ." Her hand came away from mine and she pressed the backs of her knuckles against her brow, then her mouth. She frowned deeply and shook her head. Terror dawned in her eyes. "Oh, Miss Cross."

"What is it, Irene? What happened to disturb you so?"

From the south wing came sounds of people approaching. I heard Mrs. Wharton directing whoever it was to hurry, and then the voices of Mrs. Harris and Mr. Dunn. They must have come up the servants' staircase. Irene went very still, but it was not the south end of the corridor that held her attention. No, she was craning her neck to see over her shoulder, into the north wing that disappeared from view after turning the corner off the gallery. Her hand found mine again and squeezed, and once again she tremulously whispered my name.

And then it struck me. Niccolo had been playing his cello for Vasili. Now there was only silence coming from the north wing.

When Mrs. Wharton and the other two reached us, my own voice trembled. "Mr. Dunn, please find Detective Whyte."

An eternity seemed to pass before Jesse appeared, though it could only have been a few minutes. My parents arrived before him, coming from their bedroom.

"I thought you were sitting with Vasili," I said when they reached the gallery. Did I sound accusing? I must have, for my mother pulled back and my father's eyes sparked with defensiveness, as did his tone.

"He fell fast asleep again, and we saw no harm in leaving him for a few minutes. We found his alcohol, you see, and brought it to our room to hide it."

"Both of you?"

"Emmaline, I didn't wish to leave your mother alone with Vasili given his state of mind, and neither did I wish to send her across the house alone. We were about to return when we heard people rushing by our door in the corridor."

"Is something wrong, Emma?" My mother only then seemed to comprehend the scene before her. I had managed to help Irene to her feet, and she and I stood together at the center of the gallery, my arm about her waist. I feared if I released her she would not be steady enough to stand on her own.

"Has anyone seen Niccolo?" I asked, rather than answer Mother's question.

"He was playing in his room. . . ." Furrows deepened between my father's eyes. "He must have grown tired of playing."

Irene let out a whimper, and whispered, "No . . ." Her legs threatened to give way again and I tightened my hold on her. "He . . . he . . ."

I dreaded hearing the end of that utterance. "Don't, Irene. Wait for Detective Whyte."

His footsteps thudded on the runner of the main staircase, and in a moment he came along the corridor, his face gripped with concern. I quickly looked about at the others and realized Mr. Dunn was no longer among us. My father must have realized it too, for he strode past and continued into the north wing.

Jesse breathed hard when he reached me, as if he had run from across the house. "What happened, Emma?"

"I think it's Niccolo. Something has happened to Niccolo." To confirm my guess, Irene cried out and sagged against me. I wished to bring her into a room where she could sit, but I also wanted to know what lurked in the north wing. "Mrs. Harris, would you take Irene into the sitting room, please?"

The maid passively let me pass her into Mrs. Harris's plump arms, but when the cook attempted to lead her out of the gallery, she stiffened and refused to budge.

"I knocked on his door. I had extra linens for him. When he didn't answer I thought he had gone below. I never thought . . . Oh . . . it was awful. . . ."

I caught Mrs. Harris's eye and nodded, and the woman gently but firmly led Irene away. Irene could tell us what she witnessed later, after we had seen with our own eyes the sight that had greeted her upon entering Niccolo's room. I exhaled and met Jesse's gaze.

"You should wait here," he said, but with little conviction. He knew I would follow.

My father reappeared at the other end of the gallery. He leaned to grip the railing, and his head drooped between his shoulders. It seemed a struggle for him to push out even a few words. "Jesse. Come quickly. You're needed."

Jesse strode toward Father and I followed. My mother held back with Mrs. Wharton. At the end of the gallery, where the north wing began, Vasili's door stood open. He half leaned, half sagged against the lintel, his face even whiter than when I'd last seen him and a sheen of perspiration gleaming across his brow. His eyes were red and had a wild look about them. A sharp waft of spirits reached my nose. He glanced at us only briefly before dropping his gaze to the floor. He didn't look up again as we passed.

Jesse reached Niccolo's door first. It stood partly ajar. Before he could reach out to open it wider, Miss Marcus's door opened and she stepped out. Upon seeing Jesse she clutched at the lace of her plunging neckline. "What are you doing here?"

"There may have been another incident." Jesse pushed at Niccolo's door, but hesitated on the threshold.

There were footsteps behind me. My father only now must have realized I had followed Jesse into the wing, because he called out, "Emmaline, don't!"

But it was too late, I had already reached Jesse and looked over his shoulder into the room. In the far corner, on the other side of the bed, Niccolo sat slumped against the back of an armchair, with his Montagnana cello propped before him. One of its strings had been yanked free and wrapped around his neck.

* * *

Jesse flung himself into the room and over the bed. He leaned Niccolo's body forward and set to work while my father, Miss Marcus, and I looked on in horror. The instrument's C-string had been yanked from its fine tuner on the tailpiece, ripped forcefully by some kind of tool, pliers perhaps, that gouged the cello's varnished surface, leaving a whitened scar across the grain. The string had been wrapped twice around Niccolo's neck and twisted until the metal cut into his flesh.

I had seen strangulation before, yet, nauseated, I looked away, unable to bear the sight, or the thought of such a fate. The man's own instrument, a vehicle of his murder. He had not fallen, or taken his own life, or dozed off under dangerous circumstances. He had been deliberately, blatantly killed. And as with Claude Baptiste, the manner of death seemed to convey some kind of message.

Jesse untwisted the string and worked it free of Niccolo's neck, leaving behind a thin band of blood. The act left Jesse's own fingers bleeding. He attempted to lean the torso gently back against the chair, but with a shocking suddenness he instead kicked the cello out of the way and dragged the body onto the floor. Aghast, I thought perhaps this third death was simply too much for my friend to bear. I should have known better.

I hurried to him, only to stop abruptly at the foot of the bed. I cried out and fisted my hands against my mouth. Though as white as sun-bleached bone, Niccolo showed none of the sure signs of death. His lips, though blanched, were not blue, and as I watched, blood trickled from the cut in his neck where the string had been.

I sank to my knees beside Jesse.

"Arthur, help me lift him onto the bed," Jesse shouted.

My father, unaware of what we were seeing, halted between the door and the bed. "Jesse, there's nothing you can do. . . ."

"Damn it, Arthur, come and help me. He's still alive."

From the threshold Miss Marcus shrieked. Father rushed to us and together he and Jesse lifted Niccolo. I hurriedly flipped back the coverlets, and after they placed him on the bed I pulled the coverlets and satin spread back up to cover him. My knees wobbled, and I dropped onto the mattress beside the unconscious man.

"Will he live?"

"I can't say, Emma." Jesse put a hand on my shoulder. "It's a miracle he's alive at all. But if we can't get him to the hospital . . ." He shook his head and didn't complete the sentence. He didn't have to.

Mrs. Harris volunteered to stay with Niccolo. Having had nursing experience in her youth, during the War Between the States, she was Niccolo's best hope until Jesse could arrange for him to be moved. Carl was to remain in the room as well, and Jesse armed him with Mother's fire poker in case whoever wished Niccolo dead returned for another try. In the meantime, every occupant of Rough Point was under strict orders not to go anywhere alone, or to leave someone else alone. It was as much for their protection as Niccolo's.

Jesse had us assemble in the dining room. The group felt so much smaller now, diminished in both size and spirit. Only Mr. and Mrs. Wharton, my parents, Vasili, Miss Marcus, and myself were left. Vasili threw himself into a dining chair and dropped his head onto his folded arms.

Jesse stood at the head of the table. Mrs. Harris had tended and wrapped his fingers in small bandages. He held them out. "I need to see everyone's hands."

Josephine Marcus had been quiet—no, utterly silent—since the discovery that Niccolo had survived his attack. Now she blurted, "Our hands? Why? Are you once again accusing us? You were here in this house. You should have been protecting us." Though her voice carried a sob, no tears fell from her eyes. I thought she had finished, but she rose and swept the length of the table to where Mr. Dunn and a still shaken Irene stood at attention. Miss Marcus's arm shot out, her forefinger aiming at Irene. "You! You were the last person in his room. You with your linens and towels. You would have had access to Claude's room as well." She twirled to face Jesse. "*Here* is your culprit. Look at *her* hands and leave the rest of us alone."

I had let Patch out of the kitchen, and now he growled in response to Miss Marcus's vehement charge. I expected Irene to put up an immediate protest, but instead she merely held out her hands for the rest of us to see. There were no marks scoring her fingers or palms, no evidence of having wrapped the cutting cello string around a man's neck. Her hands wavered and her throat convulsed, but she spoke steadily enough. "I am innocent, Detective Whyte."

Jesse nodded, then repeated his order. Vasili's head came up, though he looked as if he could barely maintain even a semi-upright position. He let his palms fall open on the table. Everyone else held out their hands as well—everyone but Josephine Marcus. Jesse ignored her, his features tight as he moved around the table, stopping to examine each palm closely. He even studied mine. I understood. This was an official investigation and he could not leave any possibility open to question. I also understood the pain that constricted his features. Miss Marcus's implied charge that he shirked his responsibility to keep everyone safe had cut, deeply.

But if Jesse had failed, hadn't we all? We had agreed never to be alone anywhere in the house, or if we were, to lock our bedroom doors behind us. Both Niccolo's and Vasili's doors had been open and the two men had been alone. My parents should not have left Vasili. If they hadn't, would Niccolo now lay unconscious and close to death? Or would the culprit have feared detection and stayed away? Had they unwittingly provided a convenient opportunity?

Then again, why Niccolo and not Vasili? *Had* the former dancer truly been sleeping, or . . . ?

He had been drinking again, as evidenced by my parents' having to confiscate one of his bottles. And he had been unable to control his violent outburst in response to my questions.

"Miss Marcus, your hands, if you please." Jesse had checked everyone else. She huffed and thrust out her hands. Her nose flared and contempt poured from her very bearing.

"There," she said. "You see? Nothing. Now what, Detective? Who is your suspect? No one, I'll wager, because you are useless. You might as well leave us all to our deaths—"

"Josephine!" Mrs. Wharton's admonition rendered Miss Marcus silent. "You're not helping one bit. Now is the time to cooperate, not make wild accusations."

"The detective is the one making wild accusations," the singer countered.

"I have made no accusations, Miss Marcus," Jesse said harshly. I could see his patience was wearing thin, but also each caustic word the woman spoke hit dead center at his core. Still, he wasted no more time in cosseting her. "Miss Marcus, you were in your room when Signore Lionetti was attacked. Why?"

A shake of her shoulders pulled her up taller. "I was freshening up."

"And you heard nothing from the corridor?"

"Not a peep."

Jesse studied her a moment. "You were also freshening up

the night Claude Baptiste was murdered. In fact, the broken pipe in your bathroom preceded his death. It created a distraction and sent the guests scattering to their rooms to change. What do you know about that pipe?"

"Nothing. What could I possibly know about plumbing? I was a victim of the handyman's incompetence. And Mrs. Wharton was with me afterward, helping me change my gown."

"Mrs. Wharton helped you change, but then returned to her own room to do the same. That left you alone for some time before dinner."

Miss Marcus sank into the nearest empty chair at the table, yet her defiance didn't waver. "In that case, with the exception of the Crosses and the Whartons, everyone was alone for some time before dinner. Even you, Miss Cross," she finished with a lift of her eyebrow.

I didn't reply. I was too busy calculating how much time we'd all had before dinner that night, and whether it seemed feasible that Miss Marcus had entered Claude Baptiste's room before descending to the dining room. I concluded that, given the cause of death, she would have had ample time, and sufficient strength. The way Jesse had described the drowning, anyone, man or woman, would have been capable of pulling the Frenchman under.

What about Sir Randall? Could Miss Marcus have slipped outside, made her way through the kitchen garden to the Cliff Walk, pushed Sir Randall over, and been back in the Great Hall in plenty of time for Niccolo's performance? Again, I wondered about the strength necessary to send a man plummeting to his death. But a woman, especially one as designing as Miss Marcus, would have had the advantage over an elderly gentleman like Sir Randall Clifford. He would not have expected an attack, and the element of surprise would have aided his attacker greatly.

And Teddy Wharton's grassy shoes? Perhaps that had been nothing more than ill manners.

Niccolo's near fateful attack raised a new question about strength. He had lived, Jesse determined, because the C-string, while cutting into his flesh and causing him to pass out, hadn't been twisted tight enough to cause immediate death. Had we not found him, he would surely have asphyxiated, but the botched attempt had bought him time. Had the perpetrator not possessed enough strength in his or her hands to sufficiently tighten the string?

It seemed a possibility.

"The fact remains," Jesse was saying, "that all evidence points to the killer being someone in this house—someone who has been in this house all along. Whoever attempted to murder Signore Lionetti was probably wearing gloves, thick ones, and if so, I will find them."

"So you're still saying one of us killed him?" Teddy Wharton swallowed audibly. "That one of us killed two men and tried to kill a third?"

Jesse replied with a pointed stare. Teddy Wharton paled to his hairline and turned to his wife. "Pack your things, we are leaving."

"We can't leave yet." She huffed with impatience. "We'd never make it home."

"Better we slide around in the mud than sit here waiting to be next."

His wife shook her head. "We've had this discussion, Teddy. I understand your wish to leave, and if you are set on going, then do so. I am staying."

I circled my mother and went to Mrs. Wharton's side. "Maybe Mr. Wharton is right."

She regarded me for a long moment. Then she said in a low murmur, "We must speak alone."

I frowned in puzzlement but she said nothing more. Jesse

announced that he would make another search of the house, this time for the gloves that might have played a role in Niccolo's attack. He ordered us all into the drawing room, including Mr. Dunn and Irene. Miss Marcus opened her mouth as if to protest, but apparently changed her mind.

As everyone else filed out of the room I couldn't help coming up beside her. "I would have thought you'd be more upset than this, Miss Marcus. You and Niccolo have seemed to be especially close."

Her gaze held sheer poison. "And what would you know of it, Miss Cross?"

"I know the two of you argued recently." I dispensed with discretion. "I saw you—and heard you—outside in the piazza."

Fiery color stained her complexion. "Wh-what did you hear?"

"I heard Niccolo ask if perhaps you wished he were dead." I raised my eyebrows. "Do you?"

Her hand came up and I winced, bracing for a blow that didn't come, though her hissing words lashed out at me. "Why, you conniving little witch. How dare you eavesdrop on my private conversations? You have no idea what you're playing with. Arthur might be a Vanderbilt but you, Miss Cross, are a guttersnipe with no more sense or decorum than a garden worm."

Patch darted to us and barked, but Miss Marcus took no notice. She flounced away, the ruffled train of her tea gown brushing at my own hems as if to sweep them—or me—away with the trash. She left me quaking with ire and seething with suspicion. In my distraction I hadn't noticed that Mrs. Wharton had also remained behind. She appeared now at my shoulder.

"Well, what did you expect, after what you said to her?"

The jarring ring of the telephone in Uncle Frederick's office startled us both and forestalled any reply I might have made.

Jesse rushed into Uncle Frederick's office and shut the door, while Mrs. Wharton and I waited in the dining room, anxious to know the details of the call. In the meantime, she and I returned to our discussion about Miss Marcus.

"Do you really think Josephine is a murderess?" she asked me.

"She held grudges against all three of them. I saw it firsthand. Jesse only needs to find a pair of gloves among her things. . . ."

"Do you think whoever attacked Niccolo simply tucked those gloves back in among his or her things?"

I started to reply, then, confounded, blew out a breath. "I don't know what I think anymore."

"Well, I shall tell you what I think. Let us sit."

"We're supposed to go to the drawing room with the others," I reminded her.

She dismissed this with a shrug. "Jesse won't arrest us for delaying that order, will he?"

I conceded her point and we turned our chairs to face each other. Rain streamed in thick rivulets down the mullioned windows while the shrubbery beneath swayed this way and that as if held by the roots and shaken. Mrs. Wharton leaned forward and spoke just above a whisper. "I've detected a pattern to these killings. An artistic sensibility."

"You mean because Niccolo was attacked with part of his own instrument?"

"Not only that. Randall was murdered at the cliffs—cliffs made of stone and earth, and where saplings take root in the crevices and grow. Stone, earth, wood—these are the tools of a sculptor. And Claude drowned in a saltwater bath with a pebble lodged in his mouth. These are the tools of an actor's trade, and as a stage director, he would have instructed his actors to gargle with salt water after rehearsals to preserve their voices, and put pebbles in their mouths to learn to enunciate more clearly. And now, yes, as you said, Niccolo was nearly strangled with his own cello string."

"Then . . ." I gasped as the pattern became clear to me. "My father . . . if he were to be next . . ." I shuddered as possibilities took monstrous shape in my mind. "Perhaps poisoned by his own painting chemicals. And Vasili . . ."

After a moment's hesitation, Mrs. Wharton shrugged. "I'm afraid I haven't the imagination to envision how one might do away with a dancer. Or an opera singer, for that matter. Or"—she shuddered—"an aspiring writer."

By that last she meant herself, and I placed a hand over hers. "If your husband leaves, you should give serious thought to accompanying him."

"Are you certain my husband is innocent?"

The question startled me into remembering that I *had* entertained the notion that Teddy Wharton killed Sir Randall. There had been the matter of wet grass clinging to his shoes the night Sir Randall went missing, following close on the heels of his obvious anger at finding his wife alone with the Englishman. Yet I had found nothing significant linking him to the other two victims.

That didn't stop me from asking, "Do you fear your husband?" I watched her face closely as she formed her answer.

She took me aback a second time. "Yes, at times I do. But not because I believe him guilty of murder. I fear I no longer fully know my husband or understand the darkness that is slowly taking over his mind. He is no longer the man I married."

"Because of his melancholia."

She nodded. "With each passing week he sinks deeper and deeper into himself, and the gap between us widens."

"Do you fear he might hurt you?"

"I don't think he would . . . Still, his behavior can be unsettling."

"He was not fond of Sir Randall, that much was obvious," I said. "But what about the others?"

"I honestly don't know what he thought of Claude and Niccolo, if he particularly thought of them at all. He went along with me rather docilely at first, and later with growing resentments that made no sense at all. I suppose he stopped trusting me, not that I ever gave him reason to doubt me."

I made a decision, and said, "I noticed grass on Mr. Wharton's shoes the night Niccolo played for us. He had obviously been outside. Why wouldn't he have changed into house shoes?"

She thought about this. "I couldn't say. I hadn't noticed."

"Were you with your husband when Claude was killed?"

"Yes, Miss Cross, I was. We were all dripping from Josephine's broken pipe and he and I went to our room to change. He helped me with the buttons on my dress." Her brow wrinkled. "Now that I think about it, Teddy finished changing before I did, and when I said I wouldn't need any further assistance he left me. I assumed he went downstairs. But—" Her eyes became circles, but then just as quickly resumed their natural shape. "No, he wouldn't have had time. I'm sure he would not have."

"And today . . ."

"I was with you and Detective Whyte. I don't know where Teddy was in the house." She gave an adamant shake of her head. "He didn't do it. He had no reason to want Niccolo dead. Or Claude for that matter, and in all honesty, though he might have resented Randall, I cannot imagine my husband doing anything so . . . so . . ."

"Dreadful?"

"Cunning or hazardous," she corrected me. "You witnessed Teddy's little tantrum when he interrupted my conversation with Randall. He often behaved so, and then whatever it was would blow over. He is reactive, but never particularly proactive. It isn't in his nature. I'm sorry to say that at heart, my husband is something of a coward. He would not have risked pushing a man off that footbridge, not when there might be any chance he himself could fall."

She sounded so positive, I found myself trusting her judgment. "Then we are back to Vasili and Miss Marcus."

From the Stair Hall came a *thump-thumping* as someone apparently dragged an object down each step. A moment later a voice called out, "I'm leaving now, Edith. You can either come home where it's safe, or you can take your chances here—without me."

Chapter 15

"Edith, I'm really leaving," came another shout from the Stair Hall, followed by the sound of that same heavy object being dragged across the floor. "The footman is bringing a carriage around now. You have ten seconds to make up your mind."

Mrs. Wharton sighed and went to the doorway. "I'm not leaving, Teddy, and rest assured you won't get very far. All you're going to succeed in doing is jeopardizing the welfare of a carriage horse. And shame on you for sending Carl out in this weather. You're endangering his health as well."

Mr. Wharton's disembodied voice, for I could not see him from where I sat, took on a whining note. "What about *my* life, Edith? And yours?"

"I'm not going to argue with you, Teddy. Good-bye for now, and good luck. Try telephoning should you happen to make it home." With that Mrs. Wharton pivoted and returned to me.

We both jumped when Jesse abruptly opened the office door and stepped out. "Eavesdropping, ladies?"

"We, uh . . . No, though not for lack of trying." I smiled apologetically. "We were hoping you'd have new information. Thank goodness the telephone lines have been repaired."

"For the time being. The problem stemmed from a line near town. It's been temporarily patched, but might not hold. I was able to request a telegram be sent overseas to both James Clifford and Sir Randall's solicitor."

"To discover the identity of *AC*?" I asked.

"That's right." Jesse gestured toward the Stair Hall. "What was that shouting I heard?"

Mrs. Wharton sighed. "My husband is leaving, returning to Land's End."

"What? Is he mad?" Jesse hurried into the Stair Hall, but his continuing tread signified that Mr. Wharton had already passed through to the front entry hall. Mrs. Wharton and I traded a glance and followed.

We found a dripping Carl making his way through the front door, while Mr. Wharton squeezed by him, ran hunched through the rain, and took his place in the covered phaeton Uncle Frederick kept in his carriage house. The suitcase was already on the seat beside him. He had obviously had Carl carry it out first. The footman unbuttoned the mackintosh he wore and hung it on the coatrack in the vestibule, where it would drip on the stone tiles.

"Mr. Wharton," Jesse called out into the rain. "This isn't a good idea. I've made other arrangements, if you'll just wait."

Outside, Mr. Wharton huddled into his own mackintosh as the rain pelted him from the carriage's open sides. He flipped the reins. The vehicle lurched into motion and started down the drive.

Jesse laughed softly, without mirth. "I'm sorry I couldn't stop him, Mrs. Wharton. It's doubtful he'll make it down

Ledge Road. I only hope he has the sense to turn back before—" He broke off, reddening.

"It's all right, Detective," she said. "I hope he turns back before it's too late, too."

"What do you mean, you've made other arrangements?" I asked him.

Jesse closed the front door against a gust of wind. "I'm getting everyone out of here. Two police coaches are on their way, along with an ambulance."

"Isn't it too dangerous?"

Even with Mrs. Wharton watching, Jesse framed my face in his hands. "Certainly no more dangerous than remaining here at Rough Point. Signore Lionetti needs to be at the hospital. And Miss Marcus was correct. I have been useless in protecting you."

"Jesse, no . . ."

"We're leaving as soon as possible, assuming the coaches make it here."

In the next couple of hours the storm showed some slight signs of abating, though out beyond the cliffs the ocean continued to thrash. When the coaches finally wound their way up the front drive, they brought with them an unexpected arrival.

Uncle Frederick let himself out of the first vehicle. His head bowed and shoulders hunched to the rain, he picked his way carefully across the puddles to the front door. Once he was inside, I took his hat while Carl helped him off with his overcoat. Two police officers followed him inside. Before I closed the door, the ambulance pulled up.

"Uncle Frederick, I never expected to see you today," I said.

"As soon as I had word from Howard Dunn I started out

from Hyde Park. The weather kept me from being here sooner, though it only turned fierce once I reached North Kingstown. Good heavens, Emmaline, Howard only told me there had been an accidental death—bad enough, happening here on my property. Now I'm told it was murder, and that there's been another. Good grief, what the blazes has been going on among these people, and what the devil are you still doing here?"

"No one has been able to leave because of the storm. How were the roads on the way from town?"

"Treacherous. I suppose you don't dare travel along Ocean Avenue." He glanced over my shoulder. "Arthur! I had no idea you were here. No one told me."

"Our decision to make the crossing was rather last-minute." My father and the others spilled into the entry foyer.

"I'll wager it's a decision you've come to regret, given the circumstances." Uncle Frederick moved past me to greet my parents. I stayed by the door and opened it again to a wind-borne spray on my face, until the doctor and nurse from the ambulance made it safely inside.

Hannah Hanson reached out to give my forearm a reassuring squeeze. Somehow, her arrival renewed a sense of hope in me. We had reunited only that summer after several years of Hannah living in Providence, but ever since we were little girls growing up on the Point together, she had been able to brighten any mood with the simple power of her smile. The rain had darkened tendrils of blond hair that floated free of her nurse's veil, and cornflower blue eyes held me in their steady gaze.

We clasped hands. "Thank goodness you're here," I said.

Dr. Kennison, whom I had also known all my life, wasted no time on pleasantries. "Has the patient awakened at all?"

"No," I said. "He's been unconscious since we found him."

"Where is he?"

"Follow me." I led them upstairs to Niccolo's bedroom. Mrs. Harris slipped out, but Carl had returned with us and Dr. Kennison asked him to remain.

"I'll need help getting him into the ambulance," he said. Then he opened his medical bag and leaned over the patient to check his vital signs. He let out a sigh. "His pulse is weak." He examined the wound along Niccolo's neck, shaking his head all the while. "It's a miracle he survived this. Miss Hanson, will you and the footman please bring up the stretcher?"

I waited with Dr. Kennison until Hannah and Carl returned bearing the wood and canvas litter. They placed it on the bed beside Niccolo's inert form, and together the doctor and Hannah rolled him until he lay on the stretcher on his back. My father came into the room then.

"I'll help you carry him down." Father and Carl each took an end of the stretcher, while Dr. Kennison walked alongside them. Hannah and I lingered in the room.

"Does Brady know your parents are here?" she asked.

"Not yet. The telephone connection has been tenuous, so I've been unable to send a wire. I'll try again this afternoon."

"If you like, I can send it." Color blossomed on her round, pretty cheeks.

"I know the two of you have kept in touch," I said. "I'm glad, Hannah. Very glad."

She shook her head. "We're friends. But . . . I mustn't keep Dr. Kennison waiting."

I walked her downstairs. "We'll all be leaving Rough Point now. I'm not sure where we'll be staying but—"

Jesse stood waiting for us in the Stair Hall. "There is no longer any reason to leave. Come with me."

"I'd better go. I'll see you soon, Emma." Hannah gave me a quick hug, and then, ducking against the rain, made her way out to the ambulance.

Frowning my questions at Jesse, I allowed him to precede

me through the Great Hall into the drawing room. All but my father and Rough Point's four staff members were present. Jesse bade me sit, and I squeezed in between Mrs. Wharton and my mother on the settee. Miss Marcus sat across from us in one of the armchairs. Uncle Frederick sat beside her, and the two police officers who arrived with him stood behind their chairs.

Vasili paced the room with a scowl. "I wish you would cease being mysterious, Detective Whyte."

"Detective Whyte enjoys his sport." Miss Marcus gave a derisive snort. "It makes him feel important."

My ire rose and must have been obvious, for Jesse caught my eye and very calmly shook his head, a slight, humorless smile playing about his lips. From the front hall came the sound of the door closing, and moments later my father entered the room. "You wanted to see everyone again, Jesse?"

"Please, have a seat." Once Father complied, Jesse moved to the center of the room. "I wanted to let you all know that although you may leave Rough Point, there is no longer any urgency to do so. In fact, I advise you to remain here until the roads are drier and safer."

This announcement was met with momentary silence, and then a chorus of voices spoke at once, firing questions. Uncle Frederick's was loudest among them. "You've discovered the identity of the murderer, then. Well, sir, who is it?"

"Does this mean Niccolo woke up and told you who attacked him?" Mrs. Wharton sounded desperately hopeful, but I knew Jesse would disappoint her.

"Let me explain." He held up his hands and waited until the room quieted. "A discovery was made here thanks to a wire from Sir Randall's son. We found his diary, hidden in his room. However, that only led to more questions, prompting me to order another wire sent to England only this morning as soon as I could use the telephone. I needn't have. It seems

Sir Randall's solicitor had already contacted James Clifford with information unknown to his client, concerning a recent change to his father's will."

Vasili dragged a hand through his hair, standing it on end. He looked worse than ever with his sunken, reddened eyes, colorless features, and his clothes a mass of wrinkles. "Is this to lead somewhere?"

"It is." Jesse paced a couple of steps and stopped. "It seems James Clifford's and my wires crossed in transit. For even as I sent mine, his arrived with information regarding his suspicions about his father's death and the identity of a certain individual possessing the initials *AC*."

A gasp interrupted Jesse's narrative, and I glanced over to see Miss Marcus flushing and pressing her hand to her mouth. Before I could make sense of this, Mother asked, "And who is this individual?"

If I didn't know Jesse to be the straightforward, sensible police detective he was, I'd have accused him of drawing out the moment for dramatic effect. At length he said, "Sir Randall Clifford's wife."

"But . . . his wife is deceased." Mrs. Wharton looked mystified, as did the others. "And her name didn't begin with *A*. Randall told us her name was Minerva."

"Yes, you must be speaking of his first wife," Jesse said. "In his wire, James Clifford was referring to his father's second wife."

"What do you mean, second wife?" Father let out a bark of laughter. "Trust me, Jesse, if Randall had remarried, we would all know about it."

"That's true." Mother looked scandalized, close to devastated. "We were his closest friends. If there had been a wedding, Randall would have wanted us all there." She turned an appeal on the others. "Edith, wouldn't we have known?"

Mrs. Wharton gave no answer, but merely returned Mother's

stricken expression with one of her own. Vasili gazed out the French doors into the covered porch and beyond, where the storm continued to dwindle. He shook his head as if Jesse had taken leave of his senses and was wasting everyone's time. I continued to watch Miss Marcus carefully. Her face was splotched and ruddy, and she emitted little coughs that made her nose run and her eyes tear. I went to the brandy cart and poured a glass of water from the pitcher, kept fresh each day.

"You seem upset, Miss Marcus," I said as I handed her the glass.

The others ignored me, all except Jesse, who watched us closely. Father spoke again.

"Well, Jesse, are you going to enlighten us as to the identity of this mystery wife? Surely James Clifford is mistaken."

"James Clifford might have been, but I highly doubt Sir Randall's solicitor could have gotten such a detail wrong. The legal name of the woman in question is Anna Markstrom Clifford."

"I've never heard of such a person." Mrs. Wharton turned to my mother. "Did you ever hear of Randall speaking of an Anna?"

"Let me be more specific." Jesse moved to stand directly in front of Miss Marcus's chair. "Sir Randall's second wife's full maiden name is Anna Josephine Markstrom, more commonly known to the world as Josephine Marcus."

Chapter 16

Jesse's revelation brought the others instantly to their feet, their voices creating an incoherent din. I retained my place on the settee, however. As soon as Jesse first mentioned a second wife, and I observed the effect of those words on Miss Marcus—or Lady Clifford—I guessed the truth.

Events fell into place. The bitterness between Sir Randall and Josephine Marcus and why he took her belittlement so much to heart; the contention between Miss Marcus and Niccolo, who obviously loved her and wished to marry her—it all made sense now. I suspected Claude died, not because he refused to cast Josephine Marcus in his production of *Carmen*, but perhaps because he somehow learned the truth about a marriage she had taken great pains to conceal.

These thoughts passed through my mind in the time it took Jesse to restore order to the room. Slowly, one by one, the others resumed their seats and fell silent, waiting, undoubtedly, for Jesse to make sense of the past few minutes.

He explained, "According to the solicitor, Sir Randall and Miss Marcus eloped recklessly after a drunken interlude.

Ever since, Sir Randall regretted his action and wished to be rid of his new wife." Miss Marcus made a sound of outrage, but Jesse shushed her with a fierce look. "The marriage humiliated Sir Randall. He felt ashamed and didn't wish his son to find out, not to mention the price James Clifford would pay should it become known his father married an American opera singer. It doesn't take a genius to know that James Clifford's prospects, both socially and politically, would have suffered greatly. He is a member of the House of Commons and wishes to rise in his career. That gave Miss Marcus the weapon she needed."

Jesse paused and went to the brandy cart to pour himself a glass of water. He drank deeply, and continued. "Part of Miss Marcus's blackmail was the stipulation that Sir Randall write her into his will—generously. He was also to maintain her in a lavish lifestyle, supplying her money whenever she asked for it. What she did not know was that he attached two conditions to his will: If she were to remarry in the event of his death, or if evidence of infidelity should come to light, all monies reverted to James."

All eyes turned toward Miss Marcus, who openly wept. "I didn't hurt anyone . . . I swear I didn't. . . ."

I looked away. None of this surprised me, nor did I find it particularly difficult to believe given all I had learned about Josephine Marcus. Still, I found it painful to witness the utter fall of someone I had admired only days ago.

"Oh, Josephine, how could you?" A tear trickled down Mother's cheek. "And Niccolo? All he did was love you. He wished to marry you, and you . . ."

"He pushed too hard," I said. When the others gazed expectantly at me, I went on. "He was running out of patience and insisting Miss Marcus reach a decision about their relationship. He must have pushed too hard and she . . . she made her decision to end it with him. To end him."

"That isn't true." She turned a feral expression on me, filled with resentment and fury. Her tears continued to fall, but to me they seemed the tears of someone who had just realized her luck had run dry. "You have no right to say such a thing. I didn't hurt Niccolo. I didn't hurt anyone."

"Perhaps she knew about Randall's stipulations." Vasili's knuckles whitened where he fisted them against his thighs. "She attempted to kill Niccolo because her infidelity would have disinherited her, as would their marriage."

"Or perhaps Niccolo somehow found out about her marriage to Randall, and he threatened to make trouble for her." My father spoke more to himself, as if trying to make sense of the details. "He might have even guessed she killed Randall."

"I didn't!"

Mrs. Wharton was shaking her head. "I'm finding this all too difficult to believe."

"Thank you, Edith," Miss Marcus said vehemently. "Thank goodness someone has faith in me."

"I didn't say that, Josephine. I don't know what I believe right now."

"Miss Marcus." Jesse gestured her to stand. When she didn't budge he nodded to the two policemen standing behind her chair, silent all this while. They stepped closer and from behind each grasped one of her forearms.

She flinched and tried to pull free. "Unhand me!"

"Miss Marcus—or perhaps I should call you Lady Clifford—you are under arrest for the murder of Sir Randall Clifford, and are under suspicion for the murder of Claude Baptiste and the attempted murder of Niccolo Lionetti."

The officers tugged her to her feet, but her knees wobbled and she sagged back into the chair. Her head lolled to the side and her eyes rolled back in her head. I stood and crossed to her.

"Miss Marcus . . . Miss Marcus." I tapped her cheek lightly with my fingertips. "Miss Marcus, wake up."

Her eyelids fluttered a moment and then opened fully. She looked about, blinking at first, and then gave her head a shake. "Oh, I . . . I must have fallen asleep. Forgive me. I was having the most horrid dream. . . ."

I straightened and looked down at her. "It was no dream, Miss Marcus. We know who you are, what you have done, and you are under arrest." With that I stood aside to allow Jesse and his men to once more raise her to her feet. She swayed again but this time the officers maintained a better hold on her.

"This way, love," Officer Eubanks said.

"No . . . please!" The officers were already conveying her—half walking and half dragging her—out of the room and into the Great Hall. "Edith, Beatrice, help me. Surely you cannot believe this." She craned her neck to peer over her shoulder just in time to see my mother and Mrs. Wharton stare down at their hands. Miss Marcus's features twisted. "You cannot do this to me. I am Josephine Marcus. Damn you all, I am Josephine Marcus!"

Her pleas, alternating with oaths, echoed in the Great Hall, only growing fainter as they apparently reached the front hall and vestibule. Mother pressed her hands to her ears to block out the sound and wept. My father, Vasili, and even Uncle Frederick studied their shoes as if ashamed by what had just occurred. Jesse signaled to me, and I followed him into the Great Hall.

"I'll need that cigarette stub you found on the lawn," he said, and kept walking. I trotted to keep up and climbed the stairs beside him.

"So you were right that whoever killed Claude wouldn't have needed a great deal of strength. But such was not the case with Niccolo, was it?"

"That's right. Gloves or no, Miss Marcus obviously doesn't possess enough strength in her hands to complete the job. She rendered Signore Lionetti unconscious and injured his neck, but hadn't tightened the instrument's string enough to prevent air from entering his lungs once she let go."

We paused on the half landing. "What if he never regains consciousness?"

He drew a breath. "I've seen it before, where oxygen deprivation led to permanent coma and eventual death. In which case, there will be a third murder charge against her. But the fact that the attempt failed reassures me that we've caught our culprit. A man would most likely have been successful."

We resumed our climb, and at the top turned and crossed the gallery to the north wing. I trailed Jesse into Miss Marcus's bedroom. He began opening drawers.

"What are you looking for?"

"These." He pulled a stack of gloves from one of the top drawers in the bureau and waved them in the air.

He spread them out on the bed and I moved closer to examine them. I traced my finger over a delicate lace mitt. "None of these would have protected her hands from the friction of that string."

"What about these?" He chose a tan kid glove that buttoned up the side and would have reached mid-forearm.

I studied the smooth leather and shook my head. "Not thick enough. Besides, there's barely a sign of wear, much less evidence of handling a coarse metal wire. She probably dispensed with whatever gloves she used. Perhaps she found a pair of work gloves somewhere in the servants' domains."

Jesse frowned, obviously not convinced. "I'm taking them into evidence anyway. I'll have to question the staff if they ever saw Miss Marcus in that part of the house. With the way the kitchen is positioned, it would have been difficult for anyone to slip by Mrs. Harris unnoticed."

Minutes later I retrieved the cigarette stub Mrs. Wharton and I had discovered beyond the kitchen garden. It had dried to a brittle morsel, the bits of remaining tobacco threatening to scatter on the slightest whiff of air. I returned to Jesse, waiting in the corridor, and handed it to him in the tea leaf tin in which I had stored it. "All this does is suggest whoever killed Sir Randall might have smoked a cigarette along the way."

"Yes, but doesn't Miss Marcus indulge in the nasty habit? I look at this as one more link in the overall chain of evidence." He smiled. "I'm terribly glad you don't smoke, Emma."

I wrinkled my nose. "I find nothing appealing in deliberately drawing smoke into one's lungs." Indeed, I had come very near to suffering the dangerous effects of smoke inhalation during the summer, and I had no desire to ever revisit the sensation.

After Jesse left Rough Point an uneasy sensation settled over me. It's not that I had any reason to doubt Miss Marcus's guilt. Every bit of evidence pointed in her direction, including her own words and actions here at Rough Point, and before. I didn't doubt she took advantage of Sir Randall's affections, not to mention an elderly man's loneliness, to corner him into an ill-advised marriage. I didn't doubt that money constituted her entire motive for doing so.

And yet, doubts, of an inexplicable and ungraspable nature, continued to plague me throughout the rest of the day.

When I returned to the drawing room after seeing Jesse off, the others were discussing their immediate plans. While the storm showed signs of finally moving away, the rain continued. As Jesse had pointed out, there was no longer any reason for a hasty departure from Rough Point.

"We'll decide what we're going to do tomorrow," my father said from his place on the sofa beside my mother. "If that is agreeable to you, Frederick."

My uncle conceded with a nod. "I'm just relieved this matter has been resolved. To think of such an act committed in my own house. I'd like to unload this place as soon as possible." He eyed the group ranged around the room. "I don't suppose there are any takers among you? I'll offer a good price."

It was all I could do to school the disapproval from my expression. How could my uncle worry about the sale of his house in the face of these dreadful events, and hope to sell Rough Point to the very people who would most wish never to see this house again?

My other instinct, however, was to laugh at the irony of his suggestion. My father, as an artist, could barely afford to keep a roof over his and my mother's heads. I was quite certain Vasili, no matter how talented a dancer, had never made anything approaching a fortune even at the height of his career. That left Mrs. Wharton, who certainly could have afforded Rough Point, but who already owned a home in Newport, nearby Land's End.

I might have exercised restraint in reacting to Uncle Frederick's thoughtlessness, but the others didn't. A chorus of groans broke out, and my uncle sighed sheepishly. "I thought not."

"I still can't believe Josephine did all these horrible things." Mother slipped her hand around my father's arm and he patted it absently. "I would never have suspected such a thing."

Mrs. Wharton was nodding her agreement. "I can't believe it either. Josephine is many things, and not all of them pleasant, but a murderess? I feel as though I'll never trust my judgment when it comes to people again."

"There is so much evidence against her, it cannot be otherwise." Vasili eyed the brandy cart. His fingertips shook.

"I wish Randall had confided in us." Mrs. Wharton got to her feet and began pacing, as I had observed her doing previously in times of stress. "Why didn't he? Josephine clearly took advantage of him and made him very unhappy."

"He was ashamed, obviously," my father said. "What man wouldn't be, under the circumstances?"

"Jesse said his son would have been humiliated by the marriage," my mother pointed out. "Randall hid the truth for James's sake."

"Yes, but from us?" Mrs. Wharton looked less than satisfied. "We would have kept his secret, he had to know that."

Vasili's head reared up, and he seethed in Mrs. Wharton's direction. "What difference does it make? He told us, he didn't tell us. Either way he is dead. Claude is dead. And Niccolo—we don't yet know, do we? The past means nothing now. There is only the future, without our friends."

Mrs. Wharton abruptly ceased her pacing, held immobile by Vasili's ire. "I'm sorry," she said miserably. "You are right. It is just that . . . something about this simply doesn't feel resolved. I don't know. . . ."

I felt the same, and like her I could not explain my reservations.

In the middle of the night, I came fully awake and stared into the near blackness of my room. A certainty beat through me with the rhythm of my racing pulse as images tumbled through my mind. The cigarette stub, the damaged cello—circumstantial evidence that, when taken alone, proved nothing, but when placed beside Miss Marcus's words and deeds, became damning. Or were we merely seeing what we wanted to see on the surface, without digging deeper to get at the truth?

Josephine and cigarettes . . . Josephine and Niccolo's cello, created by a master . . . Claude and the rug in his bedroom.

Something about each of the scenarios involving all three deaths struck me as wrong. All, all wrong.

At the foot of my bed, Patch stirred and then crawled up the mattress until his moist nose nudged my chin. A low whimper begged the question: Is something wrong?

"Yes, dear Patch, something is." With one hand settling on his warm neck, I wriggled my legs free of the covers and sat up. "Come on, boy."

I made my way downstairs, using the scant glow from a moon obscured by clouds to guide me. Rain pattered at the windows, no longer relentless but steady nonetheless. The house was silent but for the ticking of numerous clocks, a sound that went unnoticed by day but now seemed deafening to my ears. At the bottom of the stairs I paused to listen for any sound not made by nature or mechanics. A footstep . . . a breath . . . I needn't have worried. Patch waited patiently beside me. Had I not been alone in this part of the house he would have alerted me immediately.

Quickly I traversed the distance through the dining room to my uncle's office, all the while praying the repaired telephone lines had held. My hopes were rewarded, and the night operator put through my call. The ear trumpet reverberated with the ringing on the other end . . . ringing and ringing, until losing hope, I very nearly ended the call. But I heard a click and then a voice, heavy with sleep and edged with no small measure of irritation.

"This had better be important."

"Jesse?"

"Emma?" His tone altered immediately. He sounded fully awake and doubly anxious. "Emma, what is it? Do you need me out there? I never should have left you there—"

"I'm all right, Jesse. Please, just listen. Miss Marcus is innocent."

"What are you talking about? You heard the evidence. She

had motive aplenty and more than enough opportunity. Unless you've discovered evidence pointing at someone else . . ."

"No, it isn't that. I don't know who did it, I only know who didn't. Please, can you come here first thing in the morning?"

"I'm supposed to present our evidence to the prosecutor in the morning."

"But Miss Marcus is innocent. Please, come here first. It doesn't matter how early it is. I'll make sure everyone is up. What I have to say is best said before the others. I believe once they hear, they will agree with me, and so will you."

Jesse's exasperation was palpable across the wires. I could almost see him pressing his thumb and forefinger to the bridge of his nose and shaking his head.

"Can't you just tell me now, as long as you woke me up?"

I wouldn't back down. This was too important. "It would be better to tell you in person, and with the others present."

He made no attempt to stifle a sigh of impatience. "All right, I'll be there at seven thirty sharp. See that everyone is awake and assembled. And this is assuming the rain doesn't worsen in the meantime."

The reminder of the dangers of traveling, of asking him to brave the mud of Bellevue Avenue once again, produced a pang of guilt. If anything happened to him I would never forgive myself, but if a woman went to prison or worse, was hanged for a crime she didn't commit, and I might have prevented it, I would never forgive myself either.

"Thank you, Jesse. I'll see you in the morning."

"Emma," he called out to prevent me from hanging up. "Assuming Miss Marcus *is* innocent, then you're not safe there. Please, go back to your room and lock your door. Is Patch with you?"

I smiled down at the dark and light figure lying comfortably at my feet. "He is, and he's completely relaxed at the moment, meaning there is no immediate threat. But yes, I'll return to my room now and lock my door. Good night, Jesse."

Patch and I hurried back upstairs, but once there I found the prospect of sleep daunting. I dozed, but got very little true sleep in the ensuing hours. In fact, I found myself envying Patch's deep slumber, evidenced by his steady breathing, occasional twitches, and sweet little snorts. I, on the other hand, turned my theory over and over in my mind while wondering if I had taken leave of my senses or allowed my idealistic fancies to color my judgment.

Before dawn I crawled out of bed and dressed. Doubts once more crowded my resolve, but I could not discount even the most outlandish notion if a shred of possibility existed. I knocked on Mrs. Wharton's door. She surprised me by answering almost immediately, as if she had awaited my summons. In a hastily donned robe and a mussed braid falling over one shoulder, she squinted out at me. "Emma?" Her features scrunched in bewilderment, but in the next instant her gaze became alert. "Dear heavens, what has happened?"

"Nothing," I hastened to say. "Except that I don't believe Miss Marcus is guilty, and I can tell you why. Please get dressed. Jesse will be here in a little while."

"But . . ."

I was already on my way back into the servants' wing to my parents' room, where I repeated my message, told them their questions would be answered shortly, and doubled back into the main corridor toward Vasili's room. A faint glow kissed the watery horizon beyond the Great Hall windows, but shadows draped the gallery, so that I felt rather than saw my way across.

At the other end I knocked softly on Vasili's bedroom door, waited, knocked again. Finally, I tried the knob and it turned in my hand. My first thought was that Vasili had neglected to lock his door, but since he and the others believed in Miss Marcus's guilt, he would have seen no reason to continue locking himself in at night. I opened the door and stepped in.

He lay sprawled on his back on top of a tangle of covers. I hesitated, thinking I should have my father wake him. But I needed everyone up and dressed by the time Jesse arrived if we were to have ample time before his meeting with the prosecutor. With that in mind, I crossed the room.

"Mr. Pavlenko."

Nothing. I tried several more times before reverting to his given name, loudly and inches from his ear. That produced a groan. I tried again, this time adding a firm nudge to his shoulder. He rolled to his side facing away from me. "Whoever you are, get out." One of his unintelligible oaths completed the command.

"Vasili, you must get up. Detective Whyte will be here in a little while, and you'll be needed downstairs."

He turned slightly, so I could see his pale cheek and his sunken right eye. "Why needed downstairs? He is accusing me now?"

"No, not at all." I stopped. If indeed Miss Marcus proved innocent, I might very well be coaxing a murderer from his bed. The day Claude Baptiste was killed, Vasili hadn't been with the rest of us in Miss Marcus's bathroom. He had been in his own room after spending time with Monsieur Baptiste in the upper sitting room—or so he had said. "There is new evidence about Miss Marcus."

"She is the killer."

"No, I don't believe so." I tugged his wrist until he rolled onto his back again. He threw an arm across his eyes and groaned louder than before.

"My head . . . it is exploding."

"Yes, well, that's your own fault. Please get changed—" I

broke off as I acknowledged that he was already dressed, albeit in yesterday's clothes. "Or don't, as it pleases you. But be downstairs in half an hour. I'll make sure Mrs. Harris has plenty of strong coffee waiting for you. If you're not down, I'll have to send Detective Whyte up."

His guttural cursing followed me out the door.

Chapter 17

Mrs. Harris provided us with another simple breakfast of toast and eggs, along with that promised coffee. I had left Patch in her charge, since I couldn't always depend on him to behave in any given situation. Little conversation broke the monotony of the repast, while more than a few puzzled and annoyed looks were sent my way. The latter mostly came from Vasili, who sat with his head cradled in one hand while he nibbled on dry toast and gulped hot coffee until I was certain he'd scalded his throat.

Jesse arrived at seven thirty sharp, bringing with him Uncle Frederick who had opted not to stay overnight at Rough Point. Sir Randall had been assigned Uncle Frederick's room, and the latter decided he had no wish to sleep in a bed last inhabited by a dead man. I had tried reasoning with him that Sir Randall hadn't died in the house, much less in the bed, but Uncle Frederick would hear none of it.

"More than ever I wish to take my leave of this place and never return," he told me yesterday before accompanying Jesse back to town. "Louise is quite correct. There is a troubled spirit at work in this corner of the island—a mariner who met with a violent end, perhaps—and I'll never rest easy here again."

Normally I considered superstition nothing more than hokum, but even I couldn't deny a sense that some dark force had descended on the property. And in a matter of moments I would plunge our remaining group back into a state of uncertainty and danger.

"All right, Emma, I'm here, and I've brought Mr. Vanderbilt at his insistence," Jesse said, dispensing with greetings and pleasantries. He removed his bowler and shrugged out of his overcoat, both misted to a light sheen from what had tapered to a drizzle outside. Uncle Frederick passed by him and without a word took a seat near the head of the table. "Now will you tell me what this is all about?"

"Would you like any breakfast?" I asked first.

My uncle shook his head and Jesse sent me a stare that held impatience and incredulity in equal measure. I pushed away from the table and stood. "Shall we adjourn to the drawing room?"

"No." Vasili lifted his head from his hand. "I am not moving again, unless it is to crawl back to my bed. You will speak here and make it quick."

My indignant retort was forestalled when the door to the servants' wing opened and Carl and Irene came in to clear away the breakfast dishes. I waited, my heart thumping in anticipation, until they left the room.

"Now then," I began once the door closed securely behind them. "About the matter of Miss Marcus's guilt. I have given this serious thought, and once you've heard what I have to say I believe you'll agree that she is innocent."

Uncle Fredrick neither made a comment nor looked surprised. Obviously Jesse had filled him in on the situation on their way over.

Mrs. Wharton didn't look surprised either, but decidedly skeptical. "You said that upstairs. I can't begin to imagine how you can refute so much evidence. Or why. It's not as if there is any love lost between you and Josephine, is there?"

"No, indeed there is not. In fact I rather abhor her. She ill-used a kindly gentleman, has no sense of common decency, and possesses not a shred of empathy for God's four-legged creatures. But whether or not she committed murder is an entirely different matter. I won't see an innocent person hang if I can do anything about it."

Clapping ensued—slow, loud, and mocking. Vasili's hands came together several times as his lips curled around derisive laughter. "Very noble, Miss Cross. We are all very impressed by your selflessness. But I think perhaps you have been sipping from my vodka."

"Shut up, Vasili." Father stood up for good measure and aimed a threatening glower at the man across the table. My mother reached up to grasp his forearm.

"Arthur, sit. Let's hear what Emma has to say." She offered me a smile of encouragement, as if I were a schoolgirl about to recite lines of poetry. "Go ahead, darling."

I shook away my frustrations and cleared my throat. "I'll begin with that fragment of cigarette Mrs. Wharton and I found out beyond the kitchen garden. It is next to impossible that my uncle's gardeners would have been so careless on the very grounds they keep in near perfect condition. Isn't that so, Uncle?"

"No gardener who values his position on my estate would do such a thing," he confirmed.

I nodded my thanks to him and continued. "Then my theory is that whoever pushed Sir Randall from the footbridge disposed of the end of the cigarette before reaching him."

"Yes, and that would be Josephine." Vasili leaned back and

crossed his arms over his chest. "She smoked like the rest of us. And Randall would not have suspected anything if he saw her approaching the bridge. He simply would have waited for her to join him. That gave her the advantage."

"Did it?" I admit to studying Vasili down the length of my nose with no shortage of disdain. "Do you have your cigarettes with you?"

He shrugged and reached into the pocket of his velvet morning coat, extracting a thin gold case studded with pearls. With a snap he opened the lid.

"Would you please light one?"

He regarded my request with a look of bafflement, but took one of the slender cigarettes and struck a match. A moment later a thin trail of smoke streamed from both his nose and mouth.

"Do you see how you did that?" I pointed at the smoke drifting in the air. "You inhaled deeply into your lungs, and let out a semitransparent, grayish vapor. I have observed that with each of you who smokes." I leaned with my palms on the tabletop. "Except with Josephine. When she smokes, she puffs out fluffy white clouds. It took me a good while to understand the significance of that, but it finally occurred to me that she doesn't inhale—not at all. Which suggests that cigarettes are nothing more than an affectation for her. Something she does for show because she believes, one would deduce, that it makes her look modern and independent."

"Even if that is so, what of it?" Vasili drew on his cigarette and forcefully blew a haze in my direction. "This is ridiculous."

I blinked and coughed and fanned at the air.

"No, Emma's right." Mother tilted her head as she considered. "I've noticed, too, that Josephine never pulls the smoke into her lungs. In fact I questioned her about it once and she joked that smoking gave her something to do with her hands, and she enjoyed how it often shocked the more staid members of society."

"My guess is she didn't bother to smoke unless she had an audience." I directed my next statement to Jesse. "It's very doubtful Miss Marcus would have bothered to light a cigarette if she had been on her way to murder Sir Randall."

Jesse, who had been standing all this time, dragged out a chair at the head of the table and sat. His eyes narrowed on me. "All right, so the cigarette didn't come from Miss Marcus. That still doesn't rule out the possibility that she killed Sir Randall. She had motive."

Unwilling to be daunted, I said, "Let's move on to Claude Baptiste. If you'll remember, when I removed my shoes and tested the rug in his bedroom, I detected more moisture than logically would have been tracked in by your men. Don't forget, they entered through the front door—where they left their overcoats—walked to the Stair Hall and up the steps. Their feet would have been mostly dry by the time they reached the bedroom."

"That points even more directly at Miss Marcus," he countered. "After the mishap with the broken water pipe, she must have gone directly to Monsieur Baptiste's room."

"We know she didn't." I addressed my next comment to my mother and Mrs. Wharton. "You both helped Miss Marcus change after that fiasco. You escorted her from the spraying water in her bathroom to her bedroom, where you helped her into dry clothing. Isn't that right?"

Mother and Mrs. Wharton traded nods, and Mrs. Wharton said, "Yes, that's exactly what happened. Josephine was completely dry when we left her."

"She could have wet her feet forcing Claude under the water," Vasili doggedly pointed out.

"But there were no wet footprints on the bathroom floor," I replied without hesitation.

I turned back to Jesse. He spoke before I could. "I suppose you have a theory about Niccolo Lionetti's attack as well."

"I do. First, we found no gloves in her possession that would have protected her hands from the friction of the cello string."

"She might have disposed of them directly after the crime," Jesse said.

"But why would she have brought such gloves to Newport in the first place? It's early autumn, not cold enough for thicker gloves, and judging simply by Miss Marcus's temperament and physical bearing, I am going to venture a guess that she did not ride horses. Mother, is that correct?"

"It is," Mother said, and then compressed her lips as she took a moment to consider. "I cannot remember Josephine ever speaking of horses. I certainly never saw her on horseback."

"No, nor I," Mrs. Wharton confirmed. "Not even the times we spent at Randall's estate. He kept horses, you know, and some of us did ride. But not Josephine."

"Secondly," I continued briskly, "Josephine Marcus would never, and I do mean *never*, have damaged Niccolo's instrument—no matter who she wished dead or otherwise."

"Emma, how can you possibly know that?" An edge of anger sharpened Jesse's question. "You of all people have learned we can never fully know what is in another person's heart and mind."

"That is most often true, but in this case I believe I can know of a certainty what is in Josephine Marcus's heart." Remaining calm, I walked the length of the table and stood in front of Jesse. "Her life is about music. About the making of beautiful, glorious, harmonious sound. The night Niccolo played for us, she spoke to me about how fortunate I was to hear him play. She explained to me that an instrument made by Domenico Montagnana was not merely an instrument, it was a work of art with a soul, one that mingles with the soul of the musician. A fire burned in her eyes, Jesse, a passion—not for the man, but for the music, for the heaven he created with his cello. And while he played, it was the only time I had ever seen Miss Marcus appear truly tranquil, as if the demons inside her—of which I believe there are plenty—were awed into silence."

I glanced along the table for approbation, and found it in the expressions of the others. Tears glittered in Mother's eyes, and a pained look gripped my father's face. Vasili had crushed the head of his cigarette against his plate, leaving a mess of ash and yolk, but even he compressed his lips and stared back at me with something approaching respect. And Mrs. Wharton . . .

Mrs. Wharton rose and came to me. She embraced me and kissed my cheek. "You are completely right. Josephine could no more have damaged that cello than she could have tossed one of Bizet's or Mozart's or Verdi's original scores into an open fire. Some things are sacred, and say what you will about Josephine, there is no doubt about the things she held sacred."

Jesse let out a deep sigh. "So that leaves us where we began, with three victims and a house full of suspects."

"Whom do you suspect? Me?" Vasili lit another cigarette. "Did I kill Claude, my dearest friend? Or perhaps Arthur did it?" He jerked his chin at my father. "Did you kill them for fear they'd expose your painting forgery? Perhaps it was no joke after all, but an attempt to make your fortune."

"Vasili, you can't mean that," Mother exclaimed, but Father reached for her hand and gave it a squeeze.

"Don't encourage him. The more you protest, the more he'll insist I'm guilty."

"But you *are* perhaps connected to these crimes, Father," I said. He and my mother turned to view me with horrified expressions that hastened my explanation. "Of course I don't mean you're guilty. But we never ruled out the possibility that your painting was the catalyst that set events in motion."

"I thought we *had* ruled it out," Mother said in a plaintive voice. "Why murder Claude? Why Niccolo? And why *not* your father?"

Father's shoulders slumped. "Because it's possible whoever bought the forgery is making us all pay for Randall's and my mistake—no, it was *my* mistake alone."

"Randall played a part in it too, darling," Mother said, but Father shook his head miserably.

"Only because I talked him into it. The idea was mine."

"You finally admit it," Vasili mumbled.

Mother spoke at the same time. "Yes, because that beastly art critic, Henri Leclair, said unfair and untrue things about Randall's work."

"And now Randall is gone." Father collapsed forward, elbows on the table and his head in his hands. His color suddenly mimicked the drab clouds reflected through the windows and the colorless ocean in the distance. If I didn't know better I'd believe he had been drinking with Vasili all night. But no, my father's malaise resulted from guilt and regret and an inability to change the past.

"Then whoever purchased the forgery on the black market traced us all the way to Newport and hired someone to come after us." Vasili drew heavily on his cigarette, which crackled as the end lit up in a burst of orange. He smiled—almost. "It could still be one of us, couldn't it? It could be you, Miss Cross."

"Don't be an idiot," my father snapped.

Vasili seemed to enjoy his game. "It could be me. It could even be our illustrious Mrs. Wharton, daughter of one of America's first families."

If Vasili expected shock or wounded denial from the lady, she disappointed him by remaining calm. "How could I possibly benefit from murdering my friends?"

"Your husband, then. He is half mad, isn't he?"

Her composure unwavering, Mrs. Wharton returned to her place at the table, lifted her water glass, and splashed the contents into the young man's face. He drew back with a yelp, then fell to spluttering and wiping at his face with his coat sleeve. "Perhaps that will help sober you."

"You are as mad as he is."

Mrs. Wharton stood over him like an avenging angel. "Say what you wish about me, but do not talk about my husband, nor any other person not present to defend himself, in such vile terms again. You make me ill, Vasili. Look at you. Drunk all day and night, turning your anger toward the very people who have supported you all these years—" She broke off at his first word of protest, threw her hands in the air, and shook her head vehemently. "Oh, save your self-pity, please. Your friends wished you to join them in Versailles. And yes, they wanted an introduction to a patroness of the arts. What of it? Whatever favor they asked of you, they had returned several times over in countless ways. That is what we do for one another. Furthermore, they didn't force you onto that train. They didn't cause the train to derail. You shame yourself with your behavior, and you shame Claude."

Vasili sprang to his feet and I tensed, ready to hurry around the table and intervene. But he hesitated, and if he'd had any intention of retaliating physically, that intention became lost in the moment. Instead he sank back into his chair, let his chin sink to his chest, and began to sob quietly. Mrs.

Wharton silently leaned over him and circled her arms around his shoulders. He tilted his head, crying against her sleeve.

"I, uh . . . if you'll excuse me." Uncle Frederick pushed stiffly to his feet and strode from the room into the Stair Hall. A moment later Father helped Mother to her feet and they trailed after him.

Jesse caught my eye. "What now?"

It was a rhetorical question, I knew, for what answer could there be? I fully believed Miss Marcus to be innocent, and that led us back where we had started, with victims and no suspect in sight. "Will you release Miss Marcus?"

I knew the answer before the question had fully left my lips, so I was not surprised when Jesse shook his head. "You know I can't do that. Not without solid proof of her innocence."

"But you do believe me, don't you?"

"I do, Emma. Now I have to find a way to convince my chief and the prosecutor. If we could only find something concrete, like those gloves, and link them to an individual."

Mrs. Wharton, still leaning over Vasili, raised her head to regard us. "You have the stub of a cigarette, a wet rug, and a broken cello string that must have been torn loose by someone wearing gloves. There must be a pattern there that we aren't seeing."

"Yes, Mrs. Wharton, that is the point. We are failing to see the pattern." Jesse pinched the bridge of his nose.

"It could still be someone from outside the house," she said. "Perhaps whoever entered Claude's bedroom hadn't come from Josephine's bathroom, but from outside in the rain. Likewise, whoever dropped that cigarette might have simply walked onto the estate from any direction, most likely the Cliff Walk."

"And Niccolo? Are you suggesting whoever killed Claude

took yet another risk of discovery by entering the house again?" Even with a black market art dealer wishing to take his revenge on my father, Mrs. Wharton's theory didn't ring true to me.

She straightened, but kept her hands on Vasili's shoulders. He seemed lost in his own world, no longer paying us any heed. "Miss Cross, Emma if I may, we are left with Vasili, me, you, and your parents."

"And the servants," Jesse murmured.

I shook my head. "What motive could any of Uncle Frederick's servants have to murder people they have never met before? And they have all been in my uncle's service for years."

Mrs. Wharton raised a speculative eyebrow. "Perhaps one of them didn't wish your uncle to sell the house."

"A rather drastic solution, don't you think? Besides, if the new owners wish to replace them, my uncle will find positions for them at one of his other estates. As estate manager Mr. Dunn is already involved in the administration of the Long Island and Hyde Park properties in addition to this one, and I believe Mrs. Harris has also worked at the Hyde Park house. At any rate, that might be a motive to dispatch Sir Randall, who planned to purchase Rough Point, but certainly not Monsieur Baptiste or Niccolo. Neither of them showed any interest in buying the property, did they?"

"No," Mrs. Wharton conceded. "In fact Claude commented that he almost hoped the production at the Metropolitan fell through so he could return to France sooner rather than later. And neither he nor Niccolo possessed that kind of money."

A memory worked its way through my speculations. "At one point, I did come upon Carl testing the locks on the bedroom doors. He said Mr. Dunn had sent him. Do you think he might have been lying?"

"Carl is a local boy," Jesse said, "and might have feared being dismissed. But I can't imagine him committing murder over a footman's position. With his height and looks and a good recommendation, he would secure new employment immediately."

Mrs. Wharton stepped slightly away from Vasili. "What if he knew Mr. Vanderbilt wouldn't write him a good recommendation?"

"Then he wouldn't be here now," I said. "Uncle Frederick, like all my Vanderbilt relatives, would not retain an employee whose work they did not deem acceptable. But if there is any question, we can simply ask him."

"Then there is still Teddy." Mrs. Wharton said this in a murmur as she stared down at the table. She traced the damask design in the tablecloth. "Teddy is not himself these days. And he was in a terrible hurry to leave here after Niccolo's attack."

Although I didn't span the distance between us, I nonetheless stretched out my hand to her. "I understand what it cost you to say that."

Jesse said nothing at first, but seemed to be gathering his thoughts. Then he regarded me. "You said there was grass on Mr. Wharton's shoes the night Sir Randall was pushed from the bridge."

I nodded.

"Mrs. Wharton, when Monsieur Baptiste was drowned, you remained with Miss Marcus to help her change into dry clothes, yes?"

She nodded with a resigned air. "That is correct."

"So your husband was presumably alone for some time following the water pipe incident."

She nodded again.

"And during Signore Lionetti's attack he was where—do you know?"

She paused, a frown etching lines between her eyebrows. "As a matter of fact, I don't know where Teddy was at the time." She turned to me. "Emma, if you'll remember, we came upon Miss Marcus on her way into the billiard room, and then found my husband sitting alone in the drawing room. He and I had that row, and he left us. . . ."

"And not long afterward," I continued for her when she trailed off, "we returned upstairs to discover Niccolo had been attacked."

Jesse raised an eyebrow. "Could they both have been in the billiard room?"

I thought back, remembering the waft of cigarette smoke and the clicking of the balls after Miss Marcus entered the billiard room. When Mrs. Wharton and I returned upstairs . . . "It had been quiet in the room when we passed by that second time. I didn't think to peek inside—why would I?"

"Then it sounds to me," Jesse said, "as if you cannot account for the whereabouts of either Mr. Wharton or Miss Marcus at the time of the attack. And we discovered Miss Marcus in her bedroom, only a room away from Signore Lionetti's. That's awfully convenient."

Jesse was right. No matter how one viewed the evidence, Miss Marcus still appeared guilty. I had only gut instinct to rely upon, and that would not be enough for the prosecutor.

"Emma, given the alternatives, have you considered that you might be mistaken when it comes to Miss Marcus?" Before I could object Jesse went on, "She might well have smoked that cigarette on her way out to the Cliff Walk. Inhaling or no, the act might still have brought her a measure of courage. Perhaps the wet rug in Monsieur Baptiste's room was merely the result of me and my men tracking in rain from outside. And the cello string . . ." He trailed off, obviously grasping for an explanation.

"We all saw her hands," I reminded him. "Even if she would stoop to damaging a priceless instrument—which I am certain she would not—she could not have pried the string loose without the aid of some kind of pliers or other tool, nor wrapped it around Niccolo's neck without thick gloves. You remember how your own hands bled after working the string free."

Jesse swore softly. "We're back to those gloves again. So much seems to hinge on those blasted things. If they even exist."

Chapter 18

Mother's suitcase sat gaping on the bed, silks and laces spilling out in bursts of color. The rain had ceased almost entirely but the clouds proved more stubborn, as if unwilling to relinquish their claim over the island. Still, present conditions promised that travel would soon be safe, and the remaining group had decided to vacate Rough Point as soon as possible.

I looked forward to returning to the orderly routines of Gull Manor. Although phone service between Rough Point and town had been restored, I still couldn't reach Nanny at home and I wondered what havoc the wind and ocean had wreaked on my kitchen garden, or whether shingles would need replacing on the house or barn, or if a small lake had replaced my cellar floor. But I took comfort in knowing such damage would prove trivial enough, for my solid old house had withstood nearly a hundred years of angry ocean waves and punishing winds, and provided stalwart shelter for Nanny and Katie.

My parents would accompany me, while Mrs. Wharton and Vasili planned to make their way to Land's End. But we still needed confirmation that the roads were drivable.

"Are you all packed?" my mother asked as she emptied a drawer in her dressing table.

I smiled. "I didn't bring much with me, so yes, I'm ready."

She paused a moment in her packing, standing with a silk scarf half unfurled from her hands. "I never thought I'd be so eager to leave a place."

"You must have been relieved to leave Paris when you did. Everything considered, I mean."

She laid the scarf on the bed amid a small pile of lace collars, hair combs, and embroidered handkerchiefs. "You're still angry with your father and me, aren't you, darling?"

"No, Mother, I'm not angry."

She lowered her chin and gazed at me from beneath her lashes.

"I'm disappointed," I clarified. I fingered the latch on her open suitcase. "I'm sorry, I can't help it. But it isn't so much Father's prank that disturbs me, it was your lack of candor after so much time away. It felt as though you'd returned in body only, but left the people I call my parents back in France."

She came around the bed and sat beside me. "Oh, Emma, if you don't wish us to leave again we won't. Your father and I can resettle in Newport—"

"No, I won't hold you here if you wish to be elsewhere. And Father needs to be part of the art world, not buried in this tiny New England town."

"Newport is hardly tiny and neither is it obscure. He made a living here before and he could do it again." She placed her open palm on my cheek and held it there, allowing its warmth to sink into me.

I enjoyed the familiar sensation, so long denied me, before lifting my face away. Firmly I said, "You and Father belong in Paris."

"Then come back with us." She beamed at me. "Darling, it would be wonderful. You'd adore Paris."

For an instant my heart leapt. From Paris, it was only a short trip to Italy . . . and Derrick. The idea barely formed completion before I rejected it. Vital family matters had sent Derrick to Italy—heartbreaking matters. I had no business intruding on his life and distracting him from his purpose there. I had to believe that when he deemed the time right, he would return to America . . . and perhaps to me.

To my mother I said, "I belong here. I would have no function in Paris."

"You could write."

"I am writing here, and someday I'll be recognized as a valid journalist—an American journalist who is unafraid to write the truth." For a moment a sense of hypocrisy dealt me a staggering blow. More than once over the past year I had taken license with the truth when reporting on hard news.

But I had done so to protect the private lives of cherished family members. I was no gossip columnist. In all other matters, when finally given the chance I would report the facts with neither omissions nor embellishments, and proudly sign my full name to every article.

"I cannot write news stories about America for Americans if I'm living in Paris," I summed up in simple terms.

Mother's lips flattened, and she shook her head. "As stubborn as your father."

"Yes, it's a Vanderbilt trait."

She touched my cheek again, then turned my chin toward her with her fingertips. She showed me a shrewd smile. "Is there another reason you won't leave Newport?"

"Well, yes. Besides my job there is Gull Manor, and Nanny, and the women we take in—"

"Yes, yes, besides all that."

Mystified, I frowned. "Such as what?"

That cunning smile reappeared. "Tell me about you and Jesse."

"Wh-what do you mean?"

"Come now, darling. I see the two of you together. The looks between you, the way you seem so attuned to each other." She pulled back to regard me. "Don't look so surprised. Even your father has noticed. We'd be delighted with Jesse as a son-in-law."

It occurred to me that my parents had no inkling about Derrick Andrews. "Mother, you're letting your imagination get away with you."

"Nonsense. Jesse's a wonderful catch. Why, I have no doubt he'll be chief of police someday, and after that, who knows? He could enter politics and become a representative, even a state senator. Just think of the future you could have with him, Emma."

No one needed to point out to me how right Jesse and I could be together. Socially, we were a perfect match. And yes, our future held a world of potential. When I thought about it in those terms, of Jesse becoming a man of influence, and me, as a journalist, having firsthand access to the machinations of change and progress, my heart raced and my stomach flipped with eagerness.

But marrying a man for his opportunities was as wrong as marrying a man for his money. I could bring myself to do neither. If something lasting, something beyond friendship were to develop between Jesse and me, my heart must race and my stomach flip for purer reasons.

Downstairs, I searched for my uncle Frederick to let him know we would all be leaving soon, if he hadn't already been told, and to invite him to Gull Manor for the remainder of his time in Newport. He would probably choose to remain at his hotel in town, but I wished to extend the courtesy nonetheless.

After checking the other rooms to no avail, I thought perhaps he might be in his office. Instead I discovered Jesse there, speaking on the telephone. As I peered in the open door he caught my eye and gestured for me to enter. I stood waiting while he finished his call.

"I spoke to Dr. Kennison," he said as he replaced the receiver on its hook. "Signore Lionetti had regained consciousness."

"Oh, Jesse, that's wonderful!" Without thinking I threw my arms around his neck. His own went around me, and I felt myself pressed to his coat front. He smelled of rain and his morning shave, and he rested his chin on my head in such a way as to tuck my face against his collar. Through it I felt the curve of his neck, and I couldn't help but notice how easy and smooth a fit we made.

Though neither of us seemed to instigate the act, we drew apart simultaneously but in no rush, putting space between us even as our arms were slower to let go. I glanced up to find him staring down at me, and for the first time I felt no burden in the sentiments he communicated silently to me, nor an urge to slide my gaze away or conceal my own emotions. For in that unguarded moment, something inside me changed . . . or *eased* is perhaps the better word. Did it have to do with my conversation with Mother? Perhaps, and if so I owed her a great debt. For I saw, finally, that I had choices, and for once I perceived those choices as a blessing rather than a curse. Two men, two very different sets of circumstances, both worthy of heartfelt consideration.

But I realized something else as well. For the past year I had felt put upon, pressured to make a choice, torn in opposite directions whether I willed or no. Now I saw, quite clearly, that the decision was mine to make—or not to make. Admitting I might have feelings for Jesse, as well as Derrick, somehow brought me a measure of control over my life most women never enjoyed, because most women had their lives handed to them by their parents and were told to make do.

Somehow, in Jesse's sincere yet undemanding embrace, I had found my equilibrium.

His breath tickled my cheek and made me smile. We released each other fully but our smiles persisted, mutually, and without the unspoken questions that might have produced an intolerable awkwardness. I gestured at the telephone.

"Was Niccolo able to say what happened to him?"

"He doesn't remember anything, not yet."

"Oh." That came as a letdown. "What did Dr. Kennison say? Will he remember, in time?"

"We can't be sure, Emma. If brain damage occurred, then perhaps not."

I clutched my hands together. "At least he's alive. We have that to be grateful for." Jesse nodded, and I asked, "When must you leave? Don't you have to be at your meeting?"

"I telephoned in and arranged to meet with the prosecutor later this afternoon. He didn't like it—neither did Chief Rogers—but I explained there were recent developments, along with the hope that Signore Lionetti might be able to identify his attacker."

"You just said he can't."

"Yes, but the prosecutor doesn't know that. At least not yet," he added with a rueful look.

"The others are preparing to leave."

"Let them. I'll know where to find them. I especially have questions for Mr. Wharton. And once everyone is gone I plan to go over the bedrooms again with white gloves and a microscope."

I laughed. "That might not be a bad idea. My parents are

moving over to Gull Manor, but I'll stay to help you, if you like."

"I'd like that very much." He hesitated, seeming to weigh his words, before adding, "I could use another pair of eyes."

"I should let my uncle know what everyone's plans are. Have you seen him?"

"With his estate manager, I would think. I saw them pass by a little while ago."

"Perhaps I shouldn't interrupt them, then. They're probably discussing how to proceed with Uncle Frederick's plans to sell the estate." The sound of distant barking sent me across the threshold into the dining room. I listened for a moment to orient myself to the direction of the noise, and said to Jesse, "I fear they're already being interrupted. I'd better go and get Patch under control. I wonder what has gotten into him now. . . ."

With a shove at the heavy door separating the servants' wing from the rest of the house, I stepped into the serving pantry. Patch's barking immediately grew louder. From here I entered the narrow corridor that flanked the kitchen, storage pantries, and the servants' hall. The butler's office sat off to my right, but upon peeking in I discovered the room to be empty. This puzzled me, for if Mr. Dunn and Uncle Frederick had business to conduct, it would most likely be in that room. I started down the corridor, following the echoes of my dog's misbehavior. The kitchen proved empty as well, but I could hear Mrs. Harris humming a tune and puttering away in the cook's pantry. I passed the servants' hall, the large room deserted and lonely. Patch stopped barking, but his low growl drew me on until I reached the dry goods pantry.

"Patch, what on earth are you—" I broke off. Patch stood several feet inside the door with his back to me, his tail pressed between his legs and his hackles spiking. Beyond him, Mr. Dunn cowered against a bank of cupboards, his fearful gaze fixed on my dog. I hurried in. "Mr. Dunn, I'm so sorry. Patch, you naughty boy. What have you got there?"

Something brown stuck out from either side of Patch's spotted muzzle. Obviously he had gotten hold of something he shouldn't have and when Mr. Dunn attempted to retrieve it, the wayward pup decided to play the bully.

"Give that to me this instant," I commanded, but Patch swiveled his head away from me and growled between his clenched teeth. "You will *not* talk to me that way, sir." I grabbed his collar in one hand and with the other hand tugged the item from his mouth. This time he relinquished his hold, and I found myself staring down at a glove.

A brown leather work glove, caked with dirt, with deep score marks across the palm.

I frowned. "Where did he get this . . . ?" I studied the dirt—mud, really—clinging to the seams and folds. "He must have dug it up from outside. Someone must have buried it—my goodness—Mr. Dunn, do you realize this must be one of the gloves—" I broke off, for as I glanced up I saw that the estate manager, too, held a glove, the mate to the one I gripped. He held it in his left hand, while with his right he opened a drawer beside him and thrust a hand inside. "Mr. Dunn?"

He lurched away from the cupboards. Before I could understand or react, he grabbed me, spun me around, and yanked me up against him. An arm clamped across the front of my shoulders, rendering me immobile. Patch barked, and something cold and sharp pressed against my throat.

"Tell him to stop or so help me, I'll prevent him from ever yapping again." When all I could do was gasp, that pointy instrument poked painfully. "Tell him."

"Patch, quiet, boy. Be quiet." He quieted to a low, grinding growl. A desperate urge to shout for help came over me, but the pricking at my throat and the thought of endangering Mrs. Harris kept me silent. "Don't hurt my dog. Please. He's just a pup, and he hasn't done anything to you."

"That's entirely up to you, Miss Cross." Mr. Dunn prodded my legs with his knee. "Let's go."

"Wh-where are you taking me?"

He said nothing but I didn't have long to wonder. He forced me back along the corridor until we came to a door. Mr. Dunn ordered me to open it. A flight of cement steps plunged into darkness. "Start down."

He released his hold on my shoulders and seized my upper arm instead, squeezing so tight the muscle throbbed from the pressure. All the while, he kept that sharp instrument poised at my throat, where a quick slash would drain my life away in moments. He shut the door behind us, encasing me in a terrifying blackness. Still, for a moment I rejoiced that Patch was safe. But no, to my dismay I felt him brush the side of my skirts and heard his toenails clicking on the step beside me.

"It's too dark," I protested. "We'll fall."

"I know the way." Mr. Dunn's breath puffed hot against my ear, and I shuddered with revulsion. "I know this damnable house better than I know the back of my hand. Now move, Miss Cross, or a good shove will send you tumbling head over heels to the bottom. But that would be messy, something I hope to avoid."

As my eyes adjusted to the darkness, I realized the cellar was not as black as I'd first thought. There must be windows at ground level. The notion that I would not be helplessly blind brought me a glimmer of hope.

We reached the bottom landing and I found myself in a small square cellar, tiled in white and paneled in wood, and meticulously clean, from what I could make out. As I had guessed, high windows, caked with mud and half obscured by damp foliage, admitted a modicum of daylight. To my left another hallway stretched and then turned out of sight, with several doors along the way. Another door stood directly opposite the stairs, and a key hung from the lock. Judging by the scoured appearance of the white floor tiles that stretched beneath that door, I guessed the room inside to be a cold larder, perhaps used to store vegetables or other perishables.

Patch came to my side and growled up at Mr. Dunn. The man released me, and I glimpsed the weapon he had held beneath my chin: an ice hook, cruelly curved and as sharp as a hawk's talon. Patch saw it, too, for he suddenly leapt onto his hind legs and snapped at Mr. Dunn's arm. He caught only his coat sleeve, but Howard Dunn recoiled as if bitten. His face turned bloody red and he swore vehemently.

What I did next came entirely from instinct. Before Mr. Dunn could use that hook on my dear little friend, I grabbed Patch's collar in one hand and with the other reached to unlock the nearby door. Inky darkness pervaded the space, but I forced Patch inside and shut him in, turned the key, then whipped around and threw my back against the door.

Mr. Dunn glared at me, but with a hovering ghost of a smile that sent chills racing along my spine. With no other alternative, I dropped the key into my bodice, knowing full well the horrid man could at any time force his way upon me to retrieve it. I only hoped to borrow time, a few minutes or however many fate would grant me, so that I might find some way to save my dog and myself. I had faced dire circumstances before, and I could at least give thanks that he carried no gun—that I could see. I also possessed a knowledge of self-defense I had used in the past to my advantage, but if I couldn't manage to overpower the man and gain the advantage . . . well, I had Patch to think about, and I mustn't act rashly.

"Clever of you." He raised his arm again, mocking me by making slow circles in the air with the ice hook. A sinister giggle bubbled in his throat while his gaze raked me with an all-too-naked intent. The door behind me rattled, and I realized it was not Patch attempting to dig his way out, but my own shaking body causing the vibrations. "Someone will find us," I said defiantly.

Another scarlet wave encompassed his face. "If you had minded your own business, Miss Cross, we would not now be in this predicament. You leave me with very little choice."

"But why? I don't understand. I defended you and the other servants when even the slightest suspicion fell on you. I could see no reason why any of you would wish to hurt people you didn't know—"

"You just summed it up," he blurted before I could finish. "*Servant.*" A burst of spittle accompanied the word. "I am no better than a servant to him, the high and mighty Frederick Vanderbilt. I am nothing more than someone to be at the beck and call of his *superiors.*"

"You are Uncle Frederick's estate agent. Surely he doesn't think of you as a servant, much less treat you like one."

"You don't think so, eh? Ah, but you didn't hear him issuing orders before this troop of miscreants arrived. 'See to their comforts, Dunn, make sure they have everything they need but watch them closely. And whatever Sir Randall wants, Sir Randall may have. We want Rough Point to make a favorable impression on the man.' As if I were some sort of butler."

I shook my head, more baffled than ever. "They didn't require a butler. Mostly they wished to be left alone. You were only here to organize things, and as for Sir Randall—"

"Sir Randall had no right to this place," he shouted, leaning so close to my face his hot breath once more assaulted my skin. I turned away, but he caught my chin in a painful grip and slid the hook beneath my jaw. "He had no right, Miss Cross. None. Rough Point is *mine* by rights."

His outburst started Patch barking, and Dunn flinched and blinked like a traumatized soldier who, hearing thunder, imagines it to be enemy fire. Throbbing purple veins scored his temples. I shut my eyes and braced for a swipe of the hook, but when nothing happened within a second or two I reopened them to find Mr. Dunn clenching his teeth.

"Shut him up," he commanded.

With my back still plastered to the door, I turned my head as far as I could to be heard from inside. "Patch, quiet, boy. Stop that barking this instant." I loathed myself for speaking harshly, for using my stern voice and making my loyal boy feel as if he had done something wrong. *For your own good*, I wished I could tell him—and vowed to tell him just as soon as we were reunited.

The barking quieted and Dunn backed slightly away, giving me the courage to not only keep him talking until some opportunity presented itself, but to satisfy my now-burning curiosity.

I spoke softly, with none of the rancor coursing like sparks through me. "How could Rough Point be yours? I don't understand."

He slowly shook his head. "No, you wouldn't, would you? Because you don't believe you have a right to The Breakers or Marble House, do you?"

"Of course I don't. Those houses belong to my relatives. Their wealth has nothing to do with me. My father hails from a different branch of the family. . . ."

"Yes, I know. You're the great-granddaughter of Phoebe Vanderbilt, daughter of the first Cornelius. She married James Cross, and brought relatively little to the marriage because the Commodore didn't believe in leaving more than a few token scraps to his daughters."

His knowledge of my background shocked me. "How do you know all that?"

"I've made it my business to learn such things, Miss Cross. And tell me, have you never once considered the unfairness of the Commodore's stance concerning his daughters? Have you not ever envisioned what your life might have been had the old vulture not been so stingy?"

Indeed I had. And I'd realized my life would have been far too similar to those of my cousins, Gertrude and Consuelo, for my liking. If my independence came at a price, it was one I was willing to pay. I lifted a shoulder. "Not particularly. I like my life as it is, thank you."

"Do you, Miss Cross?" He swiped the hook at me, missing by a scant few inches. I pressed tighter against the door and contracted my stomach muscles as I sucked in a breath. "Are you that daft, or has the family sufficiently brainwashed you to prevent you from claiming what should have been yours all along?"

My mind spun in confusion. What did any of this have to do with Howard Dunn's crimes?

As if he heard my thoughts, he began to speak. "All I wanted was recognition and at least a few of the benefits of being born a Vanderbilt." I gasped at this pronouncement, but Mr. Dunn kept on. "If Frederick and Louise are tired of this place, they can damn well give it to me. What is Rough Point to them with all their millions? Nothing! A trifle. But no, they insist on selling and adding insult to injury by forcing me to cater to the very man intending to usurp my rightful position here. Ah, but who will ever buy Rough Point with the stench of murder permeating the place inside and out?"

"Please, Mr. Dunn, I still don't understand. Uncle Frederick—"

"Yes, dear *Uncle* Frederick." Those ugly veins in his temples pulsed wildly. "Do you know how it galls me to hear him call you his niece, but refuse to acknowledge me as his son?"

A cry escaped my lips and my knees turned to water. My back slid against the wood planks behind me. Frederick Vanderbilt's son? Had I heard him correctly? The blood rushed in my ears, almost but not quite drowning out the sound of Patch's whimpering. I drew in a breath and steeled myself not to sag to the floor.

"How?" was all I could manage.

"He took low advantage of my mother when they were young. Yes, the great Frederick Vanderbilt, the businessman and philanthropist, so moral and upstanding. He would never admit to his wrongdoing, and somehow he even persuaded my mother never to speak of their . . . their . . . *relations*."

"Then how do you know?"

"Because," he shouted, then continued more calmly, "he always sent us money, and gifts at Christmas and birthdays. He paid for my schooling. I ask you, why would he do all that for another man's son?"

I had no answer, indeed, simply could not reconcile myself to the idea of the man I knew—kind, generous, intelligent—with what Mr. Dunn had just revealed. But a wave of understanding came over me. "That day . . . you said we were two of a kind. This is why."

"You know what it is to be born on the wrong side of the Vanderbilt family tree, don't you, Miss Cross?"

I nodded as a realization came into sharp focus—and with it, a possible opportunity. "Yes, Mr. Dunn, I know quite well. Bad enough they treat me like a poor relation, I'm also cast into the role of servant more times than I care to relate."

These words brought a bitter taste to my mouth, for in truth I had no such complaints against my relatives. They might not always understand or approve of me, but they had always been generous and supportive. "Even here, Louise charged me with the task of ensuring the artists didn't damage the estate, as if I am a caretaker in their employ. They toss me their castoffs and consider themselves generous, and expect me to be grateful."

He was nodding, looking gratified. "Frederick and Louise, indeed the entire family, will not escape unscathed. What I have done will put them dead center of a scandal they'll never outlive. They'll be shunned by society, because members of the Four Hundred will disdain to have such shadows darkening their festivities."

"But you sacrificed innocent lives to achieve revenge on one man," I blurted before I could stop myself.

"Innocent? They're at one another's throats morning, noon, and night. They all deserve a similar fate." His eyes became small and narrow, two gleaming pinpoints in the dim light. His voice became flat and cold. "I thought you understood. I see I was wrong."

I strained my ears, hoping against hope to hear the sound of approaching footsteps. Of course there were none. Who would think to search for me in the cellar? Jesse would probably scour the grounds before he thought to check down here. "What are you going to do now?"

"I tried to make friends with you, Miss Cross, but you brushed me off with all the arrogance of a true Vanderbilt. You've left me with little choice, but I can't dispatch you here, where you might be found before I've quit Aquidneck Island." He jerked his head toward the corridor that led deeper into the cellars. "That way." For good measure he seized the collar of my shirtwaist and tugged.

Fear sent paralyzing numbness throughout my limbs. My feet turned as cold and lifeless as if I'd trudged barefoot through snow, and my fingers hung stiff and leaden. Even so, I resolved to fight him, to deliver a vicious kick before we reached that hallway, for once there I would be virtually trapped between Howard Dunn and the stairs to the upper floor. One of the doors ahead opened onto the laundry room, but other than that I didn't know these cellars. He did, all too well. My only hope of escape lay in the staircase. He tugged me again but I braced myself against the door, ready to lash out with my booted foot—

With little more than a jiggle of the latch, the door behind me burst open and propelled me straight into Mr. Dunn. The force of our collision sent us both to the floor, he on his back and me sprawled on his torso. I felt a yank and heard a tear as his ice pick caught on my skirt. He ripped it free and raised his arm again.

A blur of brown and white streaked past me and fierce growls filled the air. Clawing my way like a crazed animal, I crawled off of Howard Dunn just as Patch sank his teeth into the man's arm. Mr. Dunn fought back, and both the ice pick and Patch were thrust from side to side. Breathless and half blinded by panic, I scrambled to my feet. No weapon showed itself in this empty, tiled room. I bolted into the storage room and seized the first object that reached my hands—a sack filled with something dense and heavy. I hefted it with borrowed strength and hurried back to the main room.

"Patch, release," I commanded. The instant he did, I swung, holding the sack by its cinched closure and striking Mr. Dunn square on the side of the head. He went limp and the ice hook clattered to the floor.

Chapter 19

The force of the blow and the weight of the sack sent me to my knees. I reached out with both arms. "Patch."

His furry body filled my embrace and I hung on tight, burying my face in the warmth of his neck. His heart beat a reassuring rhythm against me, and when I raised my head I found his loving gaze pinned on my own. My own heart swelled painfully. "You're my hero, boy. But . . . however did you unlock that door?"

A dull moan came from inside the storage room, and then a voice sputtered and said haltingly, "Emmaline? Is . . . that you?"

I was on my feet again in an instant, seeing what I had missed in the skirmish: my uncle lying inside the storeroom a few feet from the threshold. I reached the open door at the same time he gripped the lintel and hauled himself to his feet. "What happened out here? Are you . . ." He trailed off as his gaze traveled over my shoulder. His lips stretched in a grim smile. "I might have known he was no match for you."

Footsteps sounded overhead and I heard the cellar door swing open. "Emma? Darling, are you down there?"

"I'm here, Mother," I called back, but my response was drowned out by the clatter of multiple feet descending the stairs. It was Jesse and not my mother who headed the downward charge that included my parents, Mrs. Wharton and Vasili, and finally Mrs. Harris and Irene in the rear. Mrs. Harris surprised me by speaking first.

"Such a commotion I heard! The dear lad"—she pointed to Patch—"barking as if to wake the dead, and shouts and—good heavens. I told Irene to run for help and, well, here we are." She, as well as the others, looked about, taking in the scene. "Mr. Dunn!" the woman exclaimed. "Is it his heart? Shall I call a doctor?"

Mother studied the unconscious estate manager for all of a moment, then with a cry ran to me and caught me up in her arms. She practically smothered me, and my gasping effort to breathe was made more difficult by my father, who put his arms around both of us.

"We're so dreadfully sorry to put you in such danger, my dearest girl." Her cheek against mine, Mother wept into my hair and held me tighter.

"You didn't, Mother. You had nothing to do with what happened. It wasn't Father's art dealer."

"It's over now," my father said in a gravelly voice. I continued stealing shallow breaths when I could, yet I couldn't bring myself to mention my discomfort or attempt to break away, not even in the slightest. This felt . . . so very nice and was . . . oh, the very thing I'd missed these several years. I had comforted myself with my hodgepodge family of Nanny and Katie and my cousin Neily and the rest, but there had always existed a gap where my parents used to be.

Closing that gap sent tears of my own to mingle with my

mother's, and as I glanced up at my father, I discovered he had succumbed to the same sentiments, with similar results. He grinned ruefully and gathered Mother and me closer still. A warm body pressed against the back of my skirts, leaning his weight against my legs in his familiar way. In that moment I felt my family to be complete.

Commotion broke out around us. At Uncle Frederick's suggestion, Irene and Mrs. Wharton found a roll of twine and Jesse set to work binding Mr. Dunn's wrists and ankles. I took comfort in not having ended his life, but I would be lying if I pretended I didn't wish to deliver a swift kick to his side.

Curiosity, rather than a lack of oxygen, finally prompted me to loosen my hold on my parents. They did likewise, and we turned to my uncle. Jesse had just asked him to explain what happened.

"I questioned him—that's what happened." Frederick Vanderbilt spoke with an outraged sense of authority. "I was in the butler's pantry, as I have a right to be in my own home, looking through some account papers, when I came upon sets of keys that Howard Dunn would not have needed in supervising the estate this past week."

"Such as?" Jesse prompted when my uncle paused.

"Such as the key to the linen cupboard. Why would anyone but the maid need that key? In fact, my wife left the key in Irene's possession the day we left Rough Point."

"But you just said you'd left Mr. Dunn here to supervise the retreat," I pointed out.

He shook his head. "Certainly not. I left him here as my representative should Randall Clifford decide he wished to buy the estate. Howard was to draw up the papers, as well as answer any questions the Englishman might have had. As far as domestic concerns went, I had complete faith in Irene, Carl, and Mrs. Harris. They were to see to the needs of the guests."

"He replaced the towels he used to dry the floor in Monsieur Baptiste's bathroom after he killed him," I said with a gasp of realization. "That's why there didn't appear to be any missing."

"And why," Jesse said, "there were damp tracks across the bedroom rug. Dunn entered with wet feet after the fiasco in Miss Marcus's bathroom. He probably sopped up as much of it as he could, but my guess is he must not have thought we would take off our shoes to check the rug for moisture."

"He also had the duplicate keys to all the bedrooms," Uncle Frederick continued.

"I knew about that," I admitted with a sinking feeling. If only I had said something at the time—but to whom? In all likelihood, no one would have considered this unusual. "Carl used them to check that all the locks were in working order."

"There was no need for that," Uncle Frederick declared. "We keep duplicates on hand only for emergencies, in the event a guest is ill and locked inside. We would *never* allow a member of the staff to unlock a guest's door otherwise. When I began questioning him as to why he should need these keys, he struck me. Knocked me out cold and dragged me down here and into the storage room. I awoke to find your dog's tail thumping in my face as he tried to dig his way under the door."

I very nearly combed my fingers into his hair to feel for a bump. "Mrs. Harris, call for Uncle Frederick's physician, and prepare a poultice, please. But, uncle, how did you unlock the door? Surely Mr. Dunn didn't allow you to keep the set of duplicate keys?"

His eyes twinkled. "In a house this size, it's all too easy for a servant to shut a door on another and walk away. It happened once, years ago, in New York. Our young hall boy actually fell asleep in the cold storage pantry one summer.

Later he said he'd gone in to escape the heat. The housekeeper walked by, saw the door ajar, shut it, and locked it. The poor boy shivered for hours once he was finally let out. Every storage room and pantry unlatches from the inside, regardless of whether the door is locked from the outside. A detail our Mr. Dunn apparently forgot."

"Uncle Frederick," I half whispered, for here was a truth I loathed to reveal, "Howard Dunn made some astonishing accusations."

Before I could say more, Mrs. Wharton came to me and cupped my face in her hands. "I'm very grateful to find you all right." She turned to the others. "I suggest we adjourn upstairs to more comfortable surroundings. Frederick and Emma have each suffered a terrible shock."

"And so has Patch," I added, and then called up to the cook who had neared the top of the stairs. "Mrs. Harris, I believe a nice meaty bone is in order."

"I believe I have just the thing," she called back. "A lovely raw lamb bone for our dear little lamb. Just as soon as I telephone into town for the doctor . . ."

The others started up the stairs after her, but Jesse hovered behind the rest. Looking from him to my parents, I nodded for them to go up as well. Mother gave me an understanding nod, called to Patch, and linked her arm through Father's. Together the three of them climbed the stairs. Only Jesse, Mr. Dunn, and I remained, but Mr. Dunn would not be listening in on our conversation anytime soon.

A fierce light entered Jesse's eyes, and I feared he would chastise me for putting myself in harm's way once again. But instead I found myself in his arms, enfolded in a formidable embrace. I reached my arms around his waist and hung on to the back of his coat with my fists. We stayed like that for several, long moments, merely holding on and demanding nothing, making no promises, simply being what we were—two people who cared tremendously about each other, as we always had, as we always would.

"Howard Dunn is not my son." Uncle Frederick held a poultice against his head but refused to sit, pacing back and forth across the drawing room as he explained. "He once asked me, years ago when he was a child. I told him no then and I thought he believed me."

"But why was he so convinced in the first place?"

He stopped by my chair and gazed down at me. "Ordinarily, Emmaline, I would hesitate to tell such a story in a young woman's hearing. But after what you have been through, not only today but every day since you've been at Rough Point . . ." He trailed off with a questioning glance at my parents, sitting together on the settee. They nodded their permission, and Uncle Frederick continued.

"Howard's mother was a Pierson—"

"A member of the Four Hundred," Mrs. Wharton interrupted, and my uncle nodded.

"Yes, and her parents and mine were quite good friends. Carlotta and I were close in age, and in fact there were hopes that she and I might one day marry." He shook his head, a sad smile on his lips. "Lottie didn't care for me in that way. She loved another man. A vile scoundrel who took advantage of her, ruined her, and left her with Howard." He resumed pacing. "As might be expected, her family disowned her. I took pity on her—how could I not have? Poor, foolish girl. Once I came into my inheritance I began sending them money regularly, not a great amount, mind you, but enough to support them in a modest lifestyle. I also sent presents at Christmas and Howard's birthday. And I did so with Louise's blessing, I'll have you know."

"I would never doubt that for a moment," I assured him. "I know how Aunt Louise adores children. She would never want one to suffer needlessly."

"That is quite correct." For an instant, regret for his and Louise's childless state cast a sorrowful shadow across his face. "I saw to Howard's education and offered him decent employment—employment many a man would covet. But I am not his father, and I can see no reason to leave him a fortune or property that will someday be dispersed among my nieces and nephews."

He abruptly threw himself into a chair and leaned to hang his head into his palms. "Perhaps if I had, those people, your friends, would still be alive."

I rose and went to him. "You couldn't have known. None of us could have. People like Howard Dunn are filled with hatred, like an illness, but they're also very clever at hiding their symptoms. Or perhaps it's that the rest of us simply can't imagine such evil in those we've come to trust. You certainly can't blame yourself for the actions of a deluded, hate-filled individual, Uncle Frederick."

He looked up at me with a sad smile. "How wise you have grown, Emmaline. How tragic that someone as young as you should have become so wise."

By noon the last of us vacated Rough Point with the help of Jesse and two of his men. The officers having determined that Ledge Road was passable, Mrs. Wharton brought Vasili with her to Land's End, where her husband had arrived relatively unscathed the day before. Upon her release this afternoon, Josephine would join them there, although Mrs. Wharton assured me the opera singer would wish to thank me for defending her. Perhaps, but there would never be true friendship between us. We were too different. On the other hand, Mrs. Wharton and I promised to meet again soon. She had every intention of holding me to my promise to critique her work, and I looked forward to her returning the favor as I wrote my article on the retreat. As with other times in the past, this piece would deviate sharply from what I had envisioned at the outset—to say the least.

As I had predicted, Uncle Frederick returned to town, from where he could wire his wife and make plans for his return trip to New York, along with Irene and Mrs. Harris. Carl would also have a job at either the Hyde Park or Fifth Avenue house, but first he wished to visit with his parents here on the island.

There had been tense moments as I waited for my parents to state their intentions. Would they bid me a hasty farewell and be off? Were they eager to quit, not only Newport, but me, their daughter, who had made no bones about judging their behavior and doubting them accordingly? As their child, shouldn't I have trusted them implicitly?

Then again, is it any surprise murder and the deplorable weather had worked on my psyche and eclipsed my daughterly affections? Now however, my regard for them pushed through the gloom and danger of Rough Point even as the sun pushed its way stubbornly through every slight break in the clouds.

I wanted them to stay on at Gull Manor, and I told them so, and added a *please* for good measure.

"Darling, of course we'll come to Gull Manor with you," Mother declared with genuine surprise.

"Where else would we go," my father added heartily, "but home with our courageous daughter?"

The three of us, and Patch, climbed into Jesse's police buggy, for he would not hear of our negotiating Ocean Avenue—arguably the most dangerous thoroughfare on Aquidneck Island in inclement weather—without him. The telephone lines along Ocean Avenue had not yet been repaired, so I was unable to warn Nanny of our imminent arrival. I needn't have worried. Delicious scents greeted us in the front hall and set my stomach rumbling.

After hugging each of us thoroughly, thanking Jesse for bringing me home, and chiding my parents for staying away so long, Nanny explained, "As soon as the rain began letting up, Katie and I started cooking. I knew it wouldn't be long before you'd all be home."

I had never been so happy to be there, so much so I smiled down at the threadbare hall rug, the bald spots on the banister where years of use had worn away the varnish, and I barely flinched at the crash as Patch apparently knocked over something in the parlor. The others followed him in, but I remained in my front hall feeling at home and at peace. Mrs. Wharton had been right, Gull Manor *was* the home of a young woman of independent means. Not only was the place mine free and clear, but unlike Howard Dunn, I wanted nothing more. *Needed* nothing more. Not in the way of material possessions, anyway. And *that*, as Mrs. Wharton had said, was worth more than all the satin brocade and fine velvets a fortune can provide. Of all the Vanderbilts, I felt myself to be the luckiest.

Happy voices drew my attention to the parlor, but before I turned into that room, I noticed a missive lying on the mail salver on the hall table. It hadn't been there when I left on my adventures, and given the weather I surmised it had been delivered today just prior to my arrival. The Western Union stamp on the sealed page raised my guard. Bad news? I thought immediately of Uncle Cornelius, still so frail after his stroke. But no—upon opening the telegram I saw the message had traveled the wires from much farther away than New York. It had come from Italy. From Derrick Andrews.

My dearest Emma, all is well. I plan to be home in the spring. I think of you daily. Will write soon.

That was all, but it was enough to start me trembling and to drown out the voices in the other room beneath the rush of my pulse points. Suddenly, my independent, well-ordered life tumbled into chaos. I forced myself to breathe, to be calm, and to remember that I had not made my choices yet, and that one choice open to me was to make no choice at all. Not until I felt completely, contentedly ready. I folded the telegram and stuffed it into my drawstring purse, and laid that on the hall table. With a lift of my chin I took two steps toward the parlor doorway, then stopped short when the conversation I had been hearing but hadn't *listened* to suddenly presented itself to my ears.

"Ask her, Jesse." Mother's voice held an eager note. "Arthur, tell him. Give him your blessing."

Oh no. Oh, dear Lord.

Father cleared his throat. "We'd be pleased to have you as a son-in-law, Jesse."

My breath burned in my throat and a tingling like a thousand pinpricks swept up my neck and across my face. I wished to simply melt away where I stood.

After a pause, Jesse said, "I appreciate that. But the time isn't right." I could all but see the blush creeping up his face and scorching his ears. My own were flaming.

"Nonsense." This from Mother again. "There is no time like the present. I've seen the two of you together. Jesse, as Emma's mother, I can assure you it's perfect. There could be a spring wedding. . . ."

My stomach tightened into a ball of misery and mortification.

"If you'll excuse me." A creaking of the sofa was followed

by footsteps advancing in my direction. I had nowhere to hide, no time to traverse the hall to the back rooms. Jesse appeared a moment later and drew up short. "Oh, uh . . . I suppose you heard that."

As I had expected, his cheeks were aflame, the tips of his ears glowing. Poor Jesse. Poor me. I nodded and stared down at my feet. "I'm sorry," I whispered. "They mean well."

With a light touch he raised my chin. "Of course they do. And don't think I won't take your father's blessing to heart. But I meant what I said. The time isn't right. Someday it might be, and on that day I'll be here. Until then . . ."

His normal complexion returned and he grinned down at me. My misery suddenly forgotten, I grinned back, and together we made our way to the kitchen to see how we could help Katie with dinner preparations.

Afterword

While Rough Point is somewhat less well known compared to some of the other Newport cottages, it's nonetheless one of my favorites. Relatively isolated at the end of Bellevue Avenue, Rough Point for many years held a certain element of mystery, sitting on its rugged headland behind high walls and solid iron doors that blocked the property from view. Those doors have since been replaced by gates, and Rough Point, maintained by the Newport Restoration Foundation, welcomes visitors to tour the house and learn about the woman who owned it for nearly seventy years, from the mid-1920s until her death in 1993.

Although tobacco heiress and philanthropist Doris Duke was Rough Point's most famous resident and the focus of Rough Point's tours, the house was originally built by Peabody & Stearns for Frederick William Vanderbilt, son of William Henry Vanderbilt, and brother to Cornelius II and William Kissam Vanderbilt, who are both featured in The Gilded Newport Mysteries.

The house in Frederick Vanderbilt's time looked rather

different from the house we see today. The far north wing that presently houses the Music Room did not exist originally, and was instead a covered, open-air piazza. Likewise, two covered porches once flanked the open veranda along the back of the house. One opened onto the drawing room, and is now the solarium. The other opened onto what was the billiard room. The drawing room was also later expanded by the removal of the wall that separated it from the library, resulting in one large room. This is now called the Yellow Room. As mentioned in the story, the house was as Gothic and dark as any Tudor-era manor house from the English countryside, and was lightened up considerably by its two later owners. I was sad to discover the fabulous stained glass windows at the half landing of the main staircase, depicting the coats of arms of the signers of the Magna Carta, were not original but added later, by the Dukes. I will admit I took some creative license in adding a couple more bedrooms than existed in Frederick Vanderbilt's day.

Rough Point was groundbreaking in that it was the largest Newport "cottage" built up until that time, and thus paved the way for even larger and more ornate houses thereafter. Yet not long after its completion, Frederick and Louise tired of the house, and of Newport, and began renting it out before selling it to the Leeds family in 1906. They, in turn, sold the property to the Dukes in 1922. Frederick and Louise Vanderbilt never had children and, upon their deaths, their fortune was divided among their many nieces and nephews.

Edith Wharton's book on interior decorating, *The Decoration of Houses*, co-written with Ogden Codman Jr., was published in 1897. As I've indicated in the story, her marriage to Edward Wharton was not a happy one. Teddy Wharton suffered from acute depression, which began a few years into the marriage and steadily worsened, ending their travels and leading to their divorce in 1913 after doctors declared him incurable. They had no children. Their Newport home, Land's End, still stands on Ledge Road overlooking the Atlantic Ocean, not far from Rough Point. It is privately owned, unmarked, and fairly well obscured from the road by trees, at least enough to frustrate would-be photographers.